ENEMIES & ALLIES

HARPERCOLLINS BOOKS ALSO BY KEVIN J. ANDERSON

The Last Days of Krypton

Superman created by Jerry Siegel and Joe Shuster
Batman created by Bob Kane

WILLIAM MORROW
An Imprint of HarperCollinsPublishers

ENEMIES
& ALLIES

KEVIN J. ANDERSON

ENEMIES & ALLIES. Copyright © 2009 by DC Comics. SUPERMAN, BATMAN, the Superman "S-shield," Batman logo, and all related names, characters, and elements are trademarks of DC Comics. All rights reserved. Printed in the United States of America. No part of this book may be used or reproduced in any manner whatsoever without written permission except in the case of brief quotations embodied in critical articles and reviews. For information address HarperCollins Publishers, 10 East 53rd Street, New York, NY 10022.

HarperCollins books may be purchased for educational, business, or sales promotional use. For information please write: Special Markets Department, HarperCollins Publishers, 10 East 53rd Street, New York, NY 10022.

FIRST EDITION

Designed by Daniel Lagin

Library of Congress Cataloging-in-Publication Data has been applied for.

ISBN 978-0-06-166255-3

09 10 11 12 13   OV/RRD   10 9 8 7 6 5 4 3 2 1

To Mary Thomson and Cherie Buchheim

Longtime friends, fans, research experts, geeks, and genuine enthusiasts

ACKNOWLEDGMENTS

Many people helped me with this book. My special thanks to Christopher Cerasi, Steve Korté, and Paul Levitz at DC Comics; Mauro DiPreta, Jennifer Schulkind, Jack Womack, and Danielle Bartlett at HarperCollins; John Silbersack at Trident Media Group; Elizabeth Thomson for her lightning-fast typing fingers; and my eager and enthusiastic test readers Deb Ray, Diane Jones, Louis Moesta, and Rebecca Moesta Anderson for their insightful advice.

And, of course, to the genius of Frank Miller, Jeph Loeb, and Tim Sale for providing such a solid creative foundation for this story.

ABOVE THE CLOUD-MISTED SEAS AND MAJESTIC CONTI-
nents of Earth orbited a small metal sphere that was not much larger than a basketball. Its stiff antennae extended to send out a simple, monotonous message, a succession of meaningless beeps.

The Soviets had named this, the first human-made satellite, Sputnik: "Fellow Traveler." The only one of its kind, Sputnik circled at the edge of space, high above proud nations and their boundaries, oblivious to the political turmoil created by its very existence.

The late 1950s marked a new era, one of both progress and international tensions. While space travel to other planets was still an unattainable dream, the fledgling rocketry programs of the United States and the USSR scrambled for the capability to launch nuclear missiles at each other. For the first time in history, human beings had the power to destroy their world.

Crossing into the night on its endless orbit, Sputnik passed over the great slumbering cities of the United States: Metropolis; Washington, D.C.; Gotham City; Los Angeles.

But even in the darkest cities below, not everyone slept. . . .

CHAPTER 1
GOTHAM CITY

NIGHT. A TIME FOR HUNTING. PREDATORS PREFER SHADOWS and cool silence. But who preys upon the predators—and where?

The Thomas and Martha Wayne Memorial Park. A civic monument to two of Gotham City's most beloved citizens. A playground with swing sets and teeter-totters, picnic tables and baseball diamonds, fountains, statues, a forested arboretum. In better times, it had been a place where families spent lazy afternoons together.

A place for families like the one he no longer had.

Now the once-bubbling fountains were empty basins to catch windblown leaves. The dense trees in the patch of forest were skeletal and frightening, like props from a Brothers Grimm fairy tale. Penknife-scratched graffiti marred the statues, defacing honored heroes. Garbage littered the walking paths. Weeds choked the baseball diamonds.

Some of Gotham's citizens shook their heads at how the son of Thomas and Martha Wayne had allowed the park to fall into such disrepair and ill repute. With his inherited millions, Bruce Wayne could certainly afford to make the park a fine place again.

But he had other ideas.

This place attracted the dregs and bottom-feeders of society. He viewed it as a trap. As bait.

On nights when the pounding guilt and burning anger grew unbearable, when he felt the need to do *something,* when he could no longer sit in extravagant splendor within a memory-haunted mansion, he went out to watch, to hunt. He could have prowled Crime Alley, once called Park Row, or guarded the slums of the East End. Or he could come here, to the park named after his parents. In a way, it was fitting.

He was ready.

His custom-made suit was both second skin and body armor, its dark reinforced fabric molded to his muscled form, sheathing his biceps, shoulders, torso, and legs. It provided as much protection as any medieval knight's suit of armor. His gauntlets were flexible yet impervious to heat, cold, abrasion, impact. His belt contained dozens of useful devices developed by the greatest minds at Wayne Enterprises (ostensibly for purposes other than to assist him in his nighttime activities). His mask, a fearsome cowl with pointed ears, proved as intimidating as the helm of a ferocious Viking warrior, and his black cape swirled around him like the trailing shadow of a demon.

When he donned this outfit, this identity, he felt powerful, full of determination, yet silent and elusive as a specter. Many people still weren't sure whether the Gotham City "Bat-man" was real or just an urban legend, a heroic boogeyman created by a desperate populace that wanted the crime rate to drop.

The criminals knew he was real, though. And they were afraid of him.

For the past year and a half since he had first donned the uniform, his crusade had been to clean up Gotham City, a gloomy place that attracted more clouds than sunshine. Although this city had wounded him deeply, he loved it nevertheless. He saw the beauty hidden beneath the warts and scabs. The *promise.* He knew what Gotham could become, and he had to do something to help.

He patrolled the park just after midnight, a time when punks, muggers, murderers, and rapists were abroad, looking for fresh victims, fresh blood. Society's predators abounded. *He* preyed on the predators.

As he took a mental inventory of the environs, nobody saw him. They never did.

A bearded wino huddled in a stained trench coat, clutching a brown paper bag as though it contained treasure. The wino curled up under a blanket of old newspapers in the dry basin of an unused fountain, snoring softly.

Four young toughs, looking as if they had just stepped out of a government poster warning against juvenile delinquency, lounged in the trees at the edge of the arboretum, chain-smoking Lucky Strikes. Snickering in low voices, imitating moves they had copied from James Dean in *Rebel Without a Cause,* all had identical haircuts slicked back with Brylcreem. One had a pack of cigarettes rolled up in the sleeve of his white T-shirt; the others wore leather jackets.

A seedy-looking man on a park bench glanced at his watch, obviously waiting for a rendezvous. After a few moments, a disheveled stranger casually took a seat next to him, as if they were simply two men arriving in the middle of the night to feed pigeons in the park. After conversing in low voices, they exchanged envelopes.

A woman came down the path, walking away from the busy city streets, taking a shortcut through the park's winding trails.

From the shadows he made a quick assessment: not a prostitute, just a woman in her early twenties wearing a lightweight coat. Her hair was dishwater blond, long and straight but covered with a black and white polka-dot scarf; her shoes were sensible, and judging from the way she moved, she'd had a long day. As the woman moved toward the arboretum, he could see she wore a waitress's uniform beneath the open coat. A large German shepherd trotted at her side, eager for a late-night walk.

He was instantly wary. She shouldn't have been going into the park. Even the big dog wouldn't be enough to protect her.

His senses were attuned to every sound, scent, and movement. Certain something was about to happen, he crouched in the shadows, his pulse racing, adrenaline filling his bloodstream. He focused his whole world around the possibility of a hunt.

He wouldn't let it happen again. . . .

In the aftermath of a traumatic experience, some people are left with a ringing in their ears. Some have lingering pain. *He* saw the deaths of his parents. Always. More than memory, different from a nightmare.

After the movie, in the alley, a bad choice, a wrong turn . . . a man lunging out of the shadows. His father's voice was calm as he tried to reason with the mugger, his eyes never wavering from the gun.

How could the reflection of blue steel be so bright in such a dim alley?

"He just wants the pearls, Martha. Just the pearls."

"And the wallet, too!"

"All right, and the wallet." Thomas Wayne's voice was soothing, as if he were reading bedtime stories to young Bruce. At only six years of age, the boy didn't understand what was happening. His father sounded calm, protective. Everything would be all right.

The pistol shot was loud. So was his mother's scream.

Those sounds never stopped echoing in his head.

His parents had taken him to see *The Mark of Zorro*. At the time, Bruce had actually believed that masked heroes did sweep down to protect the innocent. But in that moment in the dark alley behind the theater, there was no masked avenger. No one came in response to the gunshot . . . or to Martha Wayne's screams.

The boy huddled there on the wet pavement for a long time. His parents didn't move. Doctors didn't come to save his mother and father. Police didn't rush into the alley to apprehend the mugger—the *murderer*.

Spilled blood mingled with the rainwater and slime of the street, deep red, pooling together, the last warm traces of his parents. His mother's hand was very cold by the time young Bruce heard the first siren, but the little boy's heart had gone colder still. . . .

Suddenly, in the park, the waitress screamed, startling him from his thoughts. He silently cursed himself for letting his obsession distract him at a crucial moment. Weak. Dangerous. He needed to focus!

Over near the trees, the German shepherd was barking and growling. The waitress tried to pull away, but the four toughs surrounded her, switchblades drawn, their teeth bright as they grinned like jackals. "Come on, lady, we're just asking for protection money. We'll save you from the Batman. Fifty bucks will do it."

She screamed for help. The wino roused himself groggily from his hard bed in the dry fountain. The two furtive men on the park bench looked over, clearly not wanting to get involved. They would be no help to her. No one would. No one but him.

For this young waitress, at least, a masked hero *would* come out of the darkness. For her, there was a hero to save the innocent.

He struck without warning. A swirl of the black cape to make himself appear larger, terrifying—all in complete silence. With a sideways sweep of his left gauntlet, he knocked the switchblade from the T-shirted tough's hand. The young thug yowled, springing backward as if he had touched a hot plate. "It's the Batman!"

The second hoodlum dipped a hand inside his black leather jacket, reaching for something, but another gauntleted blow sent the young man sprawling to the ground, the wind knocked out of him.

Keep the victim safe. He jerked the waitress roughly aside, out of the way of the third thug, who also reached inside his jacket. But instead of grabbing a handgun or a switchblade, the attacker retrieved something golden and shiny.

A badge.

From behind him, the waitress shouted, "Gotham City PD—freeze, Batman!"

His mind immediately clicked with the realization. *A trap!* The police had laid an ambush for *him*. The thugs, the waitress . . . undercover cops.

Time to make an exit.

The waitress released the German shepherd, and the snarling dog launched itself at him, all claws, fur, and fangs, bowling him to the ground. Using the muscles of his thighs and back, he threw off the heavy dog, but it bounded toward him again. Now the woman—the supposed victim—had a police-issue revolver in her hand and a badge of her own. The other "toughs" had regrouped and pressed closer, working together, surrounding him.

"I said *freeze*!" the waitress said. "You're under arrest."

With a flourish, he swirled the weighted, scalloped hem of his cape, knocking the revolver out of her hand, then bolted toward the shelter of the arboretum and the concealing shadows of the trees.

The police dog gave chase but was unable to bite through his armored fabric, though the weight and pressure threw him off balance. Only one way to react: He let himself trip, then purposely rolled, using momentum to take the dog with him, and shoved it away as he ran in the opposite direction.

As a boy, even with all the riches in the world and a large manor house with expansive grounds, Bruce Wayne had never owned a dog—or any kind of pet. He had not wanted to get attached to anything. Too dangerous.

Now his suit gave him plenty of options. With a crunch and a twist, applying just the right pressure from his left boot heel, he released a cloud of stinking purple gas. The stench and the smoke drove the dog away yelping.

Now, however, the wino sprang out of the fountain and drew the service weapon he had been concealing within the rumpled paper bag. The two furtive men from the park bench also came at him, carrying a net between them.

Everyone was part of the trap.

Though he raised an arm to protect himself, the thrown net caught the sharp points of his mask and his forearm gauntlets.

From the trees, a voice on a bullhorn bellowed, "Batman, this is Captain James Gordon of the Gotham City Police Department. Surrender yourself."

He saw flashing red lights, heard sirens coming from the streets outside the park—more policemen homing in on the same quarry: *him.*

He slashed the strands of the net with his gauntlet's sharp razors, pulled himself free, and began to run through the shadow-latticed moonlight.

The "wino" opened fire, and bullets splintered bark and wood from a thick-boled oak. Swirling his dark cape like a toreador to distract the aggressor, he disguised the position of his body. Bullets stitched along the flailing fabric; none touched his skin. His armored outfit would stop or slow most bullets, but a solid impact from a slug might knock him to the ground.

And then the police would be able to catch him.

He made for the trees. Though the police captain's voice had come from that direction, he had to hope a large contingent of the GCPD wasn't hiding among the closely packed trunks.

All this manpower was being wasted on *him*. The corrupt police force clearly didn't like the fact that he worked against criminals—successfully, though outside of their laws—and worse, several of his recent captures were little hoodlums who had squealed about cops being on the take, which had led to official investigations. He knew the Gotham City PD protected its own, and they didn't like to be embarrassed.

And he had embarrassed them.

They wanted to bring him down.

The two men from the park bench rushed toward him, guns drawn. He struck one of them with a hammer blow to the stomach, the other with an uppercut to the jaw. Both men fell hard.

He refused to kill—not cops, not even criminals—but sometimes he couldn't avoid inflicting an injury or two, a broken jaw, a shattered tooth. He had to do what was necessary to get away. The pain of bruises and broken bones would heal.

The pain of his parents' deaths would not.

He melted into the trees, trying to be silent, but his boots were heavy, and the underbrush made crackling sounds. Even against a background of wailing sirens and shouting police, the noises seemed incredibly loud.

But this was the Thomas and Martha Wayne Memorial Park, and it held plenty of secrets. *His* secrets. If only he could find the cleverly concealed hollow tree stump, his emergency exit.

Two uniformed policemen from the squad cars tried to cut him off, and now it was time to use his Bat-shuriken, small projectiles he had modeled after ninja throwing stars. They came into the palm of his gauntlet, each one no bigger than his curled forefinger. He threw them accurately, their gleaming black curves shaped like an emblematic bat. The pointed tips nipped his pursuers' skin, leaving behind small wounds, surprise, and a sting of pain—and a fast-acting tranquilizer he'd obtained from the cloud forests in Ecuador. The two men yelped and went down.

He kept pushing ahead. The tree stump wasn't far now.

Suddenly he came upon a man with glasses, a thick mustache, light brown hair, a police captain's uniform. James Gordon, recently transferred from Chicago and making quite a name for himself in the Gotham City PD. Apparently not corrupt. *Yet.* In a ready stance, Gordon pointed the revolver's barrel directly at the bat symbol in the middle of his chest armor.

How could the reflection of blue steel be so bright in such a dim forest?

"There are two ways this can end, Batman. You come with me now—or you die."

Policemen had so little imagination. Only two ways? He raised his black-gloved hands as if in surrender. Though Gordon was not fooled, the movement distracted him for a critical instant. A small set of bolos flew forward, tiny balls tethered by high-tensile-strength polymer threads that wrapped themselves around

Gordon's closely aligned wrists. With a reflexive twitch of the trigger finger, Gordon's gun discharged.

A quick leap to the left. The bullet smashed into a tree trunk, cutting a long, pale gouge in the fresh wood.

In an instant he had tackled Gordon, using his larger bulk and greater strength to overpower the captain. "You are wasting my time—and your own," he growled, the first words he'd spoken since donning the outfit that night. How could he make this man see that they were on the same side? "Gotham would be a safer place if you'd worry less about me and more about criminals."

Struggling, Gordon hissed at him, "I *am* stopping a criminal— it's what I do. It's what the *police* do, not vigilantes. I'll have you up on charges of assault, avoiding arrest, and terrorizing the citizens of Gotham City."

"It's the criminals who are afraid of me, not the citizens." This naive and idealistic police captain might have become an ally under other circumstances. "Think, Gordon! How many muggers, thieves, assassins have I taken off the streets? That should be *your* job. What crimes have I committed, exactly? Taking justice into my own hands when the Gotham police won't do their work?"

Though he was pinned to the ground, glasses askew, Gordon looked angry. "A criminal with a moral conscience?"

"Ask yourself who's *really* doing a better job of law enforcement. How many real criminals could your officers have caught tonight if you hadn't wasted so much manpower trying to trap me?" He jerked his masked head to indicate the police swarming through the park, all the squad cars that had converged on the street. "Those officers could have been on patrol, protecting the innocent. How many people became victims tonight because of your skewed priorities?"

Gordon appeared briefly confused by the idea—until the quick anesthetic spray beneath his nose sent him into slumberland. At least he would have something to think about. The chemical would put the captain out for an hour.

Five minutes would have been long enough.

Slipping away, he covered all traces of his passage, careful to leave no sign that even the police dogs could find in the morning. His boots and uniform were specially treated to leave no scent. He found the disguised tree stump, slipped into the underground passage, and made his way back home.

To the manor.

To the Cave.

The fine dinner Alfred had prepared for him was still warm and waiting for him as though just laid out on the tray, the dishes covered. The sardonic butler always seemed to know exactly when he would return.

It had been a frustrating night. He had stopped no crimes, saved no innocents. The hollowness in his chest remained unfilled. There was too much work to do in Gotham City, and he was only one person. He had no allies.

CHAPTER 2
GOTHAM CITY
WAYNE MANOR

THE ELABORATELY APPOINTED DRAWING ROOM WAS THREE times the size of Clark Kent's apartment in Metropolis. After the thin butler had ushered them inside and closed the double French doors, Clark and Jimmy Olsen waited for nearly twenty minutes. Bruce Wayne apparently wasn't a very punctual person, at least when it came to meeting with reporters. Clark supposed that men like him operated on their own schedules, with little regard for regular people.

Jimmy stashed his Graflex Speed Graphic camera and his leather equipment kit on the seat of a large club chair as he gawked at all the strange items the millionaire had on display. The objets d'art would have been considered museum-quality relics anywhere else, but here they were simply knickknacks.

"Gosh, Mr. Kent, have you ever been in a house like this?" Jimmy picked up an ornate bronze dagger that had actually been used by a soldier in the Roman legions. Bruce Wayne apparently used it as a letter opener.

"Don't break anything, Jimmy." Clark stood in the middle of

the room on a lovely Moroccan carpet, as if keeping a safe distance from all the antiques.

The young photographer guiltily set down the knife and opened an old leather-bound book. The pages, which seemed to be vellum, slightly frayed at the edges, were covered with handwritten text and lavishly illuminated with gold leaf and colored inks. "I'll bet Mr. Wayne spends money on antiques like I spend money on bubblegum."

The extravagance made Clark uncomfortable. How different this was from the homey Smallville farmhouse where he'd grown up, with its inviting front porch and a kitchen that always seemed to smell of fresh-baked apple pie or pot roast. Comparing his home with the lonely, empty luxury here, Clark decided he preferred his own upbringing.

He straightened his glasses and smoothed back his dark hair. His blue suit was somewhat rumpled, despite his best efforts to be careful during their train trip from Metropolis. He adjusted his tie and, for the tenth time, consulted his new Timex watch.

The French doors opened, and the butler returned, impeccable in his tuxedo. In one hand he carried an ornate silver tray, polished to a high gleam that reflected the light of the fire blazing in the hearth. Perched atop the tray was a single tumbler filled with a bubbling purple beverage.

"As requested, sirs, a Nehi grape soda for Mr. Olsen, and nothing for Mr. Kent." Jimmy took the soda pop, aligned the straw, and drew a long and thankful slurp. The butler paused at the door on his way out. "Master Wayne should be with you shortly."

Within moments another man stood at the hall doorway on the opposite side of the drawing room. He wore a flamboyant smoking jacket and exuded a kind of animal magnetism. He was about

Clark's age, with dark hair and handsome features. "Wayne," he announced. "Bruce Wayne."

Clark stepped forward, extending a hand while purposely yet discreetly catching the toe of his shoe on the fringed edge of the Moroccan rug. He stumbled, caught his balance, and pretended embarrassment. "I'm Clark Kent from the *Daily Planet*. Thank you for agreeing to this interview."

At the same time, Jimmy snatched up his camera, pressed the opening button, and pulled the focus bed down until it locked into position. He inserted a flashbulb and kept himself ready.

Bruce said airily, "My apologies for being late. This is rather early in the day for me." He looked a little bleary-eyed as he smoothed a hand down the front of his smoking jacket, then walked over to a tray where Alfred had set out a martini glass containing a clear drink in which floated a twist of lemon peel.

"But . . . it's past noon." Clark could never forget his years of getting up before dawn to do his farm chores before going to school.

"I keep late hours." Bruce sipped his martini, closed his eyes, and smiled with pleasure. "Oh, forgive my manners. Would you like one as well?"

"No, thank you, Mr. Wayne—I don't drink."

Amused, Bruce took another sip. "Exactly what I've heard about you."

Clark remembered to keep his shoulders somewhat slumped to diminish his physical size. "You checked up on *me*? I thought *I* was doing the story."

"It never hurts to know who you're up against." Bruce lounged in a high-backed club chair near the fireplace. "Too bad Lois Lane isn't doing this interview. I read that famous profile she did on—what do they call him in Metropolis? 'Superman'? A very imaginative piece."

Jimmy felt the need to defend Lois's honor (though she could have done so perfectly well herself, had she been there). "Miss Lane really should have won the Pulitzer for that article. We were all rooting for her at the *Planet*."

"Too many people found it preposterous." Bruce set his martini aside and managed to make himself look even more comfortable than he had a moment earlier. "Is it true that Superman claims to be an alien from another planet? And that Miss Lane took him at his word?"

Jimmy squared his shoulders. "Gosh, Mr. Wayne, who wouldn't? Superman flies! Bullets bounce right off his chest—I've seen it myself!"

Bruce rolled his eyes. "Technology can give someone superior abilities. No need to make up aliens. I think you're all a tad too gullible in Metropolis."

Clark cleared his throat, took out his reporter's notebook, and withdrew one of his three well-sharpened pencils. "At the moment, Miss Lane is on another assignment. The *Planet* wanted a profile piece on you, Mr. Wayne, not an exposé or headline story." He flipped to a blank page, keeping up the appearance of slight fumbling. "Could we get started, please?"

Bruce took another careful sip of his martini, though the liquid level didn't seem to diminish. "Fire away, Kent. I'm all yours for fifteen minutes, before my next engagement."

"Since you raised the question of Superman," Clark began, "I hear that Gotham has its own costumed hero—or vigilante, depending on whom you ask. The Batman. As one of Gotham City's most prominent citizens, what are your thoughts on the Batman? Is he a psychopathic vigilante or a self-styled Robin Hood? And if he is one of the good guys, why doesn't he just cooperate with the police?"

Bruce let out a very small sigh. "You don't know the police in Gotham City."

"We heard on the radio that the police tried to apprehend the Batman last night," Clark said. "Apparently, they failed, despite a large-scale manhunt."

Bruce looked bored. "That's local news, nothing the *Planet* would be interested in."

The man seemed inclined to be evasive, and Clark sensed that a stronger hand might be necessary in dealing with him. "Then let's make it relevant to our profile. Last night, Batman was supposedly lurking in the Thomas and Martha Wayne Memorial Park—a place meant to honor your parents' memory. According to the Hall of Public Records, the park has become a haven for muggers and drug dealers of late, and no law-abiding citizen would willingly go there. Now it also seems to be the nighttime haunt of the Batman. Any comment?" He held his pencil poised.

When Bruce Wayne set his martini down and straightened in his chair, Clark noticed just how muscular the man really was. His question seemed to have sparked a hint of anger. Clark didn't like to upset people, even though Lois advised him that keeping an interview subject off guard was the best way to get candid and interesting answers.

Bruce flushed as if embarrassed. "Last night's incident made it plain that I have to make a priority of cleaning the place up. I'm ashamed I allowed the park to become so run-down. Wayne Enterprises keeps me a very busy man, but that's no excuse."

Clark wasn't buying it. "Really? I've heard from other sources that you don't put much time into running the company. Your board of directors handles most of the decisions."

Bruce spread his hands. "Well, to an outsider maybe a gigantic company seems to run itself, but in truth I am responsible for hundreds of vital decisions."

In an effort to capture this vague answer verbatim, Clark began scribbling with his pencil. The lead point snapped off, and he was disconcerted by his momentary loss of restraint. At least he hadn't accidentally pulverized the pencil into sawdust as he clenched his fist. He smoothly pulled out another and continued transcribing Bruce Wayne's answer. He added, "Lex Luthor himself has been quoted as saying that he thinks you should take a closer personal interest in running your company."

"Mr. Luthor has a different managerial style." Bruce gave a casually dismissive wave. "He tends to all the minutiae of his business because he doesn't trust his subordinates. My board of directors, on the other hand, has helped keep Wayne Enterprises strong and lucrative since I was a young boy. They ran the company quite profitably while I was abroad for many years."

Clark skimmed down his list of questions and notes. "If I might change subjects, you've been called Gotham's most eligible bachelor, Mr. Wayne. Suave, rich, and single, you're practically made for media attention, yet in most ways you remain a mystery."

Bruce visibly relaxed, as though glad to be in safer territory. "I'll tell you a secret, Kent. I take my inspiration from Ian Fleming's novels. James Bond is a truly intriguing character—well dressed, cultured, leading a life full of action and romance. Isn't that something we could all aspire to?" He raised his martini glass. "Like this, for instance. A Vesper: three parts gin, one part vodka, half a part Kina Lillet, a slice of lemon peel. Shaken, not stirred." He took another appreciative sip. "Delicious discovery."

Jimmy butted in. "Gosh, you read James Bond novels, Mr. Wayne?"

"Diligently. In fact, I am such an admirer of Mr. Fleming's works that I can't wait for the American editions, so as soon as Jonathan Cape publishes them in Britain, I have a copy flown over here. I find the books highly entertaining, though I must admit that some of the Bond villains are a little outrageous."

Clark pressed, still looking for his lead. "Besides imitating James Bond, what are your other secrets? Do you emulate any other fictional characters? Our readers want to know."

Bruce chuckled. "It's difficult to keep secrets when people like you are watching my every move, Kent. Photographers everywhere, reporters, gossip columnists. I can't go out to dinner without the whole world knowing what I order or how many crumbs I leave on the tablecloth."

Obviously, Wayne didn't completely avoid media attention, though most of the articles about him were surprisingly shallow and devoid of facts. Clark wasn't sure he liked this aloof and hedonistic man. Yes, he had a tragic past and an isolated upbringing, but he also bore the hallmarks of a spoiled rich kid with more money than he could spend. Clark supposed that Bruce Wayne had never really needed to work a day in his life. A week on the Kent farm in Kansas would certainly have taught Bruce Wayne a little humility and a solid work ethic.

The butler stepped through the French doors and raised his eyebrows. "Mr. Wayne, the commissioner of police is ready for your luncheon. Shall I have the Bentley brought around?"

Bruce glanced at the gold Rolex Oyster Perpetual on his wrist. "Sorry, Kent, but I do have another engagement. Alfred, please see these gentlemen out."

"Wait just a moment, please!" Jimmy, who had been listening with rapt attention, held up his camera. "I need some photos."

Striking a casual pose, Bruce stood by the club chair near the fireplace, accustomed to having his photo taken. Jimmy adjusted the focusing bed and pushed the button, and the flashbulb erupted. He quickly unscrewed the hot bulb with his fingertips, wincing, and replaced it with another. "I'd better get a few more shots."

When Jimmy was finished, but before he could pack his camera away, Bruce extended his arm in a magnanimous gesture. "Kent, come take a picture with me. One photo with the two of us. Clark Kent with Bruce Wayne. Mr. Olsen, if you please?"

Clark raised his hands. "That's not necessary, Mr. Wayne."

"I insist." *No argument.*

Embarrassed, Clark moved to stand beside him. The two men were almost equally large shoulder to shoulder. Bruce smiled and stood close. "Make sure you send me a copy of this one, please. I'd like to frame it for my office wall."

Jimmy took one last photo in a blinding flash.

CHAPTER 3
METROPOLIS
THE *DAILY PLANET*

WITH SOARING SKYSCRAPERS, BUSTLING PEOPLE, MUSIC, and the constant noise from traffic and pedestrians, Metropolis was an entirely different world from the American heartland where Clark Kent had grown up.

Surrounded by tall buildings of concrete and glass, the *Daily Planet* offices were alive with energy, ringing telephones, chattering employees, and clacking typewriters. A harried switchboard operator made connections, plugging in wires as if she were performing emergency surgery on an octopus. On the streets below, cars honked their horns; a traffic cop blew his shrill whistle.

Clark knew he wasn't in Kansas anymore.

Since his hearing was incredibly acute, he had trained himself to tune out distractions and focus on his manual typewriter and the sheet of bond rolled into the platen.

On the trip back from Gotham, Clark had compiled his notes and impressions about Bruce Wayne, pulling together enough details to make an interesting story. Once the film was developed, Jimmy's photos of the millionaire and his imposing manor had turned out well, including the embarrassing one of Wayne acting all chummy with Clark. (Jimmy had already sent a glossy print of that one to the Wayne Enterprises headquarters.) Even gruff Perry White had pronounced three of Jimmy's shots "decent enough to use."

At his desk in the bullpen on the thirtieth floor, Clark hunched over the keys, hunting and pecking his way through the first draft of his profile article. He had learned to control his muscles and give the machine relatively delicate taps, careful never to let on how fast he could really type. His first experience writing at the *Planet* had been rather unfortunate; intent on his article, he had pounded away on the keys with such vigor that his fingers had smashed directly through them and shattered the machine. Now he was both a better typist and a better reporter.

But this profile of Bruce Wayne was hardly news. Unquestionably, the man did plenty of good work and contributed large sums to charity. His extravagant lifestyle pegged him as someone who belonged out at night, dressed in a fine tuxedo, with a beautiful woman on his arm. Clark couldn't understand why the man was so devoted to his dreary Gotham City; on the other hand, Clark himself called a dot on the map in Kansas home. No accounting for tastes.

Clark soon finished his first draft, pulled the sheet from his typewriter, and removed a sharpened red pencil from a cup on his desk. He combed over the words, marking corrections. Most reporters wouldn't bother typing a clean copy before showing the piece to the editor, but Clark wanted to make the best impression. Always. It was something Jonathan Kent had expected of him.

Clark glanced around, inserted a sheet of bond into the typewriter, and when no one was looking, retyped the whole article in a blur. With the clean copy in hand, he walked toward Perry White's office. Several pool reporters gathered around the shortwave radio set in the bullpen, always looking for a story. They monitored the various frequencies, hoping to pick up a scoop.

Passing through the bullpen, Clark gave Lois Lane a polite smile, but she grabbed the phone on her desk and dialed a number with an intensity that showed she had a hot lead. He had always found Lois both beautiful and fascinating, with her dark eyes and her long dark hair in a no-nonsense but stylish cut. He'd been shyly watching her ever since he started working at the *Planet*.

She presented an all-business attitude to anyone who doubted her while revealing her generous heart to only a few. Since Clark was still a new kid on the block, Lois had not yet decided whether to consider him a competitor or harmless (apparently the only two options, in her view). One of these days, Clark would ask her out to lunch, but he wanted to let her notice him first.

He held up his article as he knocked on the editor's door. "Here's the profile you asked for, Mr. White—everything you wanted to know about Bruce Wayne."

Perry White chomped on a cigar. His ashtray was continually full of the ugly chewed brown ends, and his office reeked of resinous, pungent smoke. "*I* don't want to know anything about Wayne, but our readers are suckers for this stuff." Perry absently brushed his fingers through the white fringe of hair at his temples. He let his cigar droop and made rough grumbling noises as he scanned the paragraphs. "It won't win a Pulitzer, but it'll sell enough papers to pay for your expense account." He waggled a finger. "You and Olsen better not submit any extravagant meal receipts."

"Why no, Mr. White. We just ate hot dogs."

"You should have let Wayne pay for lunch. He's got enough money to give you prime rib." Perry tossed the copy onto his desk. "If you add a few more quotes, maybe some titillating details, it'll lead off the section-three society page, but it's not a headline. From now on get me headlines. We're a newspaper here, not one of those gossip rags."

"Yes, Mr. White. I'll do one more draft." Clark pushed his glasses up on his nose.

Through the constant chatter and background noise in the bullpen, Clark noted a sudden urgent change among the staff reporters, indrawn breaths, excited conversation. People began to cluster around the shortwave radio, listening intently. Lois hurried to join them.

With an instinct for news, Perry poked his head out of his office. "Great Caesar's ghost, what's going on out there? And why aren't those people at their desks working?"

"I think something's happening, sir," Clark said.

"This is a newspaper, Kent. Go find out what it is."

"It's an SOS call!" snapped Steve Lombard, a reporter who primarily covered sports. "A passenger boat sinking forty miles off the coast, one hundred twenty-three passengers and crew." He looked up from the shortwave set. "It's the *Star City Queen*. One of the engines exploded, blew out the lower hull, and she's going down fast. They've called for the Coast Guard, but they're still miles away."

Clark gave the matter his full attention as he backed out of the editor's office. Perry pushed past him, no longer interested in the Bruce Wayne article. Lois was in the middle of the excitement. Her face showed clear concern as well as frustration. "It'll take rescue ships more than an hour to get out that far."

"Gosh, by that time the ship will be sunk!" Jimmy said.

"Better hope they stocked up on lifeboats," Lombard cracked, as if the situation were a joke.

Lois grabbed her purse and her notepad. "Jimmy, follow me down to the docks. Maybe we can get aboard a Coast Guard ship before they head out."

The young photographer had already snatched up his camera. "Sounds like they've already been dispatched, Miss Lane."

"Then we'll wait for them to come back, gather some information in the meantime, do man-on-the-street interviews. Let's hope this doesn't turn out like the *Hindenburg* or the *Titanic*." In a flurry she was gone.

Clark knew what he had to do. He made an excuse to a distracted Perry, mumbling something about checking his sources on the Wayne profile; then he ducked down the hall. Not a moment to lose—the people aboard the doomed *Star City Queen* must have been terrified, knowing that even the swiftest Coast Guard rescue would be a long time coming.

It was easy to find a secluded closet, where he stopped being Clark Kent and became someone else entirely.

CHAPTER 4
THE *STAR CITY QUEEN*

DRESSED IN RED AND BLUE, HIS CAPE STREAMING BEHIND him, Kal-El shot out of a window on the opposite side of the building. Right fist extended, he soared into the sky, circled the rooftop's golden sphere with the orbiting words "Daily Planet," then raced toward Metropolis harbor.

Every second counted. No time to enjoy the euphoria of flying, the freedom of not having to hide his secret identity. Martha and Jonathan Kent had raised their adopted son to be much more than a passive observer. Seeing a problem, Kal-El had to *do* something about it. It was the core of who he was.

Leaving Metropolis and the shoreline behind, he headed out over the ocean. He streaked past the diligently chugging Coast Guard boats that churned a white wake behind them. Lois had wanted so badly to get aboard one of them to be an eyewitness reporter with the rescue operations; he realized he could have deposited her on the deck right before the surprised faces of the Coast Guard sailors. But he didn't want to put Lois in the middle of a dangerous situation. She had a bad habit of doing that all by herself.

Kal-El had to think of the desperate passengers first, all those people who needed him. More than forty miles from port, the *Star City Queen* was all alone.

Except for him.

With an odd combination of super-hearing and enhanced vision, he was able to push his senses from the short-wavelength band of the X-ray spectrum out to intense infrared, and from there to the very-long-wavelength radiofrequency range, where he picked up the urgent SOS transmission bleating from the *Star City Queen*. He could even hear—ever so faintly above the wind and the stirring waves—the cries of terror from the passengers and crew.

He tightened his fist and flew faster, slicing through the salty air and across the open expanse of deep water until he found the curling plume of smoke from the burning engines. Below, in the middle of blue-green emptiness, he spotted the wallowing *Star City Queen*.

The large boat canted at an unusual angle, its lower decks flooded. Below the waterline at the level of the engine rooms was a large hole made by an explosion, and portions of the hull bent outward from the blast. The frightened passengers had congregated out on deck, clinging to the rails as the ship tilted more and more, taking on water.

He could see no other boats within range, no rescuers who might offer any help. He'd have to do this himself.

The *Queen* was an old ship, repainted and recommissioned, but Kal-El could see that she should have been scuttled long ago. Two of the white-painted lifeboats had already been set out on the water, whereupon they had immediately sprung leaks, and several passengers now splashed in the water, clinging to life preservers.

Kal-El let himself drop down, red cape fluttering as he alighted on the bow, where a gray-faced, bearded captain stared at the disaster with red-rimmed eyes. "You seem to be having a few problems, Captain. I'm here to help."

Superman's arrival startled them all. The passengers began cheering so exuberantly that several people lost their balance on the slanted deck and had to clutch their companions to keep from falling overboard.

The captain straightened, showing a fresh burst of confidence. "Superman, you don't know how glad we are to see you! I doubt we'll be afloat for more than another hour. How close are the Coast Guard vessels?"

"More than an hour away," he said. His voice became stern. "Why don't you have enough lifeboats for all these passengers?"

The bearded man seemed ashamed and embarrassed. "The owners figured it would be a waste of their money to follow the recommendations from the safety inspection, and now these poor passengers will have to pay for it."

Kal-El answered with an angry frown. He looked at the ten people bobbing in the water who had been in the sunken lifeboat; they were clinging to life rings. "I take it you don't have enough life preservers either?"

"We never expected to sink, sir," said the first mate, looking sheepish. He was even younger than Jimmy Olsen.

Kal-El's brows drew together. "No one *expects* accidents. That's why it's so important to take precautions." He dashed off and promptly returned carrying two dripping passengers he had fished out of the water from the wallowing lifeboats. After another four trips, he had retrieved all the sodden people from the waves, but they weren't much safer on the slanted deck of the *Star City Queen*.

The crowd hung on his every word. Straightening his horn-rimmed glasses, a balding businessman said, "Even if you fly us to the nearest port, Superman, you can only rescue two of us at a time."

"Maybe he can carry one of the lifeboats loaded with people," a plump woman suggested; then, lowering her voice, she said, "But the boat could fall apart on the way."

"You're thinking too small," Kal-El said as an idea came to mind, though he wasn't sure he could manage something so extravagant. "Find a way to secure yourselves here on deck, all of you."

"What are you going to do?" the captain called. "Is there a way to save my ship?"

Another thump came from belowdecks, a secondary explosion in the engine room. A cry of surprise and fear rippled through the crowded passengers. The *Star City Queen* lurched.

Kal-El nodded briskly. "Trust me. This will work." He sprang into the air, shot up high over the listing passenger ship, turned, and dove deep beneath the water.

As the cold ocean folded around him, his eyes adjusted to the dimness. Above him, Kal-El saw a stream of air bubbles gushing out of the damaged hull as water continued to fill the *Star City Queen*. The ship gave a stuttering groan like a death rattle.

Swimming upward, gathering speed and concentrating his strength, Kal-El approached the bottom of the large hull. The passenger ship seemed so enormous, and he was just one small man.

But he wasn't just a man. He was *Superman*.

Kal-El spread his hands on either side of the keel, pushing his shoulder against the metal hull. The whole ship shuddered as he heaved with all his strength. He had never lifted anything so large before, had never tried, but he didn't allow doubts to enter his mind. He would lift this sinking ship because he *had* to. There was no other option.

Holding his breath, Kal-El exerted himself, shoving the huge hulk high enough to raise the gaping engine-room hole above the waterline. If nothing else, holding it here would stop the *Star City Queen* from sinking.

But that wasn't good enough.

Kal-El kept straining. Slowly—like a spoon being pulled out of Martha Kent's jar of thick molasses—the passenger ship rose out of the water. He pushed higher and higher, until the vessel itself was airborne. Salt water streamed from its sides in a drenching downpour, falling with a whisper-roar back into the waves.

The passengers on the deck were astonished. Some cheered; some hung on for dear life.

With the ship suspended in the air, rocking slightly as if in heavy seas, Kal-El turned its bow and flew off toward the harbor in Metropolis Bay. The damaged vessel groaned and creaked with the strain, but it held together as he carried it along.

He passed directly over the Coast Guard rescue ships, which still churned across the open water as fast as they could go. Uniformed crewmen stepped out of the wheelhouses and onto the decks, shading their eyes and looking up into the sky at the astounding sight. Releasing the *Star City Queen* with one hand, Kal-El waved at them as he flew past. Surprised and confused, the crews stared, then began to cheer. The Coast Guard captains turned their ships about and began chugging back toward the harbor.

Excited and tense crowds had already gathered on the docks in Metropolis harbor. Smaller boats moved out of the way, clearing a spot in the shallower water as Kal-El came in and gently set the damaged vessel down at an unoccupied slip on the wharf. He surfaced again, dripping wet, and landed on the wooden dock. The elated captain of the *Queen* threw him a thick hawser, and Kal-El pulled the boat closer to the pilings, lashing it firmly in place.

At the edge of the crowd he saw Jimmy Olsen dutifully taking photograph after photograph. Lois pushed to the front, eager to be first to talk with the rescued passengers and crew. Kal-El was glad she would get her big story, and he raised a hand to greet her. Their eyes met, and when Lois returned his wave, he would have sworn that she seemed much more interested in interviewing him than the captain or crew. Though he would have loved to do her a favor, he didn't consider it fair to give her such obvious special treatment. She was an excellent reporter and could do very well by herself. Later on, Clark Kent would be sure to congratulate her.

Emergency crews arrived to help the shaken passengers. All of the rescued people applauded Superman. Many began jabbering about their experience; some of them cried. Kal-El stayed on the docks long enough to receive their thanks, smiling politely but uncomfortable with all the attention. He had done his good deed, and that was all that truly mattered to him. Although it was difficult to show modesty after carrying a giant passenger ship across the sky, the Kents had taught him to be humble.

With a wave—and a last wink at Lois—Kal-El flew into the sky. He had to get back to the *Daily Planet,* change clothes, and return to his desk before anyone noticed he was gone. Clark Kent had an article due.

COMMUNISM IS THE GREATEST MENACE WESTERN CIVILIZA-tion has ever faced," declared Lex Luthor, prominent American industrialist and one of the world's richest men.

Leaning across the rough pine table inside the administration cabin, the brawny Soviet general chuckled. "And you capitalists want to destroy the working class by denying the fair distribution of wealth." He grinned, exposing square teeth.

"I prefer to keep my own wealth, thank you." Luthor leaned back in the distinctly rustic and distinctly uncomfortable chair. "We're both satisfied with our propaganda, General." He was perfectly comfortable speaking in Russian, having become fluent in eleven different languages before he turned his genius to nonlinguistic pursuits.

General Anatoly Ceridov folded his sausagelike fingers together. The two men were alone in the Siberian work camp's headquarters—nothing more than a primitive hut, but it was the best meeting place the Soviet KGB officer could manage.

Ceridov had ice-blue eyes, a squarish face, and rough skin, either from standing too long in the frigid Siberian wind or from using too harsh an aftershave. His reddish hair was carefully slicked back with a perfumed hair tonic. Considering that he lived in one of the most godforsaken areas on earth, his obvious vanity was both peculiar and incomprehensible.

The general wore two obsidian—rather than gold—rank stars on a red epaulet, denoting that his rank carried both great power and great secrecy. No one outside the innermost levels of the KGB knew of Ceridov's projects, or his existence. But Lex Luthor did.

Ceridov extracted a silver cigarette case from a uniform pocket. He snapped the case open and extended it invitingly. "Cigarette, comrade Luthor? American tobacco is quite a luxury."

Luthor gave a withering answer. "I can always get American tobacco."

His cordial gift snubbed, the general snapped the case shut. "Ah, but you cannot get real Russian vodka." He went to a corner of the wood-paneled room, where an empty diesel barrel had been filled with packed snow, in which rested an unmarked bottle of clear, oily liquid. Without bothering to ask, Ceridov poured two glasses and handed one to Luthor. "We have many plans to discuss, and vodka makes even weighty problems seem lighter."

Luthor took a sip and found the taste of the fiery alcohol rough and harsh. He despised wasting valuable time on social niceties, since he knew full well how much his time was worth. (He had, in fact, done the calculations himself.) "I'd prefer to get down to business. Immediately."

He had already taken incredible precautions to keep their meetings secret—a private jet with no filed flight plan, flying below radar so that even the Distant Early Warning–line guard stations did not detect him. Now he took control of the meeting. "General, as the weapons stockpiles increase on both sides, so does *our* power and influence. The USA and the Soviet Union must remain equally matched so that you and I can continue to build our respective arsenals. A cold war thrives on tension."

Ceridov drained his glass. "The very best kind of war: no shooting, but a great deal of money being spent on both sides."

Only Luthor understood the delicate balance he had to achieve. He was not just an important businessman, not just a wealthy man, he was also a *smart* man who played chess on a global scale. He owned a sprawling mansion in the swanky Lake District north of Metropolis and more secondary homes than he could remember. He could have a gorgeous woman on his arm whenever he pleased. He could buy the finest things anyone might imagine.

But such triumphs and successes had begun to bore him. Instead, Lex Luthor craved things less tangible: power, obedience, and respect. Once he set his mind on those goals, he treated them like any other business proposition. He created a perceived need, then set out to become the only man who could fill it.

Ceridov had a similar aim in the Soviet Union. While the pair might have seemed to be rivals, their shared focus made them convenient allies. Each man worked behind the scenes in his own hemisphere. LuthorCorp and its military-industrial subsidiaries reaped profits hand over fist, and the black-star KGB general became extraordinarily influential in the Communist Party.

Luthor had recently completed the construction of a new base on an island in the Caribbean, for which he had used mostly expendable workers—much like the Soviet gulag slaves here— to do the hazardous parts of the job, particularly in constructing the small power reactor on the island. Many of the workers, especially the weak and less valuable females whom he had placed in the most hazardous activities, had succumbed to lethal radiation exposure . . . which had the added benefit, in Luthor's view, of ensuring that they could not reveal the existence or location of the base. Yes, indeed, chess on a global scale.

"Unfortunately, comrade Luthor, you Americans have tipped the balance of power by developing a super-weapon that we cannot match. I have read reports of your 'Superman' in Metropolis. They say he can leap tall buildings with a single bound, that he moves faster than a speeding bullet."

Luthor tried to cloak his annoyance with a mocking laugh. "You of all people should know not to believe propaganda! According to the newspapers, he also claims to be an alien. Personally, I'm not convinced."

"But I have seen the photographs and read the interview he gave to Miss Lois Lane. Who is this man? How does he get his powers?" Ceridov's ice-blue eyes narrowed. "More important, how will you keep him under your control? He is a loose cannon, and a powerful one at that."

"Don't worry about some costumed man showing off abilities that belong in a circus act. He's a freak of nature."

The general brooded in silence for a long moment. "If I learn you are lying to me, that he is a product of your own secret eugenics program . . ."

"Like the Soviet eugenics program?" Luthor smirked wryly. "I know you've been trying to breed your own superman for years."

Ceridov seemed embarrassed by this. "Your program appears to have been more successful than ours." He poured himself a second glass, then offered the bottle to Luthor, who had taken only one sip. "More vodka? It will keep you warm."

Luthor rubbed his hands together briskly. Although Ceridov had offered him a fur parka as soon as his private jet had landed, Luthor still wore his business suit. "Why not just heat this cabin instead?" He knew that a modern scaled-down nuclear reactor provided ample power for the whole gulag and the industrial operations in the adjacent quarry. "We're in the middle of one of the largest untouched primeval forests in the world—can't you spare a few sticks of firewood?" He indicated the old-fashioned potbellied stove that sat in the corner.

"It will do no good. The wood from these forests around the meteor crater is . . . tainted, somehow. The fire burns *cold*."

Luthor scoffed. "Nonsense."

Ceridov opened the stove, and Luthor noted that while a fire was blazing inside, it generated no warmth. The general added a log from the firewood stack against the wall and shut the stove again. He didn't even need gloves to touch the metal. "If only I had the manpower to investigate the mystery. Fortunately, our beloved premier is bound to arrest more Soviet scientists soon, charge them with crimes against the state, and sentence them here to my gulag. Then, perhaps, I will have the luxury of conducting research."

Luthor had noticed an odd smell in the headquarters cabin— wood smoke with a spoiled, vinegary undertone. "The wall paneling? And this table? Made from the same local trees?"

The wood grain on the polished table, as well as the tongue-and-groove paneling that covered the wall, had strange, hypnotic swirls that drew Luthor's attention. The patterns were quite un-settling. Though he was not a superstitious man, Luthor thought he saw hints of ghostly faces in the whorls, loops, and lines that stained the wood—screaming faces. He shook his head, sure it was some trick of Ceridov's.

"Our workers cut down the trees, chop the firewood, and use the lumber. Sometimes it is difficult. Saw blades shatter. Trees fall and crush woodcutters. Our teams have a very high fatality rate."

Ceridov drained his vodka and shrugged. "It is fortunate that we have an inexhaustible supply of workers."

"Let me see these workers and your quarry." Impatient, Luthor looked at the rectangular face of his wristwatch, a white-gold Cartier Tank. "I've flown halfway around the world not to see *you*, General, but to observe the operations here. We've put a great deal of effort into this boondoggle, and I have yet to be convinced of its potential."

"Then come look at our excavations of the meteor impact site." Ceridov pulled on his heavy jacket. He opened a desk drawer and withdrew a Russian *ushanka*, the familiar fur hat, which he proudly placed on Luthor's bald head. "My gift to you. This will keep your brain warm."

"My thoughts keep my brain warm."

Ceridov opened the wooden door to the watery sunshine of a late Siberian spring. "The crater is very large. You will be impressed."

CHAPTER 6
THE *DAILY PLANET*

WITHOUT KNOCKING, LOIS MARCHED INTO PERRY WHITE'S office and dropped a newspaper on his desk, folded open to section 3 and Jimmy Olsen's photo of Bruce Wayne. "This isn't *news*, Chief. It's entertainment. What's so interesting about a playboy who flaunts his wealth and then tries to soothe his conscience by doing charity work? You shouldn't have sent Clark to do a puff piece."

"Wasn't meant to be a puff piece." Chomping on his cigar, Perry picked up the newspaper and perused the article again.

Lois pushed the paper back down so he had to give her his full attention. "I've got a better story to pitch. Forget Bruce Wayne—*Lex Luthor* is a different breed entirely. I want to do a profile on Metropolis's own rich industrialist, and you can bet your ass my story won't read like something written by the LuthorCorp public relations department."

Perry raised his bushy eyebrows. "Luthor doesn't give feature interviews. He likes his privacy too much. We've tried dozens of times."

"*Superman* doesn't give interviews either, and I managed to pull *that* off."

"Good point." Perry fiddled with his cigar, pondering. "You just have a bee in your bonnet because Luthor invited Steve Lombard to cover that flamethrower demonstration last month instead of you." He actually chuckled, and a hot flush came to her cheeks.

Lois had submitted requests to LuthorCorp to attend the big-ticket military demonstration, but Luthor had turned her down flat. "Lombard is a *sports* reporter. What credentials does he have to cover such an important story?"

"Lombard is also a man, and you're not."

Lois harrumphed, knowing that Perry had put his finger on the reason, though she hated to admit it. She knew full well the difficulties a female journalist faced every day. "Then he might as well have asked for Kent." She tried to summon scorn into her voice, but Clark was a decent reporter and so endearing with his small-town innocence that she couldn't think ill of him.

Lois leaned over the desk. "I have it on good authority that there's been a recent and very disturbing shakeup among the employees of LuthorCorp. Lex Luthor has been rapidly, but very quietly, getting rid of dozens of older men and *all* the women on his workforce, even though they've been a vital part of his military production lines for years. Tomorrow I'm meeting with a confidential source who'll tell me what Luthor's really doing in his weapons factories. My guess is he's got a whole boneyard of skeletons in his closet." She smiled at him. "By now you should know to let me follow my instincts, Chief. How many other reporters have gotten an interview with the Man of Steel?"

Perry sighed and leaned back in his creaking desk chair. "Go ahead, Lois. See if you can dig up any dirt on Luthor. Once you make up your mind, no force in the world can stop you—not even Superman. But be careful!"

She agreed quickly, but after hearing him give her the go-ahead, she wasn't really listening.

BACK AT HER DESK, LOIS SMILED TO HERSELF AS SHE REMEMBERED how she had gotten her big scoop on Superman.

Sure, Clark Kent had been the one to break the story about the strange flying man clad in blue and red. Clark, a country bumpkin fresh off the bus from Nowheresville, Kansas, had arrived at the *Daily Planet* offices when Lois, like every other reporter in town, was scrambling to get the story. In a single day, the mysterious hero had saved an airplane from crashing, foiled a robbery at an art museum, and saved five children and a puppy—never forget the puppy!—from a burning tenement. But nobody knew who he was or where he'd come from.

And Clark had waltzed in with a finished report, a front-page article that gave the amazing details of all the hero's exploits. He had meekly asked for a job at the paper, and Perry gave it to him on the spot. Clark Kent—with his self-effacing sense of humor, his chivalry, and his bumbling kindness—had somehow scooped Lois Lane.

While Clark's article introduced Metropolis to the mystery, Lois had given them the *man*. She had been the first to speak with him, had pried out answers to the most intriguing questions. . . .

On that terrifying, wonderful day, Lois had been hot on the trail of jewel thieves who'd stolen the famed traveling exhibition of exquisite Buccellati jewel-encrusted cups from the Siegel Museum of Precious Gems and Geological Oddities. The thieves had peppered the air with a barrage of bullets while innocent bystanders dove for shelter.

Lois had joined the chase, racing along in her 1951 white Ford convertible. The police were desperate to catch the robbers, the thieves were desperate to get away, and Lois was desperate for her story. She meant to scoop the whole world with an up-close-and-personal eyewitness account. She gunned the engine, swerved to pass a slow-moving car, and closed the distance to the fleeing robbers. She yanked her head to one side when a bullet drilled a spiderweb crack through her windshield and punched a hole into her car's beautiful red upholstery. She didn't slow down.

The thieves reached the Twelfth Street Bridge, a monstrosity that sprawled over the sluggish green-brown Metropolis River. On the other side, once the robbers got into the lower-end slums, a rats' nest of alleys clogged with grocers' carts and festooned with laundry-draped clotheslines, they would be able to elude pursuit. On the span of the bridge, the jewel thieves shot at the lead police car, striking its front tires. The car spun out, and the closely following squad cars swerved and dodged; one cop car scraped the guardrail, sending sparks flying.

Lois was driving too fast, intent on the chase. She slammed on the brakes to keep from plowing into the halted police cars, laying a smear of black rubber on the metal gridwork of the bridge. Her bumper smashed through the guardrail, and the shrieking metal slowed her momentum. But not enough.

Her convertible pushed through, its front wheels rolling into space, and the undercarriage caught on the edge. Lois held her breath as the snappy convertible teetered slowly, tipping her inexorably toward the river. Lois let go of the wheel and scrambled into the back seat, clawing her way toward the trunk in an attempt to keep the car balanced for just a few more seconds.

The other cops jumped out of their vehicles and rushed to help, but Lois knew they'd never get to her in time. She absolutely hated being the damsel in distress! The thieves, laughing and shooting at random in celebration, raced over the bridge and escaped into the maze of the slums.

Metal groaned as the convertible pitched forward, its heavy V8 engine dragging the front down and off the edge of the bridge. Lois scrambled from the back seat, seized the folded canvas of the convertible top, and tried to pull herself onto the trunk. So close! Two policemen had almost reached her, hands outstretched, eyes wide as saucers.

The car dropped off the bridge.

Lois found herself falling, then screaming, more in disbelief than panic. She didn't have time to panic. She was plummeting toward the river, and when she hit from this height, the sluggish water might as well be cement.

Suddenly she was in the arms of a man who simply scooped her out of the air, a red-caped stranger who could *fly*! Her stomach lurched and so did her heart; she didn't seem to weigh anything at all.

Below, her car plunged into the river with a ferocious explosion of spray, but Lois was being gently carried back up to the bridge. The air seemed remarkably still, and her world had focused to a tiny space, just her and this amazing man who was simply *there* exactly when she needed him.

Lois's heart pounded, and she looked up into the face of this hero, realizing that she was the first person ever to see him clearly, since all the earlier photos had been blurry. He was classically handsome, square jawed, with beautiful blue eyes and dark hair with a sassy-looking curl that hung over his forehead. His smile was warm and generous. He could have been anybody, yet he exuded a kind of strange familiarity.

He flew up toward the bridge, where the gathered policemen watched in slack-jawed wonder. "Please watch your driving more carefully from now on, all right, Miss Lane?" the flying man said.

"You . . . you know my name?" She struggled not to stutter, trying to remember how to be a real journalist, instead of behaving like a woman who had just survived a terrifying brush with death.

"I've read some of your articles. You're a good reporter."

She laughed despite her awe, unable to grasp this surreal conversation. "So the great costumed hero of Metropolis reads the *Daily Planet*?"

His face displayed a slight frown as he returned her to the edge of the bridge, setting her on her feet. "That wasn't a product endorsement."

Her arms had automatically looped around his neck for a better grip, but once she touched down on the solidity of the bridge, she could barely stand. Nevertheless, her journalistic instincts kicked in, and she blurted before she lost her chance, "Now that you've rescued me, I'd like an interview, whoever you are." Her tone suggested that *he* owed *her*.

"I don't speak to reporters, Miss Lane. That would be unfair to your competition."

"It's unfair to the people of Metropolis! You seem to be fighting for the forces of good, but how can we know? If you keep secrets, people will suspect that you have some sinister purpose."

That made him pause, even though he seemed anxious to go after the jewel thieves. "You make a fair point. Maybe the people of Metropolis do deserve a few answers. Shall we say eight o'clock tonight, at your apartment?"

"You know where I live?" Lois was taken aback in spite of her triumph.

He responded with a mysterious smile. "Of course." Then he flew off into the sky, dwindling to a speck above the skyscrapers, in pursuit of the thieves. Naturally, he rounded them up in due course, dropping the men like a weekly trash collection at the precinct station, but by then the jewel heist had become a much less important part of the story for Lois.

If possible, that evening had been even more surreal.

As the appointed hour approached, Lois grew more and more nervous in spite of herself. She spent the entire afternoon deciding what to wear, though she didn't normally waste valuable time making herself gorgeous to impress a man (even though this particular one *had* saved her life). Was he expecting to have dinner with her? Should she light candles, open a bottle of wine or champagne? Did he even drink wine or champagne? Who could know the answer to that? *She* would . . . and in just a short time. She watched the door, watched the clock.

"I'm here, Miss Lane." He stood on her open balcony, startling her. Of course—a man like him wouldn't use the front door!

She regained her composure, surprised that her voice sounded so normal. "Do you often peep in on single women like myself?"

"That wouldn't be proper."

She smiled. "Exactly what I expected you to say." She indicated the davenport. He declined both wine and champagne (no surprise) and got right down to business. He remained standing in her living room, his red cape moving in the slight breeze from the open balcony door. Lois urged him, "Please have a seat."

Moving with a flash of endearing awkwardness, as if he didn't know how to be casual, he walked to the davenport, adjusted his cape, and sat down. Lois took a seat on the cushion next to him, as close as she dared, and picked up her notepad and pencil, crossing one shapely leg over the other. She was pleased to see from a slight widening of his blue eyes that he noticed.

She cleared her throat, pretending to be all business. "First things first. What do we call you?"

Lois thought it was a straightforward question, but his brow furrowed. "You mean like a stage name? I haven't really thought about it."

"You have many amazing abilities, and you certainly seem like a real hero. Someone super . . . *Superman*! I like that, unless you'd prefer something else?"

"No, I like it, too, Miss Lane." She was surprised at how pleased his approval made her feel, and she moved a little closer to him, trying to be nonchalant. He didn't notice . . . or maybe he did.

"What's the significance of the symbol on your chest and cape? Is that the letter *s*?"

He touched his chest. "It's a symbol with its own meanings. But yes, it could be seen as the letter *s*."

She sighed, trying to disarm him with charm. "Is this how it's going to be, then? Evasive answers to direct questions?"

His eyes sparkled. "It depends on the questions."

"What's your telephone number?"

"It's unlisted."

"I figured as much." As Lois scribbled a note to herself, she continued her questioning. "One other thing. Why do you wear your red trunks on the outside of your pants? Isn't that a little backward?" Her lips quirked in a smile.

"Oh, now, Miss Lane," he said, blushing. "I thought this would be a serious interview."

"Just trying to break the ice. All right, I'll be serious. Tell me more about these powers of yours. What, exactly, *can* you do?"

Superman explained that he could fly (obviously), that he had super-strength, that he possessed certain other powers, many of which were just emerging. He seemed a bit mystified about them himself.

Lois was fascinated, even forgetting to take notes. "And how did you come by these powers? A radiation accident? A scientific experiment? Vitamins?"

He laced his fingers together, holding his hands in his lap as if the answer was a difficult one for him. "No, you see, I . . . I don't exactly come from Earth. I'm from another planet, a place called Krypton."

Lois stared at him incredulously. "An *alien,* you mean?"

"Do I look like an alien?"

Lois recalled the rubber monsters she'd seen in the movies. If he was telling the truth, she had her hands on the story of the century. The hard part would be deciding which headline to use. No, she thought, the hard part would be convincing people of his claims. "Do you realize how preposterous this is going to sound to my readers?"

"Preposterous?" Superman crossed his muscular arms. "You mean like a man who can fly? A man with heat rays that lance out of his eyes or X-ray vision?" She couldn't argue with that.

"X-ray vision? Does that mean you could see right through my dress if you wanted to?" The question had sounded coy and demure in her mind, but when she said it aloud, it sounded stupid. She blushed furiously, kicking herself for letting her guard down.

"Again, Miss Lane, that would be an improper use of my powers. I was raised better than that."

Of course you were. "Who raised you? Where do you come from?"

"I had good parents, a wholesome childhood, in an average but beautiful town, the real heartland of America."

"Can you be more specific?"

"It's better if I'm not. I have to keep *some* of my secrets, Miss Lane." He just gave her a mysterious smile. "And now I think I should be going. It's a big city. Somebody always needs rescuing." He had such sincerity in his voice that she didn't doubt him for a minute.

He had already started for the balcony by the time she jumped to her feet in alarm. "Wait—how do I get in touch with you again?"

"I'll know when you need me, don't worry." Waving good-bye from the edge of the balcony as Lois followed him out into the open night air, he added cryptically, "And say hello to Clark Kent for me. I'm sure he'd love to hear your advice as a reporter."

"I—wait . . . Clark?" She had struggled to think of a compelling last line, something that would make him remember her, something that would make Lois Lane sound like a person he'd want to know better. She certainly felt giddy and smitten—and embarrassed by it!—but he had rescued her from death, holding her firmly in his muscular arms, so she had good reason to have intense feelings about him.

But what did Clark Kent have to do with anything?

"Promise me I'll see you again!" she called.

"That's a promise," he said with a smile, and then added teasingly, "unless you stop getting yourself in trouble."

"I won't!" She waved as he silently sprang from the balcony. Instead of falling, he shot up into the air, waved good-bye, and vanished into the night.

Lois stared after him, reeling, swept off her feet twice in one day.

Afterward, it had taken an unheard-of *three hours* for her to compile her notes and draft a story. The story of the century: "Superman: A New Hero for Metropolis."

Lois Lane had always been a reporter to watch; after publication of the Superman article, she was the reporter every other newspaper envied. Suddenly every paper wanted to feature Superman, but he never stopped to talk with reporters after his heroic deeds. Lois hoped she hadn't disappointed Superman with her article, but she hadn't had the opportunity to talk with him again (though she did make a habit of leaving her patio doors open in the evening, just in case he decided to drop by).

In retrospect, she should have won the Pulitzer for that article, but mocking skeptics had laughed at her "absurd and undocumented claims" that Superman was a "strange visitor" from a planet called Krypton.

Now, as she thought about it, Lois remembered Perry's cautions about following up the Lex Luthor exposé. The notoriety she had gained from her Superman interview suddenly put her in a different league, made her work even harder as a reporter, though it hadn't yet earned her a raise.

This story would be different. Superman was clearly a hero, but Luthor came from a different mold entirely—she would have to approach her story with a certain amount of healthy trepidation. She could do it, though. After all, how could a story about Lex Luthor be any more problematic than getting the scoop on the greatest hero in the world?

CHAPTER 7
SIBERIA
ARIGUSKA GULAG

IN THE WAN SIBERIAN DAYLIGHT, THE STAIR-STEP LEDGES OF the quarry excavation emphasized the crater made by the Ariguska meteor strike in 1938. Joseph Stalin had kept the Soviet Union under such a tight cloak of secrecy that very few Westerners knew about the devastating impact.

Lex Luthor was one of those few.

At around the same period, two decades ago, several large meteors had peppered Earth and astronomers were baffled as to what had caused the sudden spate of high-velocity space rubble. Here at Ariguska, where the Soviets had established a large gulag for political prisoners, General Ceridov had found fascinating and unusual mineral fragments that could only be attributed to the massive meteorite itself.

When the Ariguska object had hit, the dense pine forests had been flattened outward for miles, like ripples in a pond when a rock is thrown into it. In the two decades since, the regrowth had come in stunted and twisted, as though the soil itself was tainted. Fish caught in the forest lakes were often horrifically mutated and always poisonous. Crops did not grow. Even the small garden plots planted outside the gulag fences yielded only inedible horrors.

The impacting meteorite had tunneled deep and shattered, spraying fragments of itself throughout the strata. Now, in an ever-expanding pit, the workers quarried out the dirt and discarded the bulk of the useless rock, sand, and soil, searching for the core meteorite mass.

Luthor stared at the quarry operations, at the hundreds of sweating workers who were watched over by guards in olive-green woolen uniforms. Each guard carried a workhorse Kalashnikov AK-47 assault rifle. The sullen prisoners toiled with picks and shovels, filling rusty metal carts. As the diggers worked their way toward the main mass, they left a wide corkscrewing ramp. Debris was hauled away and dumped in ugly piles of naked rock in the tainted forest.

"Impressive, is it not, comrade Luthor?" Ceridov made an expansive gesture.

"This operation has been under way for . . ." Luthor calculated. "A year?"

"Seventeen months. And in that time we have excavated a substantial amount of meteor mineral." They walked to the edge of the open pit, and Luthor looked down at the pathetic wretches laboring in it.

"How long do the slaves last?" Luthor asked.

"They work until they die, then are replaced by others who also work until they die. We have a large enough pool of replacements. Look at how much they have dug out!"

"Such a large open quarry is a bit obvious," Luthor warned. "Some high-flying spy plane could easily photograph it."

"They will see nothing more than a large quarry. However, our workers are about to begin constructing a dome to cover the bottom of the quarry when we expose the main meteorite mass."

Luthor observed a commotion among the scrawny captives. Guards rushed to a man holding a jagged green lump that gave off a faint intrinsic glow.

Ceridov signaled the guard. Red-faced from both excitement and exposure to the cold air, the man came puffing up and saluted smartly to the general as he extended a glowing emerald fragment about the size of a baseball.

Ceridov held it in his hands. "Give that worker an extra cup of water tonight as a reward." He offered the fragment to Luthor, who did not move to take it.

"That glow . . . it could be a form of radiation."

"You are a cautious man." As if to show his bravery, Ceridov squeezed the lump, holding it up. "Prolonged direct exposure to the meteorite emanations *does* have unpleasant effects on human physiology." He shrugged. "Small exposures, though, are harmless . . . to the best of our knowledge."

"The best of your knowledge!" Luthor accepted the meteor fragment with lingering reluctance and prodded the rock suspiciously. "What sort of physiological effects?"

Ceridov guided Luthor away from the quarry edge to a low bunker with extremely thick concrete walls, not far from the steaming coolant tower and containment dome for the camp's power reactor. The bunker's windows were reinforced with bars, its doors covered with two-inch-thick metal sheeting.

"A fallout shelter?" Luthor asked. It looked as if it could withstand an A-bomb blast.

"It is not to protect those inside, but to *contain* them. Listen. They are restless today."

Luthor could hear a roaring, thudding sound like a blacksmith hammering an anvil. But it wasn't a blacksmith. Something pounded on the metal doors while growling loudly enough to be heard through the thick concrete walls.

The KGB general explained, "When certain workers are heavily exposed, they *change*. Their bodies grow. They become much less human. They have extraordinary strength. Our geneticists are investigating the effects for our eugenics program. Some of the best Soviet minds have come to study them. You Americans have your Superman, comrade—the Soviet Union needs its own."

Luthor could hear clear evidence of amazing strength just by listening to the damage the former workers were doing to the reinforced bunker. His mind was racing with ideas about how to exploit the properties of the odd green meteorite: as a power source, a medical treatment, a means to transform workers into a superpowerful force of his own. He would have his LuthorCorp labs run a full analysis on the specimen. "And?"

Ceridov seemed embarrassed. "Unfortunately, these mutants burn up a lifetime of strength within only a week or two, and then they die." He added, as if it was an afterthought, "Our studies remain incomplete, since the beasts have also killed four of our best researchers."

"And what happens to the bodies after the mutants die?"

"If we can remove the cadavers before the others tear them to shreds—not a trivial operation, I assure you—the specimens are dissected."

"I would like to see one. Just how . . . extreme are the physical alterations?"

"Quite extreme." General Ceridov took him to a nearby building made of concrete blocks, and he shoved aside a metal door. The interior was dank and full of shadows, kept at a very cold temperature. Wisps of steam curled around two large misshapen bodies lying on slabs, waiting to be autopsied.

Luthor stared. *Extreme indeed.* They no longer looked human at all. Seeing the horrific changes, he looked uneasily at the glowing green rock in his hand. "I would like a lead-lined box to contain this, please, for my journey home."

CHAPTER 8
GOTHAM CITY

THE HEADQUARTERS OF THE LARGE CORPORATION WAS A shining steel tower, a gleaming monument in the heart of Gotham City. Wayne Tower's modern architectural design stood out amid the downtown's lesser, yet still imposing, Gothic monstrosities.

On Tuesdays, Bruce attended the main board of directors meeting in the glass-enclosed boardroom. Wayne Enterprises was so widespread, with so many divisions, investments, interests, and facilities, that no single discussion could cover all aspects. But once a week the ten directors were supposed to discuss the most important issues that concerned the company as a whole. Although the administrators expected little from him, Bruce insisted on sitting in nevertheless. Because he owned the controlling share of the company, they had to tolerate his presence.

Bruce took care to pretend a certain lack of interest at each meeting. Outside of these Tuesday gatherings, though, he watched the men far more closely than they realized. They would have been very surprised to learn how much he already knew about them.

"On today's agenda, Mr. Wayne," began Scott Thomson, vice

president of administration and marketing, "is the redesign of the Wayne Enterprises logo. Our corporate logo is the face we show to the world. It symbolizes all we do, and we have received input from all the division heads. But now we very much need your input." With his smooth, deep voice, he made the matter sound exceptionally important, to mollify Bruce.

Sitting at the head of the long conference room table, Bruce could think of many matters that were more vital, but he simply smiled. "Show me the designs. I assume the marketing department has narrowed the field down to the best?"

"Of course, Mr. Wayne," said Larry Buchheim, vice president of the propulsion systems division, with a nod. Buchheim rarely had good news to report, always insisting that he needed a budget increase (though whenever Bruce secretly inspected the ledgers he found surplus funding).

Thomson stepped over to four easels at the far end of the room, which his underlings in marketing had prepared. As though he had rehearsed it for a scene, he unveiled the potential logos one at a time.

The first design was a complicated affair with ornate and virtually unreadable letters that spelled out the entire phrase "Wayne Enterprises—Hope for Gotham City and the World." The next was a confusing amalgam of a missile, a medical caduceus, a sheaf of wheat, a lightning bolt, and a clockwork gear—which apparently symbolized the diversity of Wayne Enterprises. The other two designs were equally unimpressive and even less memorable.

Bruce frowned. "Do we want people to stare in confusion whenever they pick up one of our products? Our company logo should be an *icon,* something streamlined and memorable that people instantly associate with Wayne Enterprises. The choices you've given me are all muddled."

"Simple, you say?" scoffed Paul Henning, the VP of manufacturing. "Would you prefer a big W perhaps?"

Bruce shook his head. Though this was purportedly the most prominent item on the agenda, he knew they had most likely concocted it only for the purpose of making him feel "useful" during his weekly appearance.

For the last several years, he had cultivated his public persona as a dashing playboy, the rich heir who loved cocktail parties, beautiful women, and the nightlife. Clark Kent's recent profile in the *Daily Planet* had bolstered that perception. Bruce flaunted his riches, all the while being generous to the point of childlike innocence. Unfortunately, though the disguise successfully kept people from thinking of Bruce Wayne and Batman in the same sentence, it also gave him an air of incompetence. Though he was chairman of the board and the sole heir to his parents' vast fortune, the ten directors had taken it upon themselves to "shelter" him from the day-to-day business.

At the end of each fiscal year, the corporate balance sheet was healthy, and thanks to the advent of the Cold War, many subsidiaries of Wayne Enterprises had landed government contracts to provide urgently needed military supplies, services, armor, and vehicles. Only LuthorCorp had a greater number of direct contracts with the U.S. military.

Paying little attention to the new logo designs, Bruce gazed around the table at these men. After the death of Thomas Wayne, the original set of directors had been excellent regents to watch over the company. Bruce's father had been a well-known surgeon as well as an innovator and inventor. He had created a new type of iron lung that saved the lives of tens of thousands. The money from those patents had gone directly back into medical research.

Vivid in Bruce's memory was the time when the head of one

of Gotham City's well-known crime families had been shot and severely wounded. Thugs in business suits had brought the bleeding man to Wayne Manor, pounding on the door late one night and pushing their way in when the door was answered. They didn't want to be seen at a hospital.

Understanding the wounded man's need, Thomas Wayne did not hesitate to operate, no matter who he was. Instead of viewing the men as criminals, instead of noticing the threatening bulge of handguns beneath the blood-smeared business suits, Thomas saw only an injured human being. He worked using the expensive dining room table as an operating surface and succeeded in saving the crime boss. He urged the thugs to take the man to a hospital for further treatment, but they had carried their boss away into the night with only grunts of thanks.

Some months later, an anonymous two-million-dollar donation had been made to the Wayne Foundation. Bruce remembered how upset his father had been, claiming the money was dirty, since he knew exactly who the donor had been. But as he wrestled with his conscience, Thomas had also realized how much good he could do with the untraceable money. Therefore, he built a new cancer wing at Gotham General Hospital. His father found it ironic and gratifying to think of how many lives the crime family was inadvertently saving. Once, when he didn't know Bruce was listening, Thomas had told his wife, "I don't like using money from such people, Martha, but I suppose it's better for their souls than simply lighting a candle in church."

As a skilled surgeon, Bruce's father had an acute awareness of how capricious death could be. He had loved his son and his wife ferociously, and he had made certain his family was well cared for. He'd left very detailed instructions in his will, and his ironclad testaments and codicils had directed Wayne Enterprises for years.

The original handpicked board of directors had been close friends of his father, men who owed their lives to Thomas Wayne in one way or another. Newly orphaned and alone, young Bruce had gone off to boarding school for years, and those directors had carefully and honorably watched the company.

But Bruce had been gone for a long time, wrestling with his own demons, learning how to become more than just a man, building his skills, his mind, and his body—paying little attention to his fortune. More than twenty years had passed. Directors, and whole departments, had changed dramatically. These men now were two or three times removed from the ones Thomas Wayne had hired. The directors thought more about profit than about the great dreams of a skilled surgeon gunned down in an alley long before his time.

Several years ago, Bruce had returned to Wayne Manor to dust off the cobwebs, pull the sheets from the furniture, and turn the long-empty house into a glorious mansion once again. But he'd still needed time to prepare himself for his real work—to develop his armor, his weapons, his entire plan.

Obsession was not enough. With Wayne Enterprises, he had resources as well. Although he spent his nights protecting the innocents of Gotham City, becoming a caped and masked avenger—like Zorro in that last wonderful movie, at a time when Bruce had been so young and innocent—he also had to protect his parents' legacy.

While the board members assumed they had the time and freedom to run the company as they wished, Bruce was watching them. Always watching. This was the only thing he could do for his parents now. Wayne Enterprises was *his,* and the directors would be reminded of that—when the time was right.

The oldest of the directors, a thin, quiet, and extremely intelligent man named Richard Drayling, sat silent during the meeting. Come to think of it, the man had said nothing the previous Tuesday either. Bruce pretended to ignore him but quickly picked up on Drayling's mood of simmering anger and discomfort. He occasionally cast a sharp glance at Bruce, his disappointment palpable. A great battle seemed to be going on in his conscience.

Although Drayling, the director of materials science, had worked with Thomas Wayne and respected him greatly, it was abundantly clear that he did not approve of Bruce's aloof playboy behavior. It was also clear that Drayling had no great love for the other board members.

Bruce interrupted a droning report from the director of chemistry applications. "Mr. Drayling, I sense that you have something to say."

Drayling sat up stiffly, looked at Bruce, swept his gaze slowly over his fellow directors, and sighed. "Very perceptive, Mr. Wayne. Yes, I do." He reached inside his suit jacket, paused for just a moment with eyes closed, as if gathering his strength, then withdrew an envelope. He set it on the table in front of him.

"This is my letter of resignation from the board of directors of Wayne Enterprises." He stood as if carrying a great weight on his shoulders. "This is no longer a company I can believe in. It is better if I'm not a part of it, and it's time for me to retire."

Bruce was surprised by the brash move. Despite his careful study of the actions of the board members, he had not expected Drayling to leave. Something else was at the root of it. "No further explanations?"

"Not at this time. As you'll note in the letter, my resignation is effective immediately. I'll be going now."

The remaining directors expressed their surprise and disappointment, but not too convincingly. The tenor of the overlapping conversations sounded more like relief and farewell rather than any attempt to persuade Drayling to change his mind. The old man didn't seem to hear any of it as he turned and left the meeting room with pride and dignity.

Disturbed, Bruce pocketed Drayling's letter of resignation. He would read it in detail later. Right now, he studied the reactions of the other board members, and he learned from them.

"We should get back to business," Henning said into the awkward silence, glancing down at the agenda, as if resignations were a weekly occurrence.

"The dinosaurs are finally extinct," someone muttered with a snicker; Bruce couldn't tell who had spoken.

"We should get him a retirement gift," added Frank Miles, one of the research VPs, to a chorus of muttered approval.

"We have prepared the annual report for you, Mr. Wayne," said Terrence McDonnell, the chief financial officer, with a smile. He proudly handed over a glossy report that boasted impressive color photographs and a specially commissioned painting on the cover: a handsome Bruce Wayne standing in front of the monolithic Wayne Tower. The design and printing of this one report had probably cost enough to feed Gotham's poor for almost a year.

He remembered to remain aloof, despite his troubled thoughts. "Thank you. I'll glance at it when I get a chance."

"We're very pleased you've decided to devote your energies to charity work," said Shawn Norlander, VP of pharmaceuticals and medical applications. "Not only does it put the best public face on all our activities, it's also closely in line with what your father would have wanted."

Norlander sounded sincere, but Bruce knew that most of the directors looked upon his charity work, extravagant society functions, and huge donations as a ball and chain, despite the tax deductions—unnecessary expenditures that could have been better used to build new factories, make more extensive investments, or provide bonuses to management. Nevertheless, the directors let Bruce manage his charities without complaint, as if they were throwing him a bone.

Bruce slipped the flashy report into his briefcase. "I have to cut this short today, gentlemen. I'm holding an important charity gala at the manor tonight with quite a few celebrities. We expect to raise hundreds of thousands of dollars for polio research, and Eleanor Roosevelt has promised to come. Marilyn Monroe and Arthur Miller may even be there."

"Interesting. I'll try to make it," Buchheim said, but Bruce knew the directors usually made excuses.

"I'll expect to see some of you there," Bruce added with an undertone of warning, which he then turned to a flippant suggestion. "Draw straws if you have to."

"You know you have our full support for your humanitarian activities," Thomson said in an irritatingly sycophantic tone, trying to mollify him. "In any case, you are the best spokesman for the company, Mr. Wayne."

"I suppose I am," Bruce answered, lifting his chin. "And it's quite a full-time job. Please be sure to show me a list of candidates for Mr. Drayling's replacement. Thank you again for the report, and"—he gestured gravely toward the easels—"let's try a little harder on those logos for next week."

AS THE CHAUFFEUR DROVE HIM HOME FROM WAYNE TOWER, Bruce went over the flashy report the directors had given him. None of the information was new to him. Though they believed Bruce to be an indifferent manager—an impression he had actively cultivated—he familiarized himself with every department, scrutinized every project, analyzed every budget.

Two questions continued to weigh on him: *Why* had Drayling resigned? And why *now*? Bruce had tried to intercept the man to talk to him before he left Wayne Tower, but Drayling was gone, his desk cleaned out beforehand, his office dark. He would have to dig deeper, seek out the man so they could have a real conversation in private.

Back inside the Cave, surrounded by shadows, he found that his concentration always improved. This was far more than just a cave—it was a nerve center from which he kept watch and truly observed what work he needed to do to clean up his city. The cave roof high overhead was jagged with sharp stalactites. He had electric lights, surveillance cameras, an extensive library, all the information he could possibly need at his fingertips. Communications systems monitored police radio bands. The sophistication of his whirring, cutting-edge computer banks surpassed anything the U.S. government would admit existed. Part of the Cave was a chemistry lab; another grotto held an engineering bay and a machine shop. Small periscope cameras were hidden at strategic points on Gotham's prominent buildings, their images viewable from his command center.

Since he needed to be present at the gala reception above, he didn't plan to go out hunting, and so he had not taken the time to don the uniform. But the persona was always there. The Batman within gave him a different perspective, helped him think clearly and make difficult but necessary decisions. The dark suit remained on its stand nearby, always there as a reminder.

So many crimes in Gotham City were not obvious, and virtually the entire police force was corrupt, especially under Commissioner Loeb. Graft and blackmail ran rampant. Strong-arm tactics were used against anyone who accidentally witnessed activities best unseen.

He activated the high-tech cameras and receiver screens. As the cathode-ray tubes warmed up, he observed a black and white image fed directly from the boardroom of Wayne Tower. Hidden microphones had captured every word uttered since his departure and recorded everything on reel-to-reel tapes, gathering information. Now he watched the recent recording of these men, who had thought their conversations secret once Bruce left for the day.

Surprisingly, the directors did not seem concerned about the loss of Drayling. The conversation was more about Bruce and his increased interest in running Wayne Enterprises.

"Do you think he's been meddling more lately?" asked Dennis Huston, vice president of applied technologies.

"Maybe he's started believing the title on his office door," answered Frank Miles with a snort. "We'll just have to deflect him. Point him toward a new crusade, find a famine in Mongolia or something. He's like a magpie—show him a bright and shiny object, and he'll chase it. Then we'll be able to do the real work without any interference."

Bruce was not surprised by the scorn in their voices; he'd been hearing it every week, but lately he had suspected that something truly fishy was going on, and Drayling's resignation had convinced him even more.

Alfred had to clear his throat a second time to make himself noticed. "Excuse me, Master Bruce. This evening's first guests will be arriving within the hour." The butler frowned disapprovingly at his rumpled clothes. "You might wish to change into more appropriate attire."

"I see your point." Bruce rose, switching off the monitor. He would review the recordings in much greater detail later. He turned to the butler. "Alfred, you knew Richard Drayling well."

"Well enough, sir. He was an acquaintance of your father, and he and I have remained in touch. He is, after all, the last member of the 'old guard,' as it were."

"He resigned today. He said something vague about not believing in the company anymore, but I get the feeling that something's *happened*."

Alfred frowned deeply. "I'm very sorry to hear that. He was a good man, one of the last good men on the board."

"I agree, but I don't think he respected me. My public persona fooled him completely."

"You are quite convincing, sir."

"Thanks." Bruce frowned. "But you were his friend, Alfred. Talk with him. Find out if he'll tell you more about his reasons, and see if he'll have a private conversation with me. Discreetly."

"Discreetly. Of course." Alfred cleared his throat. "But this evening, sir . . . the party?"

Bruce gazed at the empty cowl of his uniform with its empty eye sockets, the stylized and frightening bat silhouette. He heaved a deep sigh at the thought of the party he had to endure upstairs. "Time to put on my other mask."

CHAPTER 9
THE *DAILY PLANET*

CLARK KENT PICKED THE WRONG MOMENT TO GO TO THE watercooler. He bent over to fill a conical paper cup, and an air bubble belched up from the bottom of the tank. He straightened just in time to see Perry White lugging a swollen canvas mailbag across the bullpen.

When he spotted Clark, the editor in chief turned directly toward him. "Kent! Today's your lucky day. I need somebody to take over the 'Lorna for the Lovelorn' column."

Clark nearly dropped his water. Lorna Bahowic, who wrote the *Planet*'s personal advice column, was a spinster in her forties, thin, with mousy brown hair. Hundreds of letters arrived weekly from people begging her for help with their love problems. Lorna had also just gone into the hospital for gallbladder surgery and would be recovering for at least a month, maybe two. Clark had already sent her a small flower arrangement and a "get well soon" card.

"But, Mr. White, I—I wouldn't have the foggiest idea how to give advice on relationships."

Perry whistled loudly. "Lane! Kent needs your help understanding women and their problems. You're a woman. Give him suggestions on how to write Lorna's column."

Lois turned, clearly annoyed by the editor's whistle. "And just because I'm a woman, that means I'm an expert on women's problems? I'm a reporter, Chief, not a psychiatrist."

"Besides, surely all the letters aren't from women," Clark pointed out. "A few must come from men—"

"We usually don't publish letters from whining men. It can be embarrassing. The two of you have worked together before, and I need that column."

Clark made a last-ditch effort without much hope. "But, Mr. White—the Korean War Veterans parade is today!"

"Olsen can cover that. I just need pictures."

"And the ribbon-cutting ceremony at the new observatory—"

Perry snorted. "No excuses. *You're* the reporters, *I'm* the editor." He lobbed the bulky mailbag, which Clark caught easily. "And this is your assignment. We'll still run it under Lorna's byline. Nobody needs to know she's in the hospital."

Lois bustled past, purse already on her shoulder, pulling on her jacket. "Sorry, but I've got an interview scheduled. Confidential source about LuthorCorp, remember? Clark, you're on your own for this one." Then her expression softened, and she smiled at Clark. "All you really need is a soft heart. You're halfway there already. And I promise I'll help—just not right now."

"I'll give it a hundred percent—I always do," Clark managed forlornly, not needing X-ray vision to realize that the satchel contained hundreds of letters, each one written by a sad or tormented person. The only saving grace was that he would get to spend more time with Lois, working closely on the column.

He had admired her from the first day he'd walked into the

Daily Planet with his original story about Superman. Lois was smart, funny, talented, and beautiful—a girl as different from anyone in Smallville as the moon was from the sun. Lois carried an *energy* around her, as if Metropolis itself charged her like a power substation. He felt like a small-town boy whenever he was with her, and he couldn't help but blush any time she paid him attention.

With a sigh, Clark carried the heavy sack of letters back to his desk and thunked it on the floor beside his rolling chair. He pulled out the letters one by one, opening them, reading the problems, and setting them aside. He was quickly overwhelmed.

I'm sure my husband is cheating on me. Should I confront him? Should I forgive him?

My boyfriend keeps hitting me, even though I know he doesn't mean it. My friends tell me to leave him, but I love him. What should I do?

We've been going steady for three whole months—will he ever propose?

My husband doesn't like my cooking. . . .

Letter after letter left him mystified about basic human nature. He could bend girders with his bare hands, outrace a speeding locomotive, fly from one side of the country to the other faster than the most advanced fighter jet. He could grab Lois Lane out of the air as her car plunged off the Twelfth Street bridge. He could whisk victims of a school bus crash to the hospital faster than any ambulance. He could carry a sinking passenger ship to the docks in Metropolis Bay. He could hunt down jewel thieves, stop kidnappers.

But this? He had no idea.

My boyfriend won't look at me anymore. He didn't even notice my new $20 hairdo.

We've been trying to have children for five years, but nothing's worked. Should we adopt? My husband says there must be something wrong with those babies, otherwise why would the mother give them away?

For the rest of the day, Clark felt he was reading the same basic letters over and over. These people posed difficult questions and had deep emotional problems that couldn't be solved by simply twisting steel or outracing a bullet.

He thought about going to visit Lorna in the hospital, to ask her advice on giving advice. How did she deal with this every day? Clark tried to imagine the conversation in the sterile hospital room, with him awkwardly attempting to discuss love with an older spinster who, despite being single, still knew a lot about the human heart.

In fact, everyone seemed to know more about emotions than he did.

Clark had a deep-seated desire to help people, and he had never questioned his own motives or feelings on the matter. To him, it was the obvious thing to do whenever he saw someone in need. Until today, he had always felt he could overcome any challenge, but now he thought perhaps he was wrong. Helping people overcome emotional pain and suffering was obviously a lot more difficult than exhibiting feats of strength.

Still, in a different way, by answering these letters and writing the "Lorna for the Lovelorn" column he would also be doing something important for people in need.

But he couldn't do it alone.

T HE LUTHORCORP ANGLE. LOIS HAD AN INSTINCT FOR these things.

She'd arranged to meet her source for coffee at a Canal Street diner. Blanche Rosen was a forty-eight-year-old widow whose husband had been killed in the Korean War. Though she had worked on various factory assembly lines for twenty years, and the last five at LuthorCorp with an exemplary job performance record, Blanche suddenly found herself jobless. Lex Luthor had systematically removed all of his female and older male employees and put "a man in a man's job."

It had happened previously in American industry, particularly after World War II. With the overseas war wrapped up and all the men returning home, many women had found themselves booted out of the factories and sent back to become barefoot and pregnant homemakers.

But with no such flood of returning soldiers now, LuthorCorp's deliberate action really stuck in Lois's craw. Worse, Blanche Rosen's surreptitious message strongly implied that something more sinister was going on. Lois was doing some digging, but so far she couldn't find anyone else willing to talk. In fact, she could find few of the fired LuthorCorp employees *at all*.

Very fishy indeed. She couldn't wait to hear what Blanche had to say.

Lois waited in a bright red Naugahyde booth. Exactly on time, an older, severe-looking woman arrived and took the seat across from her. She wore a nice dress, perhaps her best, the one reserved for temple on Saturdays. Her voice was gruff, no-nonsense. "Are you Lois Lane?"

"Yes, I am. I'm the one who can get your story told, Mrs. Rosen."

Blanche nodded. "It's not only *my* story. There's a lot of women and men just like me from LuthorCorp, but most of them aren't alive anymore."

Lois was shocked. "Are you saying Lex Luthor *killed* them?"

"In a manner of speaking. Hazardous duty, no safety procedures or equipment, harmful radiation exposures . . . 'Caribbean vacations.' I'm one of the last few left, mainly because I'm a tough old bird."

Lois took out her notepad, her expression intent. "I'm all ears, Mrs. Rosen."

The waitress came over. Both women ordered coffee, but Blanche also asked for a pastrami sandwich and potato chips. With only the briefest hesitation, she added, "And wrap up a second one to go." She clung to her pride as she looked across the booth at Lois. "You don't mind, do you, newsgirl?"

"A girl's gotta eat." Lois felt a tug at her heartstrings. "But you have to sing for your supper."

Blanche looked around the diner, studying the other customers. She lowered her voice. "How do I know *you're* not in Luthor's pocket?"

Lois let out a laugh. "That's not an image I want to think about. My journalistic credentials should speak for themselves." She leaned across the table. "Frankly, Mrs. Rosen, Lex Luthor makes my skin crawl. I've been face-to-face with him. I've seen him smile. Ever see a snake smile? There's nothing behind it. *Nothing*."

Blanche slurped her coffee and heaved a long sigh. "The things I've seen, Miss Lane. LuthorCorp and their munitions factories, the military bases, the test flights, black programs that don't show up on any official paperwork. I had a security clearance, and I performed the most delicate work . . . and now look at me. Crumpled up and discarded like a chewing gum wrapper—practically living on the streets, without a job, without a pension, my husband's death benefits almost gone. It's a damn shame, I tell you. Forget what Senator McCarthy rails about—*this* is un-American! This is not what my family left Germany for."

Blanche paused to take a large bite of her pastrami sandwich as soon as it arrived. Lois stole a potato chip and pressed for more information. "What kind of work did you do, exactly? And what's this about a 'Caribbean vacation'?"

"Reactor assembly. Luthor has his own island, complete with a small atomic power reactor."

Lois began scribbling in shorthand as quickly as possible. "Is that where he works on his secret projects for the government?"

"Miss Lane, the government doesn't know *half* of what Luthor does. That uncharted island is a test bed for some of his most dangerous technology. Once Luthor's weapons systems function, he'll sell them to the U.S. military for ten times his investment."

"So how did you get involved?"

"He invited some of his employees to help build facilities there and do the technical work. He hired Cuban locals to do the heavy construction of remodeling an old fort into a new base. Many of those men and women were just like me, divorced people and widows living on a shoestring without much to keep us here in Metropolis. When we got the offer to spend a few months in the Caribbean, who were we to complain? At the time, it didn't occur to us that we were the employees Luthor considered the most expendable . . . the ones who wouldn't be missed."

Lois nodded, letting the woman continue.

"But then they started getting sick. The Cuban work crews left, and we didn't see them again. I heard something about their boat sinking in open water, all souls lost. On the island, those poor men and women in charge of installing reactor fuel rods and coolant systems fell terribly ill, and Luthor—such a generous man!—took them to his own hospitals back on the mainland. He said he would provide the best possible medical treatment." She set down her sandwich as if she'd lost her appetite. "They're all dead now."

The cheery waitress came back to fill their coffee cups.

"Apparently there was a radiation leak. All their hair fell out—I heard Luthor make jokes about them being bald." She shook her head. "I haven't shown any symptoms yet, but Luthor swept all of us under the rug."

The story made Lois's blood boil. "Do you have any proof of this, Mrs. Rosen?"

"They took everything from me. I have no records, no photos, nothing tangible. But you'll find everything you need in the LuthorCorp munitions factory in the barrens outside of Metropolis." Her eyes lit up. "And I can tell you how a smart, resourceful reporter might be able to slip inside and take a look around."

CHAPTER 11
WAYNE MANOR

GOTHAM CITY'S MOST ILLUSTRIOUS CITIZENS ATTENDED Bruce Wayne's famous parties, and ample front-page coverage in the *Gotham Times* society section went without saying. Sparing no expense, Bruce always centered these soirees around an important humanitarian cause; though most of the celebrities and important personages attended just to be seen, they also brought their checkbooks.

"Wayne Manor is, after all, my father's house," Bruce had once told the lovely reporter Vicki Vale for a feature article. "Thomas Wayne devoted his life to helping people, and I intend to honor his memory."

"You can't possibly remember him very clearly, Mr. Wayne. You were only six years old when—"

He had been tempted to cut off the interview then and there, but instead he interrupted and said, "I remember him, Miss Vale. I remember him well."

The guests arrived in limousines that glided into the porte cochere. They displayed their most expensive formalwear, furs, and jewels. The glitterati included Gotham's most prominent citizens, as well as celebrity guests: movie stars, singers, and sports personalities, including Rock Hudson, David Niven, Buddy Holly, Paul Anka, Sugar Ray Robinson. The quiet, revered star of the show was Eleanor Roosevelt, the former first lady, who had turned her considerable energies to supporting the cause of polio research.

Though he'd changed promptly into his finest tuxedo, Bruce did not step through the entry doors until he considered himself fashionably late. His aloof nature was well known, and the guests had started without him.

When he finally descended the grand staircase, moving with an air of casual mystery, all conversation stopped. A few—the first-timers or the nouveau riche—applauded politely until Bruce alighted in the main hall and held up one hand for silence, the other for a drink. Alfred appeared immediately with a tray bearing a martini glass and his specially mixed Vesper (in reality, a bit of lemon peel and chilled ice water).

"Ladies and gentlemen, welcome to my humble home." There was a quick titter at the old joke. "Tonight I offer you an opportunity to be generous—to raise funds for polio research. Countless poor children around the world are crippled by this awful disease. The medical research and new vaccine of Dr. Jonas Salk shows great promise, and we must not let him lack for resources." He nodded toward Eleanor Roosevelt, who stood stoic and proud, like visiting royalty; she applauded loudly, though her gloved hands muffled the sound.

The former first lady cleared her throat and spoke in a strong, confident voice that might have been used in a Shakespeare performance. "You all know my personal reasons for wanting to rid humanity of this terrible scourge. My wonderful husband would have congratulated Mr. Wayne for his efforts. And I congratulate you all for being here. Please help fight this disease with the weapons you all wield—your checkbooks." The audience responded with a ripple of laughter.

Bruce stepped forward to conclude his speech. "Let us show Mrs. Roosevelt the generosity and vision of Gotham City. Tonight we can make our mark on the world—a mark that begins with a dollar sign."

"Bruce, dear, you have more money than all of us combined," purred Selina Kyle, dusky, lithe, and beautiful as she came up behind him as if to take possession. "For the cost of this party, you could have made a substantial donation of your own."

Bruce lifted his glass to salute the beautiful socialite. "I intend to do both, Miss Kyle. After you all make your donations, Wayne Enterprises will match the total, dollar for dollar. So if you'd like to make *me* dig deep into my pockets, then dig deeply into yours."

A squawking chortle emanated from a dapper, rotund man, whom Bruce instantly recognized as Oswald Cobblepot. "At that rate, he'll fund a cure for polio in a single night."

"Don't worry, Mr. Cobblepot, I'm sure we can find other worthy causes." Bruce bowed slightly. "All of you, please enjoy yourselves."

Alfred ran the manor household and serving staff like a militia. No tray of hors d'oeuvres was allowed to circulate half-empty; glasses of wine and champagne always had to be filled. Cuban cigars and Turkish cigarettes were offered in ornate silver cases.

Bruce worked his way through clusters of the rich and famous, shaking hands, trying not to spend too much time with any one person or group. Selina Kyle slipped her arm through his and walked along smoothly beside him. Her well-trained society voice carried perfectly. "We really should see each other more often, dear. You know, we are absolutely *perfect* for each other." She rolled her *r*'s as she talked. He had never been able to place her accent precisely.

Despite the temptation, he expertly cut her out of his sphere and slid into another clutch of the well-to-do, pleading an important bit of business with the city treasurer (though he had met the man only once). Selina accepted the brush-off with a flirtatious smile and a promise that they would talk again soon.

The conversations generally had nothing to do with polio, extending well beyond the concerns of Gotham City. Bruce repeatedly heard the excited buzz about the so-called Superman from Metropolis. Gotham police commissioner Loeb, a corrupt man at the top of a blue pyramid of corrupt officers, delighted in talking about strangeness in another city rather than the problems of his own. He lost no opportunity to make disparaging comments about the inept Metropolis police.

"But Gotham has its own costumed maniac." Cobblepot chomped down on his ebony cigarette holder. "Maybe the Batman has alien superpowers, too, eh, Commissioner? That would explain why your men can never catch him." He let out a nasal snicker.

Loeb's face darkened. "Superman's a hero, saves children from burning buildings in broad daylight. The Batman slinks around at night, evades arrest, and assaults on-duty officers. He's nothing but another criminal. We have twenty-nine pending charges against him, and that's just for starters. He's Gotham's number-one most wanted."

Cobblepot took a long draw, then tapped a stem of ash into a silver tray as he let out his birdlike laugh again. "You're just upset, Commissioner, because you can't make the Batman pay you a bribe."

Loeb bristled. "I will not be insulted by a petty gangster in an ill-fitting top hat and tails!"

Now it was Cobblepot's turn to take umbrage. He screwed a monocle into his eye to inspect the commissioner as though he were an interesting specimen. "I am a respectable nightclub owner, sir."

"Respectable!"

"And what is *your* opinion on the Batman, Mr. Wayne?" said an unmistakable breathy voice. Bruce turned from Cobblepot and Loeb to see that Marilyn Monroe had shown up, accompanied by her new husband, playwright Arthur Miller.

"He baffles me, Miss Monroe. Why should the Batman spend his nights lurking in alley shadows when he could be at a cocktail party instead?" His flippant comment drew polite laughter from the nearby listeners. "Speaking of which . . ." He raised his now-empty "martini" glass. "Time to freshen my drink."

He melted away again, seeking Alfred. The butler was handing a leather jacket back to Rock Hudson, ushering him genteelly out the door. The heartthrob actor had to leave early due to his shooting schedule. As they watched Hudson's sports car swirl away down the drive, Bruce asked quietly, "How much longer, Alfred?"

"The evening has barely begun, Master Bruce. Chin up."

"All for the greater good, I suppose," Bruce said, then lowered his voice again. "Are you marking the glasses carefully when you collect the empty drinks?"

"Indeed, sir. You'll have plenty of new specimens for your crime lab—*tomorrow.*" He emphasized the word with a scolding tone. "Tonight, you must play your part and socialize with your adoring public, no matter how difficult it may be for you."

"Yes, Alfred."

With a wry expression and freshened faux-Vesper, Bruce returned to the social fray. The people were laughing and drinking and smoking in a background drone, a blur of sensation and sound and smell. He made them all feel welcome.

Trays strategically placed about the halls and exit received checks and envelopes of cash donations. It was a bright and glittering party, one of his best, judging by the amount of money raised for charity. The members of Gotham's high society would consider it a triumph. Even Eleanor Roosevelt seemed to be enjoying herself, and Bruce spent a generous amount of time talking with her. She sat alone at the side of the room, watching the people who seemed too intimidated to engage her in casual conversation.

Bruce, though, was a gracious host. Mrs. Roosevelt sipped her soda water. "Thank you for this evening, Mr. Wayne, but you don't need to bother with me. I know you have many social obligations. I'm doing just fine, thank you."

"Why, you're no bother at all, ma'am. We wouldn't be here if not for your work. I'm just helping to rid the world of an awful blight on humanity." At least this was one blight he might be able to eradicate completely, forever.

She shooed him away. "Now, you go on and talk to your other guests. You're making me all teary eyed."

He bowed politely and went to attend his party. Through every excruciating moment, Bruce maintained his cordial smile. He had an innate aversion to being relaxed in public, but he had a flair for looking comfortable in almost any social setting, while his sharp eyes and ears picked up on every bit of knowledge that might prove useful. It definitely made his detective work easier.

He didn't view the event as a party so much as a chance to gather data on some of the wealthiest people in Gotham society so that he could analyze the information in his secret lab tomorrow. For tonight, he had his role to play.

CHAPTER 12
THE *DAILY PLANET*

THE NEXT MORNING, LOIS LANE STRUTTED INTO THE *DAILY Planet* office as she always did, head held high, heels clicking a confident staccato. She flung open the glass doors into the bullpen with her typical saucy "What's news, everybody?" (countered by the just-as-usual daily groaning at her corny joke).

At his desk, Clark was buried in letters, still not sure which ones to answer or how. When she noticed him, she paused, her face showing a sudden and unexpected warmth. "Were you working all night on that, Clark?"

"Oh, hi, Lois. I went home, but I didn't stop thinking about it. I'm a fish out of water with this stuff." He shrugged his big shoulders helplessly. "I sure could use your advice."

She hesitated, as if on the verge of turning away with a dismissive "Not my problem," but then she stopped. "You're a sweet aw-shucks kind of guy, Clark, but I wouldn't call you an expert on women. I don't know what the Chief was thinking giving you that assignment."

"He *did* suggest that we work together."

Lois plainly heard the hopeful lilt at the end of his sentence.

He showed her a few of the toughest letters. "What kind of advice can I give these people?"

Lois read the handwritten pages with an eagle eye, face tightening and frown deepening. She finally slapped them down on the desk. "I see what you mean. These women don't really want to do the work to solve their problems. They just want someone to commiserate with them. If you give them an honest answer, they won't want to hear it. So you've got to give them the *right* answer instead."

Clark was confused. "The right answer isn't the honest answer?"

"Trust me. Just look at the letters. *This* one"—she pointed sharply—"and *this* one. Her boyfriend keeps beating her, and she goes back to him every time? I'd like to give that guy a knuckle sandwich myself, see how he likes a taste of his own medicine." She sighed. "Then again, even if she left him, that woman would probably find someone just the same, or worse. I know the type, Clark. If they knew how to find the strength within themselves to see their own worth, then they wouldn't let men take advantage of them, much less write letters complaining about it. Unfortunately, they've gotten themselves in up to their necks, and they just expect some hero to swoop in and magically save them."

Clark baited quietly, "You mean like Superman?"

"He's the exception." Lois was obviously embarrassed, but a bashful smile crept across her face. "If only there were *more* exceptions like him." She covered her blush quickly. "Do your best, Clark. You're good at showing compassion. Just be yourself."

"Would you read over the draft before I turn it in to Mr. White? I . . . I'll buy you a cup of coffee."

She smiled. "It's a deal."

Clark watched her go, not sure whether or not he had actually asked her out for a date. He faced his task once more, wanting to do a good job. He still didn't understand these problems . . . but he knew someone who might. Someone who would also understand just how lost he was—and why.

His mother had always helped him out when he couldn't understand the nuances of life from a human point of view.

Mind made up, he went directly to Perry's office. He straightened his tie, smoothed down his shirt collar, then knocked on the door. "Excuse me, Mr. White, I'm feeling a little under the weather. I'd like to take the rest of the day off, please."

"I need your column by tomorrow, Kent—no excuses!"

"You'll have it, Mr. White. I'll be back at my desk in the morning, I promise."

CHAPTER 13
WAYNE MANOR

A PLAYBOY LIKE BRUCE WAS EXPECTED TO SLEEP IN AFTER a party, and the doors of his bedroom suite remained locked for hours. While armies of housekeepers and cleaning staff restored the manor to its quiet grace, however, he got up early and descended through a secret passage to the Cave, where he could do his research.

First off, he stood before a table where Alfred had arranged a line of empty, dirty glasses from the night's party. The butler had been careful to collect at least one item from each guest, and now every specimen sat on a handwritten card identifying the user.

Getting out his packets of powder and a thick brush, Bruce quickly and gently dusted the smooth surfaces. The fingerprints came out quite clearly, and Bruce spent an hour photographing them so that he could add them to his detailed library and catalog the results. By now his fingerprint collection must have rivaled that of the Gotham City Police Department. He had no way to tell when, or if, the information might become vital for an investigation.

But his mind was elsewhere, focused on a much more challenging riddle.

Ever since the first appearance of Superman, Bruce had been intrigued by the man's amazing powers, and the previous night's party gossip had only sharpened his interest. Now he hunched in his large chair and pondered. Next to the blinking lights of his computer banks with spinning reel-to-reel tapes, a set of rounded cathode-ray tubes projected images and information.

He watched newsreel footage of Superman's exploits; he studied photographs, newspaper clippings, eyewitness accounts. Even though most photographs were motion-blurred due to Superman's incredible speed, the hero wore no mask, as if confident that his identity would remain a secret.

Bruce could not understand how a mere man accomplished so many amazing things. Superman had hefted a huge passenger ship with ease and set it down safely in the Metropolis harbor. As the rescued passengers filed onto piers toward rescue teams with warm blankets and hot coffee, they were thrilled and giddy. The weeping boat captain had practically fallen to his knees in gratitude. After acknowledging the sincere thanks, Superman had simply waved and flown away. . . .

Another time, he'd burst from a burning building with a child in each arm as flames raged all around. The children were coughing and gasping but largely unharmed. The fire hadn't singed a hair on Superman's head. . . .

Bruce studied photographs of Superman cornering a group of gangsters. With their backs to a brick wall, they brandished tommy guns and unleashed a hail of bullets—which bounced harmlessly from the big s emblem on his chest.

Bruce paused the tapes, used magnifiers to study every image, but he could not figure out the trick. What sort of fabric could deflect bullets so perfectly, so painlessly? Even with the best-known bulletproof technology on his armored Batman suit, *he* still felt bullet impacts like the blows of a hammer.

What about Superman's heat vision? Some sort of laser built directly into his optic nerves?

His strength was incredible. He bent iron girders in his bare hands. The flashy blue and red uniform must have been augmented somehow—with reinforced fibers? Pulleys? Hydraulics? Bruce tapped his fingers, deep in thought.

Superman flew effortlessly through the air, but beneath the cape, there was no room for a hidden jetpack, and none of the images showed any indication of exhaust or rocket flames. Where did the man get such technology? Lois Lane at the *Daily Planet* would have had the world believe he was an alien with extraordinary inhuman powers, but Bruce didn't buy that for a second.

Carefully dividing the problem into several apparently unrelated parts, he had slipped technical challenges into the workload of Wayne Enterprises' divisions, but so far his crack scientists had yielded no answers. Even *they* could not come close to what this costumed hero did on a routine basis.

Only one other U.S. company approached the technological innovation of Wayne Enterprises. Could Superman actually be a LuthorCorp creation? An experimental soldier released by Lex Luthor? So far, the bald genius had been curiously silent on the matter of Superman, making only offhand skeptical statements about the "so-called hero" who had "walked onto the stage with his grandstanding exploits." That alone made Bruce suspicious that Luthor was behind Superman himself—or at the very least deeply engaged in an investigation of his own.

Alfred interrupted him, wearing a singed and stained laboratory coat and insulated black rubber gloves. Protective goggles hung on a strap from his neck. Leaving the household staff to continue their work, the butler often assisted Bruce in his large-scale experiments. On a test rack in a side grotto, he had fired up a set of small, self-contained rockets designed to be installed in a jetpack. The gauges recorded stresses, thrust, stabilization.

The butler shook his head. "I'm afraid that these bulky jets have the thrust to carry a person through the air, Master Bruce, but not smoothly or with any precision. Even with a more compact design, the pack would require a full-body support framework and fireproof materials, practically a suit of armor."

Bruce sighed. "That won't do. Superman moves with flexibility and speed." He had given the problem to the applied technologies division, and Director Huston had accepted the task, but he had not expected to find an easy solution. "I'm beginning to doubt I'll understand Superman's abilities any time soon. The more questions I ask, the fewer answers I get. I don't have the slightest idea how he does it or how to re-create those abilities myself."

Alfred raised his thin eyebrows. "Have you considered, Master Bruce, the possibility that Superman may be *exactly* who he says he is? That he does indeed come from another planet?"

Bruce frowned. "That's not a rational suggestion at this point, Alfred. There must be some other answer."

Alfred shucked off the thick gloves and removed his lab garments to reveal incongruously formal garb underneath. Bruce was sure that few other scientists wore a tuxedo (sans jacket) beneath a white lab coat. "It is time that I oversee the household staff—a far more difficult job than this, if you ask me, sir."

The butler hung his lab coat on a peg, pulled his jacket from another peg, and brushed off the front of the dark fabric. Before leaving the Cave, he turned. "You will be pleased to know, sir, that I've arranged to have a conversation with Richard Drayling later this afternoon, as you requested. Based on our longtime friendship, I believe Mr. Drayling does want someone to confide in. He and I are of an age, and we'll talk casually of old times, of your father . . . and of why he felt the need to resign from your board of directors."

"Thank you, Alfred." Bruce pinched the bridge of his nose, concentrating. "If there's something going on at Wayne Enterprises, then I need to know about it. Let's hope we can solve that mystery at least."

CHAPTER 14
SMALLVILLE, KANSAS

SMALLVILLE WAS HALFWAY ACROSS THE COUNTRY, BUT A man who could outrace a supersonic jet covered the distance in no time. As Kal-El flew, lighter than air and faster than the wind, his thoughts remained unsettled by reading about so many troubled romances and complicated emotions.

After crossing the Great Plains, looking down at the colorful checkerboard of crops, he found his beloved Kansas town. When he saw that the Smallville Cemetery was empty, he alighted there first, just to have some time alone.

The grave was immaculate, the vase on a stand filled with fresh-cut flowers: bright yellow daffodils and scarlet tulips, signs of spring. His father had always loved spring: planting season, time to ready the soil for a new year. Clark had been a one-man army on the farm, helping Jonathan Kent.

Now that his mother was all alone, she didn't even try to handle all the acreage. Martha had her garden, her chickens, and her house. The rest of the land she leased to neighboring farmers, the Hubbards and the Schmidts.

Kal-El knelt by the headstone.

JONATHAN KENT

FAITHFUL HUSBAND

LOVING FATHER

YOU WERE OUR GREATEST STRENGTH

His vision shimmered a little. Jonathan Kent had been a man of few, but wise, words, and now no words were needed. The silence felt comforting rather than empty. For hours and hours, Clark and his father had done their chores, baled hay, planted crops, fixed the fence line, without needing to reassure each other with incessant conversation. Their relationship was comfortable, no frills, just a solid core.

When his father did decide to make a comment, it was bound to be important. "If you don't need to say anything, son, there's no need to talk. These days, with their radio programs and phonograph records, people forget the virtues of an hour of good, quiet thinking."

Though he knew his true name was Kal-El, here in Smallville—especially at his father's grave—he would always be Clark Kent. It didn't matter what he learned about the destruction of Krypton or his biological father, Jor-El. It didn't matter that he was the only one of his kind on Earth. Here in Smallville, he would never be alone.

He ruffled his palm through the thick, lush grass of the gravesite. He closed his eyes and remained quiet, though he badly needed to say many things. Jonathan Kent had always understood his thoughts, even when they remained unspoken.

IN THE FARMHOUSE KITCHEN, MARTHA KENT WAS JUST TAKING a golden-brown apple pie from the oven. He didn't need super-senses to detect the aromatic cinnamon, sweet sugar, and tart Cortland apples. Martha's face showed her delight when he opened the front screen door. "Welcome home, son. You're just in time." She displayed the luscious-looking pie.

"You always seem to have one ready, Ma. How do you know when to make them?"

Her eyes crinkled behind her gold-rimmed glasses. "Superman always knows when people need him. How can you underestimate a mother's ability to do the same with her baking? There's coffee in the percolator and a jug of whole milk in the icebox for you." Her gaze traveled over him, and she nodded at his red boots, blue suit, and scarlet cape. "You go change clothes while I cut you a big slice of pie. That nice Pete Ross comes around to check on me at least once a week. He'd love to see Clark Kent, but it wouldn't do for him to catch a glimpse of Superman at my kitchen table!"

Clark dashed up to his old bedroom and returned seconds later wearing an old plaid shirt and dungarees. Martha was just scooping a generous slice of pie onto an aqua Melmac plate. She cut herself a much smaller wedge and settled into her chair at the Formica-topped kitchen table.

"So how *is* Pete these days?" He did his best to follow the lives of the friends he had left behind in Kansas.

"Oh, still running the general store, still talking about heading out into the world and making his fortune someday."

Clark laughed. "And still not doing anything about it?"

"That boy has never driven across the county line, as far as I know." Martha sipped her coffee. They chatted about his daily work at the newspaper, his apartment in Metropolis, the new gladiolas she had ordered from the seed catalog, which would really spruce up her flower garden.

But Martha wasn't fooled. During a brief lull in the conversation, she leaned forward and spoke in her no-nonsense way. "Something's troubling you, Clark. What is it? You didn't come here in the middle of the week just to chat with your old mother."

Clark straightened quickly. "That's not true! I missed you."

Martha set her cup down and gave him the "mom" look. "I know that's not technically a lie, Clark, but you didn't answer me."

With a sigh, he told her about his predicament with the "Lorna for the Lovelorn" column. "So many people have so many problems, and I don't know how to solve them all. I don't know what to tell them."

Martha patted his hand. "For a man of steel, you've got a heart of gold."

He was finally able to confess his deeper concern. "I'm not from Earth, I'm from Krypton—and I'm the only one of my kind. What if I never understand this world and this world never understands me?"

"Do you think any of us humans really understand each other? If the troubles of people could be so easily fixed, then nobody would be jumping out of windows, no marriage would end in divorce, no crime would ever be committed. But that isn't the world we live in, so we have to do our best to make it a better place. And believe you me, son, you do far more than your share."

Though she was trying to comfort him, she had inadvertently touched upon another thing that troubled him. "But I can do so much *more*, Ma. From the moment I first put on that suit, I've been helping people in danger, stopping criminals, preventing accidents—but people need to be saved every hour of every day. How many car wrecks have happened in the time I've been here talking to you? How many robberies? How many shootings?

"And it's narrow-minded for me to worry only about crimes

committed in Metropolis. What about the whole world? Couldn't I prevent wars? Stop slavery? Divert rivers and prevent drought? Distribute food and stop hunger? I could work every second, and *still* the job wouldn't be done." He looked at her, his blue eyes sorrowful and intense.

His mother gave him a wistful smile. "Your father used to talk like that when he saw how much work needed to be done around the farm. Thought it would never get done . . . and yet it did."

Clark shook his head and took the last bite of pie. "Here I am in your kitchen as mild-mannered Clark Kent. But what business do I have trying to lead a 'normal' life? Doesn't the world need Superman to be a hero twenty-four hours a day, seven days a week?"

Surprisingly, Martha chided him gently. "Clark, you're entitled to your own life. You deserve to know people, to observe them, so that problems like the ones in those letters you're reading won't be such a mystery to you." She couldn't resist and leaned over to kiss him lovingly on the cheek. "You have to learn to be human as well as a super hero. Pay more attention to your friends, your relationships. Spend time with your pal Jimmy Olsen. And I know you're sweet on that Lois Lane."

He glanced away, embarrassed. "She certainly likes Superman, but I doubt she notices Clark Kent."

His mother patted him on the shoulder. "Dear, you keep forgetting that they're one and the same. It doesn't matter whether you wear a suit and tie or a blue outfit and red cape. It's who you are inside. You're a good man, Clark. Lois seems to be as sharp as a tack—I guarantee you she's noticed. Give her the benefit of the doubt."

"I will. In fact, we're planning to have coffee together. If she remembers."

"Of course she'll remember, dear. How could a girl forget something like that? But as for you, young man, remember that life isn't just one emergency after another. You need to *live* and experience the joys that are around you. Don't define yourself as nothing more than a hero. Let yourself be a man, too."

He felt choked up listening to her, and he knew she was right. "Pa always told me that the harvest wasn't only about the grain we loaded and earning a living—he made me smell the fresh-cut hay, sweet as it dried in the sun, and feel the cool spray of water from the irrigators on a hot day. He would just stand there after the sun set and the night dew started to come out, and he'd take a long inhale . . . and just *breathe in* the farm and the crops and the earth itself."

"That's it, Clark. Jonathan helped me see the same thing when we were just courting." She hugged him.

"I'll pay more attention to being human and not just look for emergencies to solve. I promise."

Martha smiled. She knew one thing for certain—Clark Kent *always* kept his promises.

AS THE MAJORITY CORPORATE SHAREHOLDER, BRUCE Wayne occupied the most desirable corner office in Wayne Tower, complete with leather-upholstered furniture, mahogany desk, thick carpeting. An engraved holder with a pen and a letter opener graced the olive-green desk blotter. The few papers in his in-box were neatly stacked. Nothing was marked urgent.

Behind him, the wood-paneled wall was covered with civic awards, thank-you letters, a framed crayon drawing from a child whose cancer had been treated at the Thomas Wayne Memorial Wing. He had recently hung (partly as a joke) the framed glossy photograph of himself with Clark Kent.

No one expected a man like Bruce to keep regular hours or to spend a lot of time at his actual office. He rarely put in a full day's work—after all, a playboy millionaire had many other things to do. However, he intentionally adhered to an eccentric schedule so that no one would think twice if he came in at odd hours, stayed late or wandered the halls. It worked to his advantage now.

His suspicions about the Wayne Enterprises directors were growing; the time for quiet observation had passed. Bruce decided to take a more active role in uncovering the blight at the core of his father's company. . . .

Shirley, his executive secretary, guarded the gates with utmost professional courtesy and tact. "Will you be staying late tonight, Mr. Wayne? Shall I order you dinner?" Both beautiful and efficient, she endured his whims, produced memos whenever he felt like issuing them, maintained his stack of telephone messages, and most important, maintained his privacy.

"I'll be fine on my own, thank you. Close up, put out the lights, and go home. Have a good weekend."

As a gracious gesture, Bruce had decreed that anyone who took public transportation was allowed to leave a half hour early on Fridays. His employees had readily embraced the habit, and Wayne Tower emptied out as dusk set in. Ostensibly, he was staying behind to work on the donations from the polio benefit, which had raised $47,862. He had upped the amount to an even $50,000, then matched it from his own fortune.

Tonight, though, he had other things to do.

He waited as darkness fell and the lights winked out in the other offices. Since he couldn't begin to prowl until the building was silent and empty, he sat pondering in the dark, running through his plan. . . .

Bruce was very troubled by what Alfred had learned from Richard Drayling during their conversation that afternoon. The butler's gaunt face had shown clear distaste for the news he had to relate. "Mr. Drayling resigned because he is concerned for his family, sir. He fears for his life and theirs."

Bruce hadn't expected that. "In what way?"

"At first it was an offered bribe, a substantial amount of money. Naturally, Mr. Drayling declined. Next came blackmail, which he also brushed aside. Finally, they made overt threats."

Bruce felt a storm growing inside him. "Alfred, what are you talking about? Who are 'they'?"

The butler sniffed. "Lex Luthor, sir. He has been systematically corrupting your board of directors, getting them in his pocket. Mr. Drayling is certain that most of the others have already succumbed."

Bruce felt cold. "And what does Luthor want from them?"

"Mr. Luthor has bribed, or otherwise coerced, the directors to pass along crucial Wayne Enterprises research. Several of LuthorCorp's major technological breakthroughs originated in your own divisions."

Bruce's hands clenched into fists. "Five times in the past six months, LuthorCorp edged out our bids on large government contracts. Now I know why."

Maybe he had bided his time too long, played his part too well as a carefree heir only marginally interested in business matters. He was disappointed that Drayling had not felt comfortable enough to talk to the son of Thomas Wayne, but perhaps the older man had seen Bruce as part of the problem, no different from the corrupt board members.

He knew full well that Gotham City ran as much on graft and blackmail as it did on electricity and heating oil. During the years of Bruce's absence, the Wayne Enterprises directors had gotten more complacent and less adept at covering their indiscretions.

Alfred continued, "Mr. Drayling resisted LuthorCorp's advances out of respect for your father. When his refusal led to direct threats against his family, however, he could not tolerate the situation. Therefore, his only alternative was to resign. I explained that he should consider giving you the benefit of the doubt . . . but actions speak louder than words, if you will forgive the cliché."

With a heavy heart, Bruce understood the man's decision. "Starting tomorrow, I'm hiring private security to watch over Drayling's entire family. The time has come to show the board members that I'm not completely harmless or incompetent. Once I do some house-cleaning, maybe I can convince Drayling to come back."

But first he had to gather his ammunition and investigate exactly what the nine remaining directors were up to.

AS THIS WAS WAYNE ENTERPRISES, BRUCE COULD HAVE WALKED into the sealed Records Room and requested any folder he liked, but he didn't want to tip his hand. For the moment, he preferred that his inquiries remain unnoticed—until he had all the proof he needed. Bruce hoped that the directors, believing him to be disengaged from the day-to-day administrative details of his own company, would have let down their guard.

After waiting until midnight, Bruce slipped out of his office and made his way down the dim halls. Most of the fluorescent lights overhead were off for the weekend; only a few flickered now, shedding an uncertain light. He moved through the shadows, cloaked only in his business suit. He could have donned his Batman outfit and returned to break into the building to do his detective work, but he had a better disguise here. Bruce Wayne had every right to be in Wayne Tower.

He had full knowledge of the building's upgraded security systems; he had, in fact, studied every detail of the plans when he'd decided to install covert surveillance kits as well as adding back-door combinations to allow him to go anywhere through-out the building. He had also created a master key for himself that permitted access to any of the executive offices.

He began with Thomson's.

The metal file cabinets were locked, but he picked the locks easily. He rattled open the first drawer and shone a penlight down on the neatly labeled manila folders. Recognizing project code names, he skimmed correspondence files, private calendars, and meeting notes, then inspected some of the more problematic categories. He flipped through memos, carbon copies, photostats, and handwritten notes on legal pads, items that Thomson had not even trusted to his secretary.

Bruce's speed-reading ability was phenomenal, as was his retention, but his miniature camera was faster and more reliable, so he took microfilm shots of the pages that appeared important.

What were these men *really* up to? He needed to obtain proof of the LuthorCorp connection. He found copies of drawings for the jetpack prototype, body armor, reinforced structural suit, small rocket launchers—the projects he had quietly initiated as a surreptitious investigation into Superman's abilities. Thomson had collated all of the projects from various divisions, putting the pieces together, probably for delivery to a LuthorCorp representative.

But Bruce didn't see the smoking gun he needed. Not yet.

He prowled through each office one by one—Buchheim's, Huston's, McDonnell's, Fitzroy's. As he dug into their private records, he saw that some of these men had been embezzling the Wayne fortune, while others were using the guise of his legitimate corporation to engage in unsavory or illegal activities.

He knew it was just the tip of the iceberg.

He had spent so much time developing his Batman persona and fighting street criminals that he had ignored these white-collar thieves right in front of his face.

When he finished with his inspection in Wayne Tower, Bruce returned to the Cave with all the evidence he had gathered. He still needed rock-solid proof, not just innuendos. When he challenged the board of directors, he wanted to deliver a coup de grâce. He knew he could eventually find the proof he needed.

The night was still young, after all.

CHAPTER 16
LUTHORCORP

AN IMPOSING FIGURE IN BLACK WINGTIP SHOES AND A
gray suit, Lex Luthor stormed down the corridor of
his munitions factory. Seeing the expression on his face and the
angry flush that bloomed along his bald pate, even his personal
bodyguard Bertram gave him a wide berth.

Luthor much preferred the civilized comforts of America to the
rough and raw Siberian wilderness. He had been in a good mood
in the several days since his return to Metropolis. All of his plans
had hummed along like good tires on fresh blacktop.

And now this gaping pothole.

He took the elevator from the administrative offices down to
the manufacturing floor and walked briskly through the maze of
hallways, past laboratories, noisy high bays, assembly lines, and
shipping docks. He hadn't spoken a word since learning of the infiltra-
tor who'd been caught red-handed, and the men trailing him at a
prudent distance prompted none. As far as Luthor was concerned,
they didn't exist. He despised people who didn't respect his boundaries or his privacy. There would be an extensive shakeup in his
security department for allowing this breach; he'd have Bertram look

into the matter personally, and then he would take any necessary action. *Any* action, so long as it could be cleaned up later. Luthor despised mistakes. But that would have to wait for another time.

He finally arrived at the closed door of an employee lunchroom. Two straight-backed guards stood outside. "We didn't want to do anything until you got here, Mr. Luthor."

"At least *someone* is thinking." He flung open the lunchroom door.

Lois Lane sat in an uncomfortable plastic chair, looking completely relaxed. She had served herself coffee from the percolator. Luthor took a moment to let his rage dwindle to a semblance of calm. He liked to appear in control at all times. Gadfly reporters— especially *this* woman—were a cross he had to bear, but now it was time to do some crucifying of his own.

On the lunchroom countertops sat thermoses, packs of cigarettes, lunch pails. When the whistle blew in an hour, workers from assembly line number five would pour into this room, gobble their food, relax for fifteen minutes, and return to work. Like drones, they performed their tasks adequately day in and day out. But people like Lois Lane made him angry. She didn't know her proper place.

Seeing him, Lois flipped open her notepad and gave him an icy, expectant smile. "Ah, there you are, Mr. Luthor. Thank you for seeing me at last. As you know, I've been trying to get an interview for some time."

"How did you get inside, Miss Lane? This is a heavily guarded industrial center working on U.S. military contracts. Did you fail to see the 'No Trespassing' signs?"

Lois shrugged. "Did you fail to read my numerous requests for a meeting? Our readers want to know what you're up to."

"The American public has no business looking into my private affairs."

"The American taxpayers have *every* right to know how their money is spent. The defense of the United States is hardly a 'private affair.'"

He scowled. "Since you have infiltrated this facility, I gather you've seen with your own eyes that we are manufacturing new models of tanks, artillery shells, and missile components for the Defense Department."

Bertram shuffled forward to hand Luthor a small camera he had taken from Lois. With a stern frown, he accepted the camera, opened the back, and removed the film, unspooling it into the light. "I'm afraid your photographs didn't turn out, Miss Lane. A shame." He let the exposed film drop to the lunchroom floor, where someone else would clean it up later. He leaned closer, placing both hands on the lunchroom table. "Are you a Communist spy, Miss Lane?"

She laughed at that, pointedly ignored her camera and ruined film, and scribbled something on her notepad. "Let's not waste the opportunity here, Mr. Luthor. You're a very powerful man, and like most powerful men, you're also very mysterious. *Daily Planet* readers are keen to hear all about one of Metropolis's wealthiest and most influential citizens. For instance"—she tapped pen on paper as though considering what must have been a well-rehearsed question—"you often go on secretive trips to undisclosed locations. Why is that?"

"Your precious taxpayers aren't entitled to know my social schedule. That's why I own a private jet." Luthor turned to a different and time-proven tack. With fake self-deprecation, he pointed to himself. "I'm not a rich playboy bachelor like Bruce

Wayne, I'm not a celebrity, and I'm not some . . . man of steel—I'm just a business executive making a living."

"I agree, Mr. Luthor—you are *no* Bruce Wayne. And certainly no Superman."

He smiled with acid benignity. "That's all I have time for, Miss Lane. I'm a busy man, and my hardworking employees will be going on their shift break in a few minutes."

"Your young *male* employees." If Lois Lane had a major fault, it was a poorly developed sense of tact, and she did not know when to stop pestering.

"*My* employees. Shouldn't a woman your age be married, Miss Lane? Having children, starting a family? You aren't getting any younger."

He snapped toward the guards at the door, "Gentlemen, please escort this woman off the property. And that notebook will have to remain here along with the camera—this is a top-secret, classified facility. We can't allow any possibility of espionage."

The burly men grabbed her arms, and for a moment it looked as if she would actually thrash and struggle. But Lois apparently realized she would make an amusingly helpless spectacle as they dragged her off kicking her heels and flailing her arms. Instead, she angrily allowed herself to be marched out.

Once they had disappeared down the corridor, Luthor's composure began to crumble. Extracting his handkerchief, he wiped a single bead of sweat from his smooth brow. Yes, he was greatly relieved that she had seen only the assembly line, the tanks, the large-caliber artillery guns, the missile nose cones. All those projects were perfectly legitimate.

Not far from where she'd been apprehended, though, Luthor maintained his secure administrative room, which held a large wall map, illuminated radar screens, and the information about his isolated Caribbean island base, not far from the Cuban coast. *If she had managed to get one floor higher in her prowling,* he thought, *that nosy bitch would have seen everything.*

AFTER BEING GIVEN THE BUM'S RUSH OUT, LOIS BRUSHED herself off, regaining her dignity. "Well, that went about as well as I expected."

Blanche Rosen had been right on the money. Lois had infiltrated the facility through a delivery dock when all the men had been on their coffee break. She had slipped up the fire-escape stairwell and gone directly to the secret rooms. She had taken a roll of film already, stashed the small canister inside her waistband, and then sneaked to the lower assembly levels, where Luthor constructed his legitimate munitions for the army. There, she had allowed herself to get caught.

She returned to her rented car—another Ford convertible, but chartreuse this time—which was hidden in the trees outside the fence. Now that he knew he had a weak link in his outer perimeter, Luthor was bound to crack down. She wouldn't get inside again, at least not that way.

Lois climbed into her car and slammed the door. The white canvas top was up, keeping the interior cool. She opened her glove compartment and extracted another notebook, then quickly wrote down everything she could remember, from quotes to details. She hoped the hidden roll of film would yield enough explicit information about what she had seen inside Luthor's locked control room—the outline of the Caribbean island base, strange military plans, blueprints for exotic, high-powered weapons.

She felt in her bones that this could be the story of the decade, hopefully enough to take Luthor down once and for all.

CHAPTER 17
GOTHAM CITY

THANKS TO DRAYLING'S REVELATIONS TO ALFRED AND THE suspicious documents he had found in their offices, Bruce believed that most, if not all, of the remaining board members were under Luthor's thumb.

But he did not believe they were stupid. Arrogant, perhaps. Overconfident, definitely. Some might even be terrified. But not sloppy. They would never leave the truly damning evidence in their own offices. He had to dig deeper to find what he was looking for.

And the best time for digging deep was after dark. Night after night.

He sifted through all publicly available information about the nine men and stripped away their first layer of secrets. Then he donned his other identity and slipped out, targeting each man in turn. He would investigate until he had the necessary proof or until he was convinced a particular man was genuinely clean.

So far, no one had fallen into the latter category.

Next on the list was Paul Henning, the vice president of manufacturing—the first appointed board member who had not been personally selected by his father. Henning had replaced Willard LaBrie, a good man twenty years Thomas Wayne's senior, who had succumbed to a heart attack in his sleep. At first Henning had seemed to fill his predecessor's shoes very well, but he'd grown arrogant, greedy. He had made mistakes, and his biggest mistake was that he left *clues*.

Though Henning owned a nice house in a good suburb of Gotham City, he also surreptitiously rented an apartment under an assumed name. The secret apartment was convenient, discreet, and readily accessed by his mistress for an occasional rendezvous. At the moment, though, it was unoccupied.

The fire escape window in the apartment building had been painted shut. From his utility belt, he withdrew a tiny vial of solvent and applied it to the cracks on the sill, loosening the paint. Powerful magnets on telescoping rods dealt with the latch. Then with a slender metal probe he jimmied open the window.

Several lights were on in the surrounding apartments, and a radio's music drifted into the night. A couple downstairs argued so loudly and constantly that their shouts provided the perfect distraction. Nobody heard the slight sound of a window opening. With a swirl of his dark cape, he slipped inside, then gently slid the window back into place.

He was in the kitchen. Dark, cold. Not a single dirty dish in the sink. Everything neatly in place in the cupboards. Several bottles of bourbon, vodka, and gin stood in a row, with two clean highball glasses and an empty ice bucket. The sitting room contained a plaid sofa, a round table with a lamp, and a large radio. The bedroom held little more than a nightstand and a bed with two pillows, wrinkled sheets. The bathroom was a standard towels/ bath mat/medicine cabinet affair. The cabinet yielded nothing.

Too clean. Too innocuous. Henning couldn't be *that* careful.

Back to the sitting room for a more thorough inspection. The walls were bare. Nothing in the lamp's base.

He slid the sofa forward and found a central heating vent that shouldn't have been there, since a functional radiator stood plainly against the opposite wall. He pried loose the metal grill and discovered not a duct, but a wall safe. The man had a much deeper secret than the fact that he had a mistress.

Donning small earphones from his utility belt, Bruce extracted a sensitive gauge, and in ten minutes he had the safe open. Inside, he found corporate papers, memos, canceled checks, a ledger that revealed numerous transfers of technical documents, and blueprints for highly classified projects that Wayne Enterprises had spent years and millions to develop.

Everything had been transferred to LuthorCorp. Henning had accepted plenty of bribes, and he had kept track of them all. Perhaps the man wanted his own proof to use against Luthor if ever the bald industrialist double-crossed him. It was all the proof Bruce Wayne needed now.

Scowling beneath his mask, he reread the details to make certain, took microfilm photographs of each page, and carefully repackaged the contents.

OF ALL THE MEN ON THE BOARD, SHAWN NORLANDER SEEMED like someone Thomas Wayne would have chosen. He had a normal-appearing life, a wife and two children, and no evidence of living above his means. But that did not clear him of suspicion. If a payoff had not been enough enticement, Luthor could have threatened his family or blackmailed him somehow.

Norlander lived in a two-story Tudor-style home on a maple-lined suburban street, with a backyard enclosed by an incongruous chain-link fence. A Chrysler station wagon with lacquered wood-panel sides sat outside in front of a white-painted detached garage. A push lawn mower leaned against a wall.

He decided to enter from the back, but the fence gate was locked. The chain links rattled as he clambered over to drop with quiet grace to the concrete pad behind the house. His boots barely made a sound. He approached the back porch cautiously and found a locked Dutch door. Producing lock picks from his belt, he squatted and went to work. The dead bolt posed only a small difficulty, and the knob caused no problems at all.

Before he could open the door, however, he sensed movement outside in the yard and saw something large and faintly growling. It was a dark-furred monster loping forward under the thin sliver of moonlight. A mastiff. Only its fangs and gleaming eyes showed in the darkness. Now he understood the reason for the fenced yard.

The well-trained mastiff neither barked nor howled—it simply attacked. The weight of the huge body drove him down. As he raised a defensive forearm, powerful jaws clamped down on the reinforced gauntlet, biting but unable to penetrate the armor fabric. Everything was completely silent save for the hungry growl, like a badly misfiring engine, that continued to emanate from the beast's throat.

He punched its snout, and the dog released its grip. He pulled his arm free, but then the dog drove him back down to the porch. Claws scrabbled on the reinforced fabric over his chest.

Grabbing for the utility belt, he tried to reach his capsules. The forgotten lock picks clinked on the cement porch step, and he ducked so that the fangs barely brushed his exposed chin, striking only the cowl's dark face shield. The mastiff's jaws sank into one of the pointed false ears.

Finally finding the right compartment on the belt, knowing he had to end this brief struggle before the commotion woke anyone up, he seized the vial he sought. He crushed the thin glass ampoule in his palm and shoved the sharp, oily scent of chloroform at the dog's snout. It whiffed, snuffled, began to reel, and finally collapsed against the porch. The effects would last about thirty minutes. It would have to be long enough.

As his breathing slowed, he slipped inside Norlander's house. The kitchen yielded nothing; neither did the formal dining room. He crept upstairs, past the bedrooms of two sleeping children, son and daughter, the boy no more than six. *Six years old.* A boy who probably thought his life would never change, that his parents would always be there. A boy who might suggest going out to a new motion picture in the heart of Gotham City. A boy who might run around the house playing with an imaginary sword, pretending to be Zorro . . .

Work to do. He couldn't let himself think like that.

Bypassing the master bedroom, he crept down the hall until he found the study. He would focus his search there. Indeed, in Norlander's desk—in the false bottom of a drawer—he found documents, photos of a little girl, a bank account set up in two names, neither of which was his own. A picture of a woman the right age to be the child's mother. Not his wife.

And a threatening letter: "No one needs to know about your illegitimate daughter. She's safe, and your comfortable life is safe. Your real family won't suspect a thing. We ask only one small favor."

Digging deeper, he found more evidence of Wayne Enterprises projects being transferred: pending medical breakthroughs, trade secrets that were funneled to LuthorCorp. A juicy bribe had turned Henning; blackmail had broken Norlander; threats to his family had forced Drayling to resign.

He replaced these items exactly as he'd found them. Nobody would know he had been here until it was too late. On his way out he carefully locked the Dutch door once more.

Where it lay sprawled, the mastiff had begun to stir. He bent down and touched its fur. The beast had simply been defending its home from a sinister prowler, protecting those who meant the most to it. Exactly as *he* needed to do with Wayne Enterprises.

On the chain collar encircling the gigantic dog's neck hung a tag bearing its name. FLUFFY.

Leaving the house behind, he slipped over the fence once more and moved off into the night to his next target.

CHAPTER 18
METROPOLIS

ONCE HE GOT BACK TO HIS DESK AT THE *DAILY PLANET,* Clark Kent wrote the draft of his initial "Lorna for the Lovelorn" column, but he wasn't finished yet. First he needed to show it to someone.

"Remember I promised you a cup of coffee, Lois?" He held the typewritten sheets in his hand while he nervously pushed his glasses up with the other. "Um, would now be a good time? We can just go to the coffee shop around the corner." He waved the article. "I'd really like to know what you think."

Lois was in a rush, as always, up to her eyebrows in a big new story she was chasing. If she was on the verge of a real scoop, how could advice to the lovelorn compete with that? But she stopped, saw the look on his face, and instantly warmed to his dilemma. "Oh, Clark—you really look out of your element."

"That's how I feel." He shrugged. "I promise it'll take only a few minutes."

She gave him a quick, compassionate smile. "You buying?"

"Sure."

"Then I'm having a Danish, too." She startled him by slipping her arm through his and steering him toward the elevator. "This isn't a date, you know. Just two coworkers discussing a story."

The elevator doors opened with a ding. Clark was embarrassed. "A date? Why, no, Lois. I mean, there's nothing wrong with—"

"I'm flattered by the attention, Clark. Really, I am. But my heart's set on someone else."

The elevator ride seemed to take forever. "Superman's a hard act to follow," he agreed.

She stiffened. "I didn't say anything about Superman!" When the doors slid open to the lobby of the building, Lois hurried out, with Clark following closely.

In the coffee shop she chose one of the stools at the counter rather than the more intimate setting of a booth. A gum-chewing waitress hurried over with two cups of coffee, and Lois pointed to a cherry-filled Danish in the display case. Nearly twice her size, Clark swiveled on the stool beside her and handed her his article.

"I'm not sure the advice is correct, but I tried to listen to them, respond to how they're feeling, and give them support, one way or another. My mother told me to be compassionate. She said that as long as the advice comes from my heart, then the recommendations can't be entirely wrong."

Lois sipped her coffee and skimmed the article, talking to him as she did so. "When did you see your mother? I thought she's in Kansas."

"I, um, spoke to her on the telephone."

Lois's darting eyes danced back and forth along the lines of text, and he watched her nod slightly to herself. She slowed, read more carefully, and handed the pages back to him. Her smile of approval meant more to him than he could have ever expected. "Not bad, Clark—and I mean that. Not only is it what readers want, but it's good advice, too."

"Thanks, Lois. It was so hard to choose among all those letters. Everyone seems to have a different problem."

Lois tapped her fingernail on one of the paragraphs. "This one's a little thin, though—the man in love with a coworker who doesn't seem to know he exists. I think you should tell him to do little things . . . open doors, ask for her advice, bring her coffee or a newspaper. He doesn't need to win a football championship or put an end to world hunger—he just has to show her that he's a worthy guy. And believe me, women *do* notice these things, whether or not it's apparent to the man."

He took a pencil from his pocket and scribbled notes in the margin while she ate her Danish. "Thanks, Lois. That really helps."

"Your heart's in the right place." She took a quick gulp, finished her cup, and waved away a refill as she swung off the stool. "Gotta go. I'm after an important follow-up to the Luthor story. Thanks for the coffee." Lois pecked Clark on the cheek and gave him a quick smile before she hurried out of the coffee shop. "Good column, Clark. Who knows, you could have a whole new career ahead of you."

He knew he was bright red from blushing.

TAKING HIS MOTHER'S ADVICE TO HEART, CLARK ALSO MADE AN effort to strengthen his friendship with Jimmy Olsen. The freckle-faced young man was delighted when Clark suggested that they catch a movie after work. Jimmy picked the movie—*Earth vs. the Flying Saucers*—and they sat together near the front, munching on popcorn, sipping cherry cola through straws.

Clark stared at the black and white images, watching the enemy aliens with their whirling saucer-like ships, their death rays. Afterward, as the two of them went for ice cream sundaes, Jimmy chattered with animation and enthusiasm about the film. He had thoroughly enjoyed it. Clark, though, was troubled by the persistent portrayal of aliens as evil monsters that wanted to destroy or enslave the human race.

No wonder many of Lois's readers had been skeptical about Superman's declaration that he was not from Earth. He had hoped to provide a shining example, to expose the silliness of being afraid of the unknown, but since he knew no other genuine aliens, how could he be sure?

Hollywood's murderous craft were drastically different from how he imagined spaceships from Krypton would have been constructed, especially ships captained or devised by someone like Jor-El. . . .

THE NEXT DAY, CLARK GLANCED UP FROM HIS TYPEWRITER AS a rush of excitement whirled through the newsroom. Phones started ringing simultaneously. "Quick, turn on the radio!" someone yelled. They all gathered around the shortwave, listening intently to emergency dispatches, alerts that were broadcast on the public bands.

"—repeat, this is a news flash! At this moment, fighter jets are scrambling to respond to a strange silver spacecraft that has appeared over Washington, D.C. Witnesses describe it as a flying saucer. It refuses to respond to radio transmissions."

Clark's glasses skidded down his nose and he pushed them back up. Jimmy was already on his feet, flushed with excitement. "Gosh, Mr. Kent—do you think it's the start of an alien invasion, just like in the movie last night?"

Lois grabbed her phone, yelling toward Perry White's open

doorway, "Chief, I'm calling my father! If anyone knows what's going on, the general will."

"Great Caesar's ghost! He's not going to stop to give interviews in the middle of a national crisis!"

She dialed furiously. "He will if he wants to keep getting birthday cards from me."

Thoughts spinning, Clark wondered if this was finally his opportunity to speak with a fellow alien, maybe even another Kryptonian survivor. He rose quickly from his desk. "Can't talk right now, Jimmy. I'm on a deadline in an hour, and I have to finish my column for Mr. White." He picked up papers and bustled out of the newsroom while the other reporters clustered around the radio.

RED CAPE RIPPLING BEHIND HIM, KAL-EL STREAKED THROUGH the sky, straight toward the nation's capital. By adjusting his senses, both seeing and listening to radio waves on specific bands, he could monitor the action. Seven USAF F-100D Super Sabre jets had taken off from nearby Bolling Air Force base, but the "unidentified flying object" had soared away from Washington, D.C., skimming low to the ground, then looping up into the clouds in a series of impossible maneuvers. The fighter pilots did their best to keep up, roaring along at top speed; they left vapor trails that Kal-El could easily follow.

If this truly was an interstellar ship, it would be capable of incredible velocities. As the sleek elliptical craft raced westward across the United States, it outdistanced the supersonic jets. But Kal-El could fly faster even than that.

The UFO raced across the Great Plains, cutting across Nebraska, then headed south. Kal-El wondered briefly if it would arrow toward Smallville. Might a fellow Kryptonian be able to detect someone from his former home in the middle of Kansas? Maybe even the remnants of his crashed ship?

Kal-El picked up on the chatter among the F-100D pilots. "So far the bogey hasn't launched any bombs or missiles, Cap. Maybe it's peaceful—over."

"And maybe it's just here to ask for directions to Venus," one of the other pilots shot back.

The squadron commander broke in. "Our orders are to pursue and intercept. We've gotten no response to our transmissions, so we have to assume that thing means no good. Listen up—when you get in range, fire at will. Acknowledge."

A chorus of voices responded. "Copy that."

"Roger."

If the alien visitor did not speak English, Kal-El wondered how the spacecraft could possibly respond. He felt a powerful need to reach the flying saucer first, before the fighter jets did anything foolish. These men might unintentionally provoke an interplanetary war.

He soared forward to catch up with the Super Sabres. One of the pilots detected him on his radar. "Sir, there's something coming up on our six! Wait . . . it's Superman!"

Kal-El streaked by, hand raised, cape now a blurry red line behind him as he shot past the lead plane.

"Roger that. He'll knock that alien out of the sky!"

"Maybe so . . . but remember, *he's* an alien, too. Over."

"Eyes front, Cap! Where did those other aircraft come from—over?"

Three larger planes now flew on a perpendicular course, peeling out in front of the strange silver craft. The unmarked private planes also intended to intercept the alien saucer. The Air Force squadron sent hails, demanding that the new pilots identify themselves, but the mysterious aircraft did not respond. The unidentified planes cut directly across the UFO's path, but the saucer zigzagged, ducked beneath them, and streaked past in an instant.

Kal-El scanned ahead, squinting, pushing with his enhanced vision to glean information about the three private craft. His X-ray vision penetrated their hulls, and through the fuselage he discerned pilots, technicians, and engineers working with analytical devices, studying screens. They all wore uniforms with a very familiar corporate logo.

LuthorCorp.

What did LuthorCorp have to do with the alien craft? Kal-El supposed that someone like Lex Luthor would be fascinated by otherworldly technology. He probably wanted to seize the silver craft for himself, and he undoubtedly had his own equipment, including unmarked supersonic aircraft, so that he could get the strange ship before the military did. Regardless, it was obvious that even these new planes had no chance of catching the flying saucer.

Kal-El put on a burst of speed, pulled ahead of the Super Sabre jets, and began closing the gap to the UFO.

As he raced past, he saw that the men inside the LuthorCorp aircraft were activating a kind of pulse beacon from a small antenna. But instead of aiming it at the flying saucer, they pointed the spike back toward the oncoming F-100D squadron.

Behind him, Kal-El heard a cry of surprised dismay transmitted by one of the pilots. "Mayday, Mayday! Flameout!"

The squadron formation broke apart and scattered, with the trailing jets circling away. The lead Super Sabre, though, began gushing black smoke from its engines as it tumbled awkwardly from the sky like a downed waterfowl. The pilot hit his afterburners, trying everything. "All systems FUBAR. Can't eject. Malfunction! Going down, going down!"

Kal-El saw the F-100D enter a deadly and disorienting flat spin, its engines erupting in a blaze of flame. One of its wings shimmied dangerously. The pilot inside was doomed.

Meanwhile, the LuthorCorp craft beat a hasty retreat, no longer pretending to chase the flying saucer, and the UFO streaked away in a completely different direction.

The remainder of the USAF squadron could do nothing to help their fellow pilot. Their own cockpit systems were also scrambled, and the pilots struggled to keep from crashing alongside their leader.

Kal-El didn't pause to think about what he should do. He had to forget about the flying saucer. Someone needed his help. He whirled about and dove toward the falling jet.

He filled his lungs and expelled a great gust of air, enough to freeze the engine cowling and extinguish the flames before the fuel tanks exploded. Then, as gently as he could, he took hold of the jet's belly, raising his hands over his head so he could support the falling deadweight, taking away the burden of gravity as he eased the aircraft toward the barren ground below.

The Super Sabre's systems were completely fried, which prevented the pilot from extending his landing gear. Kal-El brought the jet down carefully on the desert sand, set it on its belly, then tore away the canopy. He snapped the pilot's harness and pulled the man to safety, still concerned that the jet might explode.

As he stood on wobbly legs, the pilot removed his helmet and drew deep gasping breaths. He shook his head and looked back at his wrecked plane. "Thanks, Superman. You saved my life."

"Glad to be able to help. I wouldn't leave you stranded." The airman brushed himself off, looking both shaken and relieved.

Normally, such sincere appreciation would have been all Kal-El needed to hear, but he looked up into the sky, where the UFO had already streaked out of sight. The crippled squadron had sent out distress signals and requests for backup, then circled around to retrieve the downed pilot.

With bittersweet disappointment, Kal-El scanned the sky for any silver glint of the saucer, but too much time had passed. The mysterious spacecraft had vanished.

CHAPTER 19
THE LUTHOR MANSION

HE HAD SEEN ENOUGH EVIDENCE, BUT HE DIDN'T HAVE enough answers. Before confronting the members of his board, Bruce decided to go to the core of the problem: Lex Luthor.

The industrial magnate's private home was in the Lake District north of Metropolis, an extravagant fortress built along the lines of a military citadel, strikingly different from the stately Gothic architecture of Wayne Manor.

Bruce easily found an excuse for a quick trip from Gotham City to Metropolis using his Wayne Enterprises private jet. Charity functions, private meetings with potential donors, maybe even a night on the town—he didn't need to worry about a cover story.

Before departing for Metropolis, Bruce studied the blueprints (both the redacted plans on public file and the *accurate* versions that were supposedly not available to anyone), old and forgotten permit applications and rubber-stamped approvals, the landscaping layout, the architectural elevation drawings. He searched for weaknesses and considered some of the surprises that might be waiting for him. Then he got himself ready.

The ostentatious Lake District homes were surrounded by a comfortable buffer of forested land. Luthor's property was encircled by a dangerous-looking wrought-iron fence topped with spear points, beyond which stretched a no-man's-land of additional fences and booby traps.

Any man who needed so much security obviously had something to hide. Bruce Wayne knew that from personal experience.

Darkly caped and fearsomely cowled, with heavy-traction boots and armored bodysuit, utility belt loaded with a cornucopia of imaginative tools, he prepared to infiltrate Luthor's mansion.

He began his approach as soon as full darkness fell. Given the perimeter fences, he decided the best approach was from the lake. Fitting an air mask to his face and immersing himself, he glided forward underwater, creating not even a ripple—a shark now, instead of a bat.

Luthor's mansion had a private dock, but no boat was tied up to it. While closing the distance and shining a small light into the murky waters before him, he saw large metal spikes strategically submerged at the property line. These would tear the hull of any boat that approached too closely. The placid surface gave no hint of the jagged tips just underwater.

Intent on avoiding these spikes, he didn't see the fine mesh of entrapment wire that snared him. He struggled, but the elastic net drew tighter. Forcing calm, he worked one gauntlet free and produced a wire cutter from his utility belt, with which he made short, methodical work of the lethal strands. He swam free. Gradually he raised himself above the surface, coming to shore. His thick suit had been scratched by the sharp entrapment wire; a normal swimmer would have been sliced to ribbons.

He crept up from the lake, careful not to stir the dried leaves or fallen branches at the water's edge. When he reached the spiked fence, he worked his way over and through, careful to make no sound. Before taking a step, he scanned the ground carefully. He found and avoided four trip wires and a land mine trigger. He hoped that no neighbor children accidentally heaved a baseball over the fence; Luthor had a lethal prejudice against unexpected visitors.

After conducting careful surveillance for several hours during his preparations, he already knew the guards' habits. While he waited in the shadows, five armed men walked about in a standard patrol pattern. Intimidating yet inefficient. Predictable.

Luthor's intelligence was also his weakness, because he believed himself superior to most people. Since his security would baffle any *normal* man, he would think he was safe. Arrogant . . . but sloppy just the same.

The imposing mansion had sharp angles and plenty of glass, metal, and concrete; it did not at all fit with the natural wooded surroundings. The highest roof sported a small private observatory. This "home" seemed designed to convey the impression that Lex Luthor had many friends and social obligations, but the mansion was in fact virtually deserted. As the midnight hour approached, Luthor's only company was his security team.

With his dark cape helping to hide him, he circled to the wing that housed Luthor's extravagant second-floor study, which was fronted by a balcony. He suspected that the household safe and Luthor's private records would be there.

Withdrawing a sharp-pronged grappling hook, he twirled it, paying out the thin, strong cable. He let the hook fly, and it sailed upward on a gentle, precise arc. The prongs caught and lodged around the stone balustrade. He pulled the cable taut, then braced his boots against the stone wall. He felt acutely exposed, worried that a spotlight might happen to brush across the mansion's exterior. According to their unvarying patrol patterns, he had forty seconds before the guards returned.

He reached the balcony, swung himself over, and crouched in the shadows just as a guard turned the corner, walked past, and continued into the grounds.

The French doors of the balcony were locked. The interior lights were low, the room empty. He peered inside, saw no sign of Luthor. On the other side of the mansion, the observatory dome was cracked open, and the telescope within was pointed toward the starry sky.

Removing a diamond glass cutter from his belt, he scribed a circle in the inset glass near the lock and easily removed the cut section of the French door. He slithered his hand inside and turned the lock, then quietly swung open the door. He felt like James Bond infiltrating the headquarters of SPECTRE. But this was not a spy novel—this was real.

He would search the offices quickly, take what he needed, and get back out. Since this was Luthor's inner sanctum, past the gauntlet of security measures and a veritable army of guards, Luthor would be most confident of himself here. He had left important papers, files, and objects right there on the desk.

After tonight, Luthor would likely be even more paranoid.

Sifting through the memos with gauntleted hands, looking at folders and labels, he sorted out what he needed. The more he saw, the deeper the conspiracy went. He found files on each member of his board of directors, records of their indiscretions, specific descriptions of how each man had been turned into a LuthorCorp puppet, along with notes on the technical data and prototypes they had smuggled to Luthor.

With soft clicks of his miniaturized camera, he photographed everything.

After he viewed the next files, his anger grew. The Wayne Enterprises designs that Bruce had quietly encouraged for the sole purpose of understanding Superman's abilities—LuthorCorp had put the pieces together into a unified application. Luthor had developed a model of armored "battlesuits," walking robotic armor shells with enhanced muscles, built-in weapons systems, even jetpacks for brief flights.

The battlesuit blueprints, though, had been piled to the left of the desk, as if some emergency had preempted all other concerns. The urgent work that occupied Luthor was a set of memos and classified dispatches, communiqués sent by courier to the White House, to the Air Force, to the chiefs of agencies not generally known to the public. The carbon copy of a memo addressed directly to President Eisenhower sat on top of the stack. Luthor demanded that the Air Force release his "private property" from a secret installation in the Nevada desert, a classified base that the memorandum called "Area 51." Responses from the Air Force, even from Eisenhower, repeatedly denied any knowledge.

Very interesting . . .

Minutes ticked away. Glancing again around the office, he knew he should leave and not press his luck, but he felt violated and angry at how Luthor had taken advantage of a long-standing trust built into the corporate structure of Wayne Enterprises . . . how he had tried to bring down his father's company. Lex Luthor's schemes were like a set of Russian dolls, one nested inside another, inside another, on and on until any investigator would get lost.

One more thorough search of the office. Atop a sturdy file cabinet he found a small cubical lead box next to a stack of printouts, spectrographs, and filtered photos of a crystalline rock. The label on the lead box marked the specimen's origin as Ariguska, Siberia.

With his attention to details, he noted the casual placement of the lead box and the unexpected clutter of the documents. The clues told him that Luthor had devoted a lot of recent attention to this specimen. He lifted the hinged cover on the lead box to reveal a baseball-sized fragment of a crystalline substance. The irregular-shaped rock emitted a faint emerald glow.

Though he had studied geology and could readily identify many types of gems, natural crystals, and igneous, metamorphic, and sedimentary rock, he was totally unfamiliar with any substance such as this. A meteorite, perhaps?

He looked more closely at the analytical reports; LuthorCorp chemists had been unable to determine the mineral's molecular structure. The energy readings, the radioactive emissions, and the character of its refracted light were all highly unusual. Luthor's personal handwritten notes produced more questions than answers.

"Energy readings exotic, difficult to correlate. Nature of material conveys the possibility of chemical/radioactive power. How to release it? Mineral is unlike normal fissile material. Mutagenic properties—unknown, but likely. Possible uses? Not yet determined. Potential? *Unlimited*."

More mysteries opening up like Russian dolls: Strange items being held by the government inside a secret military facility in Nevada. Battlesuit prototypes based on proprietary research and development done by Wayne Enterprises. Now a mysterious, energetic mineral specimen from Siberia . . . .

Lex Luthor had already stolen so much from Wayne Enterprises, had whisked cutting-edge technological discoveries out from under Bruce Wayne's nose. Though this intriguing green rock appeared to have nothing to do with the corruption of the board of directors, perhaps it was something that Wayne Enterprises should investigate as well. It was time to balance the scales.

He lifted the lead box from the top of the file cabinet to look at the mineral more closely.

Suddenly alarms shrieked, bells rang, and spotlights blazed all around Lex Luthor's household.

CHAPTER 20
THE LUTHOR MANSION

SITTING IN THE QUIET DARKNESS OF HIS PRIVATE OBSERVA-tory, Lex Luthor spent the evening in contemplation. He kept a blank notepad near the telescope's eyepiece, both for astronomical observation and to record the innovative ideas that invariably popped into his head whenever he let his thoughts flow.

Tonight, though, Luthor remained angry and frustrated. He was not accustomed to people refusing to give him what he needed or wanted. Reasonable men did not turn down Lex Luthor's requests—yet President Eisenhower had snubbed him. Who did the man think he was?

With the observatory dome cracked open and his sixteen-inch refractor telescope pointed to the sky, Luthor continued his study of the empty, threatening heavens. The evening was chilly, and he tightened his smoking jacket of patterned silk lined with baby seal fur.

He maneuvered the telescope into position. His personal calculations had provided tracking tables, so he knew exactly where and when the blip of Sputnik would cross the night sky. It was a fad these days for people to go outside with binoculars or little toy telescopes to search for the orbiting object. Each time the Soviet satellite crossed unchallenged over American airspace, Luthor considered it a provocation. He would keep watching the skies.

Time and again, the Soviet space program had proven its superiority. At one time, Luthor had invested in the U.S. space effort, had studied the progress of the Vanguard project, had met personally with Wernher von Braun—but it all disappointed him. Vanguard was supposed to have beaten the Soviets into space, but it was now overdue and over budget. And so Luthor chose not to bother with such bumbling bureaucracy. He had decided to do something on his own, using his Caribbean island base. . . .

Now he peered into the eyepiece, adjusted the focus, and watched the stars in his field of view transform from fuzzy blobs into diamond sparkles. Sputnik would be along any moment now.

Emergency alarms startled him out of his reverie. Automatic lights blazed on in the observatory, temporarily blinding him, but Luthor was already on his feet. He recognized the pitch of the sirens, knew the location of the clanging bells. This was no bumbling intruder at the outer fences; it was an inner-perimeter security breach. He snatched up the master Handie-Talkie and held the transmit button. "Report! What's happened?"

"Intruder, Mr. Luthor," Bertram replied crisply.

"*I know that!* Have you caught him yet?"

"No, sir. We're making our way to your study now."

Luthor was already bolting from the observatory, astonished that anyone would *dare* do this to him. Such a person would have to be suicidal. "Make certain he's alive when you apprehend him—I may wish to do some of the questioning myself. No need to inform the police."

He'd reached his office by the time the first security squads converged there, but the intruder had already fled. Luthor scanned his desk, saw that papers had been moved, noted the circle of glass cut out near the French door lock. A chair had been overturned, presumably as the burglar made his rapid escape.

With sick dread, he jerked his head so quickly he nearly gave himself whiplash. The lead box containing the green mineral from General Ceridov's quarry was gone.

Astonishing—and baffling. How could any corporate spy have known about that? He dashed onto the balcony, spied the grappling hook still anchored on the balustrade. The entire property was bathed in searchlights.

Shouts from the grounds now, then barking dogs. They would tear the man apart and probably leave little for interrogation . . . or even identification. Luthor suddenly caught sight of a shadowy figure in a dark cape—some sort of *costume?*—racing along, dodging nets and spotlights, leaping expertly over land mines and trip wires, easily maneuvering through the deadly obstacle course. Whoever this man was, this burglar, this *spy,* he knew Luthor's mansion and property down to the tiniest detail.

An explosion sounded, accompanied by an eruption of dirt and smoke: One of his own guards had not been so adept at avoiding the land mines. Luthor made a disgusted sound; they could pick up the bloody pieces of the clod later.

"Hurry, he's getting away!"

The intruder kept running.

KAL-EL FLEW OVER METROPOLIS, HIS RED CAPE FLUTTER-
ing in the breeze. Below, he saw nighttime traffic lights
and the winking glimmers of bright skyscraper windows, people
attending shows, dining in restaurants, seeing motion pictures.
Staring at the kaleidoscope of night life, he tried to imagine how
magnificent Krypton must have been, how exotic, how spectacular. But Earth was his planet now, and these were his people.

He needed to make sure that Lex Luthor did not pose a danger
to them.

Kal-El himself had seen clear evidence of LuthorCorp planes
chasing the mysterious alien saucer. He wanted to look the man
in the eye and ask him why. If he had tried to do so as Clark Kent,
reporter for the *Daily Planet*, he would have gotten nowhere. As
Superman, however, he could not be ignored.

Kal-El streaked north beyond the city limits, up toward the
Lake District. He skimmed pine forests interspersed with posh
homes until he found the bright lights and incongruous modern
architecture of Luthor's mansion. It was naive to think he could
simply land on the man's balcony and talk with him, as he had

done with Lois Lane. And he would not fly overhead and use his X-ray vision to spy on Luthor's private activities in his own home. By any measure, that would have been wrong. His parents had taught him better than that.

As he approached, still trying to formulate a plan, he heard Luthor's household alarms and saw bright spotlights illuminating the grounds. With a quick scan, Kal-El watched guards responding to an emergency—a home invasion. Luthor was being robbed! Some intrepid burglar had broken through the industrialist's security and was now getting away.

With his sharp vision he saw the shadowy shape of a man in a dark costume, cape, and mask. The caped figure expertly dodged booby traps, leaped over wire fences, and raced toward the perimeter of Luthor's property. The confused guards shouted and fired their guns at the uncertain target.

Without hesitation, Kal-El swooped down. Jonathan Kent had taught him in no uncertain terms that the law was a safety net that applied to everyone, rich and poor alike. He had foiled many robberies and heists and would do so again, here on Luthor's property. Kal-El could stop this criminal and turn him in to the authorities, without anyone getting hurt. *The law applies to everyone.*

He recognized the prowler's fearsome disguise from stories in the Gotham City papers: the Batman, a vigilante who had attacked the Gotham police and broken as many laws as the criminals he supposedly apprehended. Batman could have been a hero; he could have fought for the forces of good, but Kal-El was seeing him now for what he really was—no more than a petty criminal in a disguise. Kal-El had dealt with petty criminals before.

He landed silently in front of Batman, assuming a wide-footed stance, fists on hips, cape fluttering. "Stop!"

Intent on eluding the guards behind him in the trees, Batman halted. His eyes narrowed behind the dark mask, but his response was not what Kal-El expected: "I *knew* you worked for LuthorCorp." He was holding something in one gauntlet, hidden by his cape.

Kal-El frowned, not knowing what Batman was talking about. "I do not work for Luthor."

"Don't lie to me. And don't think you can stop me."

With a flick of his other wrist, he flung a pointed Bat-shuriken, but the tiny throwing bat ricocheted off Kal-El's chest and fell to the ground. The sharp barbs did not penetrate his blue suit, nor did the tranquilizer toxin come into contact with his skin. Batman paused only a moment before the same hand let fly a bolo string, and the weights wrapped around Kal-El's arms and torso. With a flex of his elbows, though, the high-tensile-strength cables snapped like cotton threads.

Spotlights shone through the dark trees. The guards were coming, shouting, and Lex Luthor was with them.

Kal-El did not abide thieves; Batman had to be held accountable for what he had done here. The bald industrialist would likely want to take matters into his own hands. Kal-El couldn't allow that either. He did not trust Lex Luthor to provide appropriate justice.

Bursting through the trees into the clearing, Luthor spotted the two of them standing there, facing each other. He let out an astonished gasp.

Acting on impulse, Kal-El seized Batman by his cape-covered shoulders and bounded into the air, carrying him away. "I'm taking you to the proper authorities."

Below, Luthor shouted, "Stop them! Don't let them get away!"

His guards opened fire, but Kal-El dodged the bullets as he

flew into the night, heading across the calm surface of the lake. Batman didn't struggle, didn't argue as they raced out of sight, low over the water. Instead, he said accusatorily, "How did LuthorCorp create you? Drugs? Controlled mutation? Technological augmentations?"

"Luthor didn't—"

Kal-El was startled when the other man twitched, touched a catch on his suit, and suddenly his slippery cape detached from his shoulders. Batman dropped free and plunged into the lake water below. Kal-El was left holding the scallop-edged cape while Batman dove deeper beneath the surface, fitting a breather over his face.

Kal-El's vision could penetrate the dark waters. Dropping the useless cape, he dove into the lake himself, knifing beneath the surface and stroking toward the sleek figure. Seeing him approach, Batman released a small canister from his belt, which burst open, spreading a foaming cloud of bubbles and murky dye, like an underwater smoke screen.

Kal-El couldn't believe how quickly the man could move. Though he sped through the murk, Batman had already changed direction, stroking toward the nearby shore and the dark, clustered mansions opposite Luthor's property.

Kal-El had had enough. With a burst of speed he seized Batman again and flew up out of the water, leaving a splash behind them like an erupting geyser. Batman punched him in the jaw with a blow that would have stunned any normal man, but Kal-El gritted his teeth, flew to the pebbly shore, and dropped his opponent on an empty stretch between homes. "I don't want to hurt you, but I'm not going to let you get away. You'll stand trial for your crimes."

As lake water ran smoothly from his dark suit, Batman seemed to be studying Kal-El, seeking hidden vulnerabilities. Batman said in a low voice, "If you take me out of the equation, then who'll make Luthor accountable for *his* crimes?"

Kal-El hesitated. Lois had been clear about her suspicions of what the millionaire industrialist was doing, and her reporter instincts were rarely wrong. But a crime was still a crime, and he could not ignore what Batman had done. Kal-El made accusations of his own. "I know you broke into Luthor's home. What did you steal from him? What's so important?"

"You tell *me* why it's important." Batman turned slightly, holding a small lead box in his gloved hand. "What does Luthor want with this specimen? Why is he protecting it?" He opened the lead box to reveal a shimmering green fragment of broken crystalline rock.

Kal-El suddenly felt as if a locomotive had struck him in the back. He felt weak, drained. "What . . . is that?"

"You tell me." Batman pressed forward, and Kal-El's knees threatened to buckle. His vision turned dim, and black dots swirled before his eyes. He reeled, utterly helpless on the stony shore of the lake as he struggled for breath. Nothing like this had ever happened to him before. He collapsed to his knees, fighting to stay conscious.

And in that instant Batman was gone. Among the complex shadows of the pine forest at the boundary of the estate, the other man simply disappeared, taking the glowing green mineral with him.

As soon as Batman was gone, Kal-El felt his strength begin to return, his senses restored like a rush of cool water. But he was still weak, disoriented, reeling. And astonished. How could such a brief exposure to a lump of rock affect him so greatly? What kind of secret weapon was it?

On the opposite side of the lake, the lights and commotion at Luthor's mansion continued. He heard alarms, shouts, two random and unnecessary gunshots. Soon even the distant neighbors would realize something was going on.

Kal-El scanned the forest, the isolated docks, the dark houses, but he saw no sign of Batman. The other man had completely vanished.

CHAPTER 22
THE *DAILY PLANET*

THE DAY AFTER HIS STRANGE AND UNSETTLING ENCOUNTER with Batman, Clark returned to his desk to face yet another bag of letters addressed to "Lorna for the Lovelorn." He adjusted his dark-rimmed glasses and stared warily, as if these pleas for help were also made of the mysterious green stone that had so profoundly affected him the night before.

Yet another problem his superpowers couldn't solve.

After what he had seen at Luthor's mansion, Batman's baffling comments and accusations, and the LuthorCorp planes chasing the flying saucer, Clark knew he needed to uncover the truth. He needed to be a journalist again, a *real* journalist.

He dumped the mailbag on his desk. All these letters came from people who truly wanted answers to their personal problems, but Clark Kent wasn't the one to give them. He was a *reporter,* not a counselor or a social worker. Though he carefully maintained a meek and harmless demeanor, Clark was far from passive. Straightening his jacket, he went to the glass doorway of Perry White's office and knocked politely.

Perry was reading his own newspaper, scrutinizing the headlines, chomping on his cigar. He looked up. "Kent! That first Lovelorn column of yours was lackluster. Those people want advice, not sympathy. You have to *solve* their problems, not just hold their hands."

Exactly the opposite of what his mother and Lois had told him.

"You're right, Mr. White. I don't think I'm—"

Perry cut him off. "I've been thinking, Kent—I didn't hire you to be a pen pal for our whiniest subscribers. My wife, Alice, has been nagging me to take a crack at the Lorna column herself. She's always giving *me* advice—she might as well do it for profit." He didn't seem to expect Clark to laugh at his joke. "I've decided to reassign you."

"Uh . . . thank you, Mr. White."

"Don't thank me—I want you back doing real work for this paper."

Clark jumped in, showing his initiative. "I was thinking about a follow-up on that flying saucer sighting—"

"You must be reading my mind, Kent. Get out there and snoop around before Lois gets it into her head to investigate. Since her expense accounts are always higher than yours, I want you and Olsen to check out this UFO story, especially with the new information that just came over the wires."

Jimmy hurried into the office, hearing his name. "There's more to the UFO sighting? Where are we going, Mr. White?"

"We've got reports that a flying saucer crashed in a Podunk town in northern Arizona. Could be the same one, or maybe it's all part of an invasion. The closest airport is Las Vegas, so you'll have to land there, rent a car, and drive. You're sharing a motel room, mind you. And the *Planet* isn't paying for gambling markers or topless Vegas shows!"

"No, sir, Mr. White!" Clark and Jimmy answered in unison.

"I knew you two would be perfect for this job." Perry nodded wryly. "In fact—broaden the story, Kent. Give me a full background on the whole flying saucer craze. Even the Air Force has launched an official investigation—Project Yearbook or Project Bluebonnet, something like that."

"I believe that's Project Blue Book, Mr. White."

"See? You're already an expert! I want a full investigative piece. Tell me if this crashed flying saucer has real little green men or if it has more to do with pink elephants from the bottom of a whiskey bottle." He shooed them out of the office. "Get to Metropolis airport, pronto. Lois is at an impromptu press conference Lex Luthor just called—I want you on your way before she decides to stick her nose in your story and asks to come along. Besides, there's a gambler's weekend special flight, and you can shave fifteen dollars off your plane tickets. Move!"

Clark and Jimmy scurried from the office, both grinning at their shared good fortune, though for very different reasons. "Gosh, Las Vegas, Mr. Kent! I'll bet the lights on the Strip are bright enough to attract alien visitors." The young man began gathering up his equipment. "Do you think the flying saucer is real?"

"Aliens on Earth? It's up to us to find the truth." Clark did his best to cloak his excitement. He had been seeking the same answers most of his life.

LEX LUTHOR RARELY ISSUED PUBLIC STATEMENTS HIMSELF, leaving that chore to his press relations staff. Therefore, Lois Lane was very interested when the bald industrialist called an emergency press conference. He was certainly incensed about *something*.

Knowing what she did about his shadowy activities, Lois wasn't inclined to believe what Luthor had to say; nevertheless, if he took questions, she could ask him—in public—about why and how he'd gotten rid of his female employees, about their mysterious deaths, maybe even about the unmarked LuthorCorp planes that had chased the flying saucer a few days ago, according to Superman's statement after the recovery of the crashed jet.

She was eager to hear how Luthor would answer.

Despite her persistent telephone calls, Lois had been unable to get any clear answers from her father either; General Sam Lane's military reticence had won out, despite his daughter's pestering. But the incident could not be ignored: An Air Force jet had crashed in pursuit of a UFO, and no one seemed to understand why. Had the alien ship used a secret weapon, or had the systems been scrambled by the LuthorCorp planes?

She doubted Luthor would admit it, either way.

Now, as she stood among the crowd of reporters, Luthor emerged from the front entrance of his imposing corporate head-quarters. He was impeccably dressed in a well-tailored black business suit with a thin black tie. He strode to the podium that had been set up for the event, positioned for optimum coverage, and gazed down at the clutch of reporters as though they were necessary evils. Radio newsmen proffered bulky microphones. Even a television news crew was there with an unwieldy, large camera.

Luthor had to force himself not to scowl as he recognized Lois, front and center, prepared to take thorough notes. His gaze skated past her, and he fashioned what must have been meant as a welcoming smile; it seemed to be an expression he rarely used.

He gave a pleasant greeting. "Ladies and gentlemen of the press. I have done many good things for the United States of America— and that has made me a target for evildoers and Communists. Last night an intruder broke into my *home*." As he emphasized the last word, his pale face assumed self-righteous anger. Reporters eagerly recorded his words, scribbled notes, and followed him with their microphones. "This burglar might just as easily have been an assassin. I could have been killed." He waited a beat, as if perplexed that his listeners were not as outraged as he was.

Lois seized upon the pause in the conversation. "Average people are robbed every day, Mr. Luthor. Why is this a big story?"

Luthor leaned forward, relishing his next words. "Because average people, as you call them, are not robbed with the assistance of *Superman,* Miss Lane."

His words dropped on the crowd like a bombshell. *Now* the

reporters did gasp, and photographers snapped pictures of Luthor standing there, looking smug.

He raised his voice. "Superman claims he's here to defend people. He says he wants to stop criminals—and yet, when *my* house was attacked, when *I* was robbed, he came . . . and helped the burglar get away. I saw him with my own eyes. When my security men were about to apprehend the thief, Superman flew off with him, whisked him to safety!" Luthor jabbed a finger toward the reporters, toward the TV cameras, and particularly toward Lois.

Chasing the story, looking for a big scoop, the reporters muttered about this new idea. "Why would he do that, Mr. Luthor?"

"Indeed, why would he do that? Maybe a good investigative reporter could find the answer. Ask yourselves—what is Superman hiding? What does he really want from us all?"

Offended on Superman's behalf, Lois refused to consider what Luthor was suggesting. "Maybe Superman wants to protect the innocent. It's what his track record shows."

Luthor gave a brief, utterly humorless chuckle, as if he found the very idea of altruism to be absurd. "It seems that Superman protects only those he likes. Do we really want selective justice handed out by a man who openly claims to be an alien? From a man who refuses to disclose his true identity? I look forward to what you all dig up about him."

Lois remembered the accusations Blanche Rosen had made and the corroborating evidence she herself had found inside Luthor's munitions factory. Superman wasn't the one who needed the persistent attentions of an investigative reporter. But from the predatory expressions on some of her fellow journalists, she could tell that at least a few of them would play right into Lex Luthor's plans. It infuriated her.

"And how do you explain the unmarked LuthorCorp planes that were supposedly chasing the flying saucer? Superman says he saw them with his X-ray vision," Lois blurted. "Did they have anything to do with the crashed jet?"

Luthor responded with a sneer. "Listen to yourself, Miss Lane. *Unmarked* planes. *Supposedly* chasing a UFO. All according to Superman's *X-ray vision*? I wouldn't put much stock in what Superman has to say after what I *actually saw* him do last night."

Seeing that he had achieved his desired intent, Luthor turned about and disappeared into his headquarters, ignoring the cacophony of questions that erupted in his wake. It didn't matter to her if these other reporters went haring off to uncover Superman's dark secrets—they would find nothing. Though she had only met him a couple of times, Lois felt she understood him with her heart. She had not the slightest doubt that Superman was exactly as brave and as good as he appeared to be.

Luthor, on the other hand, had plenty of things to hide.

WHEN SHE RETURNED TO THE *DAILY PLANET*, LOIS HURRIED TO her desk and pulled out the scrap of paper on which she had written Blanche Rosen's phone number and address. She had already searched through hospital records and obituaries and had found listings for several of the men and women Blanche had identified. All of them had died of "natural causes."

Since those men and women were either widowed or unmarried, without families, no one would raise too many questions. Their deaths would be quietly swept under the rug, unnoticed. No one but Lois was going to do anything about it.

She had made up her mind to get Blanche a job at the *Daily Planet*. With all her years of diligent service for the country, the woman could fill some position—in the secretarial pool, in the cafeteria, on the switchboard. And it would spite Luthor.

Feeling good about what she was about to do—Blanche certainly needed a break in her life—Lois went in person to the woman's small apartment on the Lower East Side. Driving her convertible, she followed the directions she had jotted down.

As she turned onto the right street, scanning the address numbers on the brownstone buildings, Lois had to swerve to the curb as a police car roared past her, siren wailing. With her reporter's instinct, Lois looked around, keen to see what might be happening. As she eased the car back into traffic, another shrieking siren came up behind her, an ambulance this time, its red lights flashing.

Now she followed, accelerating to keep up with the emergency vehicles, and her heart sank with dread as she began to realize where they were going. The same address she had scrawled on her notepad.

Outside Blanche Rosen's apartment building, the police car had already stopped at an angle to traffic, both doors wide open. Two officers worked to keep the crowd back. Paramedics jumped from the back of the ambulance, but the body sprawled on the street had been covered with a sheet, already turning red from seeping blood. Several old women on the sidewalk were holding each other, sobbing.

Lois quickly got out of her car and ran over to the scene, but she already knew. A policeman stopped her from getting closer, though she pushed against his implacable arm. "Sorry, ma'am—this is a crime scene. I can't let you get any closer."

The paramedics looked under the sheet; both men shook their heads.

One of the old women from the sidewalk pleaded with the

second policeman, grabbing his shoulders and looking up at him through owlish glasses. "I saw it all, Officer! You have to catch him—some terrible man ran her down in the street and then just drove off. Just drove off! He left her there on the street. Oh, poor Blanche!" The old woman looked at the policeman, then at the gathered crowd, as if someone there could give her answers. "What sort of man would do something so *awful*?"

CHAPTER 24
WAYNE TOWER

BRUCE SAUNTERED IN TWO MINUTES LATE FOR THE BOARD of directors' private Thursday session. Though it wasn't his regular day to sit in as a figurehead, this would be quite different from the average meeting. He had his own item for the agenda.

The men sitting around the boardroom table were startled by his arrival; he noticed the flash of annoyance that rippled across several faces. All of the directors had cups of coffee; some of them held lit cigarettes. An executive continental breakfast was spread upon a side table.

"Mr. Wayne! We didn't realize you were joining us. This isn't Tuesday," said Buchheim.

Thomson was a bit surlier. "We have a full agenda today, sir. If you've come about the new corporate logo designs, I'm afraid they'll have to wait until later."

Henning flicked cigarette ash into a large tray in front of him. "I can have my secretary type up a full summary of our meeting for you afterward, Mr. Wayne. That should be all you need to know."

Bruce went to an empty chair, ignoring their comments. Without sitting, he rested his briefcase on the table. "You'll make the time, gentlemen. Important matters have come to my attention."

He unsnapped his case and removed a stack of files. He circled the table, dropping a sealed file in front of each man. They gazed at the folders, perplexed and impatient. Someone muttered about the time wasted on "another charity boondoggle to save the baby seals."

Director Miles heaved a long sigh and whispered (but not so quietly that Bruce couldn't hear), "God save us from self-important millionaires." Bruce let Miles's folder fall heavily in front of him, with a loud slap.

"Wayne Enterprises is about to experience a hostile takeover," Bruce said. All nine heads snapped toward him at these shocking words. "By *me*." He calmly returned to the place he had claimed and sat down. "You can peruse these documents in detail, though you'll already be familiar with the contents." He swept a warning gaze around the table, pausing briefly on each man. "I have my own photographic copies of each."

The men opened the folders in front of them, flipped cursorily through the memos, photographs, and documents . . . then began to pay closer attention. The mood in the air changed, and they whitened in shock. Each man had a different vulnerability, and now they were all trapped.

Norlander looked up first, as if he wanted to slide under the table and hide. Huston's mouth hung open, but no words came forth. McDonnell and Fitzroy gazed at each other, tension building between them like static electricity.

Bruce folded his hands on the polished table. "I am Bruce Wayne. This is *my* company, created and built by *my* father, according to *his* ideals. From now on, we'll do things *my* way."

At once the room erupted into cries of feigned innocence,

outrage, and accusations. Bruce sharply held up one hand, and they fell silent as though shot. "Some of our best breakthroughs, our most innovative solutions, were secretly handed over to LuthorCorp. In spite of our most brilliant geniuses delivering excellent work, Wayne Enterprises has been hamstrung. *By you.* Richard Drayling resigned because he wouldn't play your game, or Luthor's. Every one of you has betrayed me."

He passed out a chart of the Wayne Enterprises organizational structure, showing himself at the top as chief executive officer. "I submitted this material to the authorities and I will decide whether or not to have you each tried in a court of law. I should have you arrested here and now. Security is waiting outside this door." He poured himself a steaming cup of coffee and took a long sip. "I could certainly cause a scandal for Mr. Luthor, but he's as slippery as an oiled eel. I'd rather beat him at his own game."

Silent as corpses, the nine men stared at him. "I'll be tendering my resignation immediately," Norlander said, breaking the silence.

"You will *not*," Bruce snapped, his eyes flashing. "Your fates depend entirely on how all of you play your parts. It would not be in your best interests to let word of your . . . 'extracurricular activities' leak to your families, to the community, to the newspapers. I will have a further, and particularly binding, nondisclosure document drawn up for all of you to sign, and as I mentioned I have provided copies of these files to Captain James Gordon at the Gotham City PD." The men muttered, fidgeted, looked away. Bruce felt, though, that the information itself was the biggest stick he needed to keep them in line.

"However, I will not press charges—so long as you cooperate." He continued. "This is how things will be until I decide otherwise. No one—particularly Lex Luthor—will know there has been a change in your activities. He can suspect nothing." His tone left no room for questions. "Each Wayne Enterprises team will operate independently. Each division will report its research results and show any designs, blueprints, and prototypes directly and *only* to me. I will tell you what plans to deliver to Luthor, which components of prototype technologies. That way I'll be in control of what he does and doesn't have."

What he didn't tell them was that he would have them deliver subtly *nonfunctional* items to LuthorCorp. Red herrings. He intended to give Lex Luthor all the rope he needed in order to hang himself.

When Bruce ended the meeting, the men couldn't leap from their chairs quickly enough. Most of them would frantically try to clean up any incriminating material they still had lying around. But it was too late.

"One moment, gentlemen." His voice was a lasso that yanked them to a halt at the conference room doorway. "Since you're all involved with Lex Luthor, which of you can tell me why he's so interested in a secret Air Force base in Nevada? It goes by various names—Area 51, Groom Lake, Dreamland. What technology is Luthor giving the military?"

Bruce was an expert at reading guilty expressions, but all of these men were genuinely mystified by the question. Nobody answered him for a moment, and finally Miles muttered, "I'm sorry, Mr. Wayne, I know nothing about it. Truly."

Bruce curtly dismissed them, and the directors fled. He would have to do his own investigating into Luthor's connection with Area 51. He remained at the long table, thinking, while cigarettes still smoldered in the ashtrays.

CHAPTER 25
MERCY DRAW, ARIZONA

THE SMALL RANCHING TOWN IN SOUTHWESTERN ARIZONA was named Mercy Draw, and a flying saucer had crashed there. Supposedly.

The town was amazingly far from any other signs of civilization. As Clark and Jimmy drove their rental car for hours, the flat desert scenery looked like . . . desert scenery. And then more desert scenery. And then more. Clark was very glad he had prudently topped off the gas tank. Though he pushed the accelerator as far down as he dared, the lonely highway rolled out for miles and miles in an endless asphalt ribbon.

When they finally reached their destination during the hottest part of the afternoon, they saw a tall, rusty windmill, a general store, a few shacks, and a saloon. Several dusty pickup trucks were parked outside the saloon entrance.

"And I thought Smallville was small," Clark said.

"It's probably one of those towns where everyone knows everyone," Jimmy said. "We should be able to find that rancher without too much trouble."

Clark went to the general store but found it empty. A handwritten paper sign taped to the door read AT THE SALOON. The sign looked as though it had been there for months.

The pair walked through the swinging doors into the dim warmth of the watering hole. The bar was so filled with cigarette smoke that it seemed to generate its own permanent acrid fog. When he and Jimmy entered, everyone turned to stare at them, marking them as outsiders, strangers, city slickers. Someone elbowed a skinny, grizzled cowboy at the bar who sat nursing a mostly finished mug of draft beer. "A couple more live ones for you, Freddy."

"Excuse me," Clark said. "We're looking for a gentleman named Fred Franklin. He's supposed to have seen a crashed flying saucer?"

The good ol' boys at the bar laughed and groaned. They all dug into their pockets and slapped down dimes in front of the grizzled beer drinker, who had just won some sort of bet. "There you go again, Freddy. They're all yours."

The man drained the dregs in a gulp and heaved himself up, wiping his hands on his jeans. His Adam's apple protruded from his neck almost as far as the brim of his ten-gallon hat. "I'm Fred Franklin." He lifted his empty mug and pointed an elbow at the bartender. "Be glad to talk to you—if you'd refill me."

Clark pulled out a quarter and laid it down on the bar surface, which was stained by many ring marks. Jimmy whispered, "Mr. White will never reimburse us for beer expenses!"

"I may have to pay for that myself, Jimmy, in order to get the story."

The bartender dutifully filled Franklin's mug, leaving a generous portion of suds on top. The rancher slurped while grinning at Clark and Jimmy. "Now, since we're best friends, tell me what you'd like to know."

The other bar patrons retired to a table, where a card game soon ensued. The ritual seemed all too familiar to them. Glancing at some fresh newspaper clippings tacked to the walls, Clark noted that Fred Franklin was a local celebrity. Mr. White wasn't going to be pleased that so many other reporters had gotten here first.

Clark took out his pad. "We've heard rumors about a crashed object on your property, Mr. Franklin. Could you please describe it for us?"

"I can do ya one better. Wanna real scoop? I'll take you out there, show you exactly where the thing crashed."

One of the patrons snickered, holding his cards close. "Just like all those other 'scoops' you gave them reporters, Freddy?"

"You hush up—these gentlemen and I are conducting business."

"We'd very much like to see the site, Mr. Franklin," Clark said.

"And I need to take photographs," Jimmy added.

Franklin shrugged amiably. "Fork over a sawbuck, and you'll have my undivided attention and exclusive access for the rest of the afternoon."

The two hesitated; then Clark pulled out his wallet and extracted a ten-dollar bill. He noted the transaction on his pad.

THE LONG AND BUMPY ROADS CONSISTED OF GRAVEL, DUST, and an endless sequence of ruts that didn't bother Fred Franklin in the least. His pickup roared along, spewing clouds behind them. Since their rental car was not adequate for the rough ranch roads, Clark and Jimmy were crowded in the cab with him, Clark's large form dwarfing Jimmy's.

"Please tell us more about the saucer, sir," Jimmy said. "Did it make any sound? Was it damaged?"

"It sorta hummed and whooshed, then tore a big trench in the dirt when it crashed. Couldn't tell if it was damaged or not." He drove along, his voice rattling in time with the bumps.

"How big was it?" Clark asked, remembering what his small Kryptonian ship had looked like. "Was it smooth or made of rough plates? Did you see any markings?"

"I can't give everything away!" The old rancher sounded cagy.

"We want to get our ten dollars' worth," Clark said.

"Oh, you will. You will!"

After passing through several rickety gates of barbed wire and creosote poles, they turned off the alleged road onto an even worse track. Clark scanned ahead with his enhanced vision but could still see nothing. Finally, at no particularly remarkable spot, the rancher ground the truck to a halt, turned off the ignition, and opened the creaking driver's-side door. Clark and Jimmy were both covered with reddish-brown dust thanks to the open windows. Franklin spat out a mouthful of grit as he swung his legs out. His boots crunched through the gravel to an area where something big had obviously landed.

The ground was churned and excavated. Deep tire tracks ran in all directions. Even the meager scrub brush, mesquite, and sage had been plowed over, leaving a ragged scar. Clark noticed burn marks on the ground, a few black oil stains, but most of the topsoil had been scraped away and hauled off.

"Hey, I don't see any crashed flying saucer," Jimmy said.

"Well, it's not here anymore," Franklin said. "Never said it was. The government came and took it away, a whole buncha soldier types. Like a military invasion, it was."

Clark could not hide his disappointment. "And this is all that's left?" Jimmy began shooting photographs anyway.

"Yep, the army beat you and all those other reporters here.

Special squad came out from Nellis Air Force Base, took the saucer, the debris, the rocks, even the dirt. *Everything.*" He sucked on his teeth.

"But where did they go?" Clark asked. "Where did they take the flying saucer?"

Franklin leaned back on his heels. "Son, they didn't exactly give me a receipt or a forwarding address. I doubt they intend to pay for all the damage they did to my place here."

Clark looked at the dusty, scrubby wasteland, where a few dead weeds and some torn-up sagebrush were drying in the late afternoon heat. He didn't notice any particular damage.

"You boys might want to check out Nellis. I worked for two years out at the Nevada Test Site. Saw four A-bombs go off with my own eyes. People from Las Vegas would drive out to the desert highways, unfold their lawn chairs, and have a picnic, waiting to see the mushroom cloud."

"And what does that have to do with the flying saucer?" Clark asked.

"You can't very well keep an atomic bomb test secret, but that's not all they do out there. I hear they got a special experimental base by Groom Lake—super top secret. Nobody admits to it, but it's there. It's called"—he lowered his voice to a conspiratorial whisper—"*Area Fifty-one.* But you didn't hear that from me."

"And how are you aware of it, Mr. Franklin?"

"Out here in the desert, you hear things. You see things." He gestured meaningfully up at the sky. "But it was an alien ship, you mark my words. Never seen anything like it. And now they've got it at Area Fifty-one."

Clark refused to give up. "Jimmy, we've come this far. We need to get something for our story."

The rancher hooked his thumbs into the belt loops of his jeans. "Say, if you really want a headline, for another five bucks I'll show you the world's largest cow pie. Got to have something to do with the radioactive fallout from all those nucular tests."

Clark heaved a sigh. "We'll pass, but thanks."

CHAPTER 26
LUTHOR'S ISLAND

THE SMALL ISLAND WAS SURROUNDED BY A CALM, DEEP BLUE ocean. The humid air sparkled in the warm Caribbean sun, filled with the scents of lush tropical vegetation. This was a far cry from Siberia.

When Luthor met General Ceridov at the concrete jetty on the island's south side, the Soviet officer reveled in all the sunshine and heat. He had eschewed his wool uniform and donned a ridiculous-looking floral-print shirt that already displayed semicircular sweat stains under his armpits. "Lovely installation. Thank you for inviting me, comrade Luthor."

For his own part, Luthor wore a khaki tropical-weight suit. "You were kind enough to show me your gulag and quarry. I'm returning the favor." Since the incident at his mansion, in which Superman had helped the other costumed burglar steal his meteorite sample, he'd felt violated. After delivering his damning press conference, he'd departed immediately for the Caribbean.

"And what is the name of this island?" the KGB general asked. "I could find it on no map."

"Luthor's Island, of course."

"Vanity?"

"Clarity. And efficiency."

"Ah, if you say so."

Ceridov regarded the warm sea and sugar-sand beaches, the overgrown jungle marred by new gravel roads, and the angular buildings that housed Luthor's facility and operational headquarters, using some of the structural remnants of a large old Spanish fort. "Ah, the tropical climate. I can see why my government supports Fidel Castro and his Communist revolution in Cuba. Soon all of these islands will be within the Soviet sphere of influence."

Ceridov followed Luthor along the jetty to the beach, where an unmarked Jeep waited. The KGB general seemed too confident, perhaps even teasing. "We will take over the world soon enough. When all is said and done, perhaps we can turn your little island into a vacation resort for party officials!" He laughed at his own joke. Luthor did not.

"Don't believe your own propaganda, General. I like my island exactly the way it is." Though undeniably charismatic, Castro seemed an unruly and unwashed fanatic, dedicated to the Communist cause with a fervor that had not been equaled since Lenin himself. Instead, Luthor had paid substantial bribes to the current Cuban dictator, Batista, finding it simpler to manipulate a man who could be bought, a man who showed a healthy and normal tendency to basic greed rather than a passion for an esoteric cause.

"My position here is secure, and I am left undisturbed to do my work. Everyone from Cuba to Jamaica to the Bahamas knows to avoid this area. I've been forced to sink a fishing boat and couple of pleasure craft to emphasize that point. The nighttime fires from my smokestacks and flames from the firing of test rockets are enough to feed local superstitions that some giant dragon lives here." He rolled his eyes at their gullibility, even if it served his own purposes.

First off, Luthor drove his guest up to the launch complex, pleased to show the black-star general what he had accomplished with his own fortune, his own ingenuity and investment. The missile launchpads bore dramatic patterns of soot and char from test blasts. When the general seemed overly fascinated with the red-painted gantries and cooled tanks filled with propellant, Luthor said, "If you think that's impressive, let me show you something much more unusual." The skin around Luthor's eyes crinkled, the closest he ever came to a genuine and unrehearsed smile.

He led Ceridov to ranks of dish-shaped projectors, and both men gazed at all the beam transmitters pointing to the skies. "These focused energy rays can shoot directly through the atmosphere and strike any incoming target. It is a perfect defense against Soviet aggression." He turned to the KGB general. "I hope you are as eager to test it as I am."

Ceridov was intrigued. "Certainly, comrade Luthor. For a long time now, I have wanted the opportunity to demonstrate our missiles in a real combat situation. Normally that would lead to the end of human civilization—"

"But with these beams, I could intercept your missiles before they cause any damage. This way, we both win."

"You would take that risk?" Ceridov's bushy eyebrows lifted. "The danger to America . . ."

"I prefer not to think of myself as just an American. I am a citizen of the world. *My* world."

During the tour of the island, Luthor intentionally kept the Soviet officer from the secluded north end, where the largest and most ambitious construction work took place. Ceridov didn't need to see any of *that*. It was a different part of Luthor's plan.

He brought his guest to the main command center, a modern structure built around the old fortress walls and a tower of ancient stone. His headquarters, control room, and offices were inside new cinder-block structures whose interior walls were painted white or seafoam green. Rather than simple hardwood planking, the floors were the most modern waxed linoleum in alternating squares of black and white. His central control room had large computer banks that displayed amazing constellations of indicator lights. These electronic superbrains had been modified from von Neumann's original designs for the sophisticated computer called ENIAC, with an added dash of Luthor genius.

"And what supplies your power?" Ceridov mused as he walked past the tall computers, regarding the flashing lights as though they imparted some sort of secret message. "Your own reactor? A new-model design, I presume?"

"The very best design." Luthor nodded smugly. "Far superior to your antique at the Ariguska camp."

"Antique! That is the most sophisticated new Soviet model."

Luthor made a bland gesture. "As I said . . ." He merely showed Ceridov the control rods and indicated the maximum power levels he could achieve using high-quality radioactive material diverted from the processing plants in Oak Ridge, Tennessee.

"And how did you build this reactor? In my gulag, we lost many prisoners to hazardous radiation exposures. Safety measures are very expensive."

"I may not have a prison camp, General, but I do have a pool of expendable workers."

"You continue to surprise me."

"As it should be." Luthor turned back to the much more interesting weapons systems. "My focused-energy-ray defense system will be complete as soon as I receive a few important components from my insiders at Wayne Enterprises. When I am ready for the test firing, will you be prepared for my signal? We have to give them a real target."

"Two of our most hawkish generals are easily provoked. General Gregor Petreivich Endovik and General Ivan Ivanovich Dubrov have long advocated a preemptive strike against America. They are my puppets. They will play right into my hands."

Nodding calmly to himself, Luthor regarded the large screens on the control-room walls, which showed live images of oblivious people going about their daily business in Washington, D.C.; Metropolis; London; Leningrad—reading newspapers, hurrying to catch a bus, walking inside skyscrapers, shopping in open-air markets, playing in parks with their children or pets.

This little "incident" would ratchet international tensions even higher, thereby benefiting both Ceridov and himself. Once Luthor successfully demonstrated his unexpected defensive system, he would seem to be a savior, after which he would sell his extravagantly expensive "death ray" to the U.S. Department of Defense. And after Luthor's energy beams had destroyed the Soviet missiles, General Ceridov would be able to demand—and get—more spending for his military, thereby ensuring a continued and profitable arms buildup on both sides.

Ceridov frowned. "Once our nuclear missiles are launched, I will not be able to recall them. You are positive that your system will be effective?"

"I am entirely confident." How dare the man suggest otherwise? "Complete and total nuclear annihilation would be bad for business."

Ceridov took him at his word. "Do you have vodka? We must toast."

"This is the Caribbean," Luthor reminded him irritably. "We have rum."

"It will have to do." Ceridov waited as Luthor extracted a bottle and two glasses from a metal desk drawer and poured them each a drink. They raised a silent toast, each man mulling over his own grand dreams.

THOUGH THEY INTENDED TO PURSUE THE STORY TO NELLIS Air Force Base the following day, Clark and Jimmy had to stay overnight in Las Vegas. Self-conscious about the expense to the *Daily Planet*, Clark drove around comparing room rates. Finally, they found a budget motor hotel with two beds, air-conditioning (which, unfortunately, didn't work), and a private bathroom: the Atomic Age Motel.

After they checked in, Clark and Jimmy were free for a night on the Vegas Strip (though both of them were somewhat intimidated by the prospect). Clark flipped through a copy of the *Las Vegas Sun* and was surprised to find a wire-service article on page seven about Lex Luthor's press conference, in which he accused Superman of collusion in the robbery of his mansion. The reporter seemed to make much of the fact that Superman had not been seen in Metropolis for a day or two and had made no public response to Luthor's accusations.

Clark pressed his lips together, upset by the implications. He had not been helping Batman escape—he'd been taking him off to the authorities. The two had never been partners in any way! How could anyone, especially Lex Luthor, accuse *Superman* of dishonesty?

Jonathan Kent had always insisted, "A man's actions say everything about him that anyone needs to know." Superman did not need to defend himself against accusations from a man like Luthor. Clark tossed the newspaper into the wastebasket and tried not to think about it anymore.

On their way out, Jimmy stopped to stare at a metal slot machine in the shabby lobby of the motel. It was adorned with a whirling model of a nucleus and a bright loop of neon light. Jimmy's small supply of money was obviously burning a hole in his pocket, and he pulled out a shiny nickel. "Okay, just once. I don't usually gamble, but . . . well, we are in Las Vegas." He held up the coin and looked with some trepidation at the seductive machine. "I should give it a whirl, right?"

"Those things are called one-armed bandits for a good reason, Jimmy."

Undeterred, Jimmy plunked the nickel into the slot, pulled the handle, and set the machine in motion. With a quick glimpse of his X-ray vision, Clark viewed the mechanism behind the small transparent windows and saw what lay in store for his friend.

The reels spun, and Jimmy stepped back as though afraid the machine might turn white hot. The blur of whirling cartoon fruit halted sequentially, and Jimmy gasped with delight as the first, then second, then third bunch of cherries thunked to a halt. A light on top of the machine blinked and a bell clanged. With a clatter, a wealth of coins showered into the spill tray: twenty nickels.

Jimmy yelped with excitement, scooped up the coins, and counted them. "A dollar, Mr. Kent—I won a whole dollar!"

"Actually, ninety-five cents. You spent—"

"I never won anything before! I can't believe it. Maybe we should go to one of the casinos. I'm hot tonight!"

"Jimmy, right now you're ahead ninety-five cents. Do you want to risk losing it?"

"Maybe I should just keep my winnings." Jimmy settled down, though he still seemed unable to believe his good fortune.

Clark allowed himself to share his friend's innocent joy, but his thoughts drifted back to the crash site of the supposed spacecraft. As Superman, he *had* seen and chased a mysterious UFO across the United States. He'd watched the Air Force jets doggedly pursue it. Now the military had taken away this crashed vessel from Mercy Draw, presumably the same one. Had there been any alien survivors aboard?

He tried to imagine what might have happened if his own Kryptonian spaceship had been intercepted by the U.S. Army instead of the humble Kents. How different his life would have been if he'd grown up on a secret military base rather than in Smallville, Kansas.

In their rental car, Clark and Jimmy drove along the Strip, passing one gaudy casino after another: the Sands, the New Frontier, and the famous Desert Inn. Clark could see that his friend was about fit to bust, as Jonathan Kent might have said.

"Look at all the colors, the lights! Have you ever imagined so much neon in the whole world?" Jimmy kept staring at the marquees. The Dunes advertised what was purportedly "The Greatest Show in Vegas"—Minsky's Follies. "What do you suppose that is, Mr. Kent? Singing and dancing?"

Clark looked at the fine print beneath. "'A daring new topless show.'" When Jimmy blushed bright red, Clark suggested instead something more their speed. "How about another movie?"

Jimmy agreed immediately. "*Invasion of the Body Snatchers* is playing. I've been dying to see that one!"

THE THEATER WAS MOSTLY EMPTY, AS THE LOCALS APPARENTLY preferred gambling to motion pictures. Jimmy sat wide-eyed, munching his popcorn, while Clark pondered the implications of this latest installment in the current "evil alien" film genre. As they left, both were unsettled (though for different reasons) by the frightening invasion of "pod-people," capped by Kevin McCarthy's paranoid tour-de-force performance at the end. *They're coming! They're coming!*

As they returned to the Atomic Age Motel, knowing they had to get up early for the long drive out into the desert, Jimmy finally asked the question on his mind. "Do you suppose there could be aliens walking among us—ones that look just like people, so we can never tell? More aliens . . . not just Superman?"

Clark automatically brushed aside the idea. "It's just a movie, Jimmy. It's supposed to scare you—for fun. It's not real."

Jimmy nodded, abashed. "You're probably right, Mr. Kent." Clark gave the young man's shoulder a comforting pat, and they walked toward their room in silence, thinking their own thoughts.

CHAPTER 28
THE CAVE

IN THE DANK SHADOWS OF THE CAVE, THE MYSTERIOUS mineral fragment emitted its own gemstone light, an eerie emerald glow, though no unusual radiation registered on Bruce Wayne's sophisticated instruments. When he passed a Geiger counter wand in front of it, the device yielded no clicks, no static. The rock shed no intrinsic heat; in fact, it felt cold and oily to the touch.

No wonder Lex Luthor was so interested in this sample. But why did it have such a dramatic effect on Superman, who seemed impervious to all other forms of attack? A simple exposure to the rock had nearly paralyzed him. Bruce had seen it with his own eyes.

After extricating himself from the debacle at Luthor's mansion, he realized that too many things simply didn't make sense—Superman foremost among them. Was the "Man of Steel" the personal watchdog of Lex Luthor? Superman had denied the accusation . . . but why else would he have raced in to protect the mansion and prevent Batman's escape? On the other hand, why hadn't he simply delivered Batman to Luthor and his goons, rather than flying off with him?

Did LuthorCorp have something to do with his superpowers? And if Luthor could create a Superman, why would he waste time dabbling with the bulky and primitive battlesuits based on Wayne Enterprises technology when those suits were clearly inferior to Superman's demonstrated abilities?

And what did this lump of green rock have to do with anything?

Bruce continued to run his tests. Researching the name "Ariguska," he discovered an isolated region of Siberia, unremarkable save for the fact that a large meteor had hit there two decades ago. Classified maps suggested, but did not confirm, that a harsh gulag was known to exist in the vicinity. Did the Soviets have some kind of mine there, the source of this rare and unusual mineral? And what could it be used for in a practical and industrial sense?

Around the United States, thanks to the burgeoning nuclear industry, prospectors were combing remote deserts and mountains using Geiger counters to locate natural uranium deposits, hoping to strike it rich. Atomic power showed great potential, and the nuclear weapons industry had a constant demand for new fissile material.

Bruce ran a fingertip along the smooth green face of the stone. Had Lex Luthor or his Siberian cronies discovered a substance potentially more powerful than uranium?

Crystalline spectroscopy had broken down the mineral's content of heavy elements as well as strange inclusions of inert atoms and noble gases—argon, neon, even krypton. Other than that, the mineral itself seemed unremarkable. But if Luthor considered the green rock so extraordinarily valuable, there had to be something more to it. . . .

Studying the unusual rock under high magnification, he detected a shocked crystalline structure, which implied that this sample had been subjected to tremendous heat and pressure—an impact or a great explosion. Perhaps this was a fragment of the Ariguska meteorite. . . .

The mineral sample wasn't the only mystery he had uncovered in Luthor's secure private office, though. Bruce wondered what kind of "property" Luthor was demanding the U.S. military return to him? Why was he so interested in Area 51? Why had unmarked LuthorCorp planes been chasing the UFO, according to Superman's statement, and what had they done to cause the F-100D to crash?

Bruce was certain everything was connected.

He looked up to find Alfred approaching with a tray bearing dinner. He set it down on one of the laboratory tables and removed the plate covering with a flourish. "A fresh salad and pea soup, sir." The butler regarded the glowing emerald mineral next to all of Bruce's analytical notes. "I noticed you seem to be in a green phase today."

CHAPTER 29
NELLIS AIR FORCE BASE, NEVADA

THE ENDLESSLY MONOTONOUS SCRUB DESERT OF SOUTH-ern Nevada looked different from the endlessly monotonous desert of Arizona . . . and yet the same. Clark drove the rental car again for hours along the eerily deserted highway. "You'd almost expect to see buzzards circling up there."

With the highway map spread out on his knees, Jimmy looked up to study the cloudless blue sky. "I'd rather see flying saucers. Then at least we'd get a story for Mr. White."

They had picked up the highway map at a filling station when they left Las Vegas that morning, heading north in the general direction of Alamo and Ash Springs. When the map proved entirely unhelpful in revealing the location of any secret experimental area, the man pumping the gas had drawn a circle on it with a callused, grease-stained finger.

"This is what you want, here—the Tikaboo Valley. That dotted line is a dry lake bed, Groom Lake, but the government took the name off all the maps. You won't find the roads marked either." He vaguely traced the spot with his finger again. "Just head out that direction and you'll find what you want—or they'll find you. They got orders to shoot to kill."

"It's all right," Jimmy had said cheerfully. "We've got press passes."

Clark had folded and refolded the map, trying to make the creases match. "Thank you very much, sir."

Now the rental car rolled past ranchland fenced in with barbed wire, where it seemed impossible that any livestock could possibly survive. Jimmy swigged from the grape Nehi he had bought with some of his slot machine winnings at the gas station. In a generous mood with all of his nickels, he had bought Clark a bottle of soda pop as well.

During the long ride, the young man regaled Clark with stories of flying saucer sightings and UFO encounters he'd read about. Nine unusual objects had been seen flying near Mount Rainier, Washington, in June 1947, and less than two weeks later the famous "crash" had occurred near Roswell, New Mexico, and all evidence of the object had been whisked away by the U.S. military.

"That sounds a lot like what happened at Mercy Draw," Clark said.

Jimmy bobbed his head. "I wonder if the army has a secret warehouse filled with downed alien craft."

A year after the Roswell incident, a DC-3 commercial airliner nearly struck a torpedo-shaped object; both witnesses were veteran airmen who had served in World War II and were not prone to hallucinations. Only a few months earlier, a Kentucky Air National Guard pilot had crashed his P-51 Mustang while pursuing a flying saucer.

Sighting after sighting had generated a public craze and much speculation about aliens. The Air Force had launched several major investigations, the current and most ambitious being Project Blue Book. Their results, though, had never been released to the public. Clark, of course, had done his homework, intrigued by the possibility that he might not be the only extraterrestrial visitor on Earth. So far, he had no concrete answers.

They took an unmarked road leading west from Crystal Springs, though the map gave no hint of its destination. They rolled along parallel to a drooping barbed-wire fence that bore unwelcoming PRIVATE PROPERTY and NO TRESPASSING signs. Miles later, with no apparent change in terrain, the ominous signs switched to PROPERTY OF U.S. GOVERNMENT, then WARNING: MILITARY INSTALLATION or DANGER: LIVE WEAPONS RANGE.

"We must be getting close, Mr. Kent."

But they were out in the middle of nowhere, and Clark could see no barracks, no Quonset huts, no installation of any kind. He peered into the distance for a guarded gate, office, or entrance station, which would have been present at any normal military installation. With his keen eyesight, he noted three Jeeps racing along a dirt road that intersected the highway, kicking up plumes of dust behind them.

"We've attracted some attention," Clark said.

"Maybe we can ask them where to go."

Another Jeep roared up on the blacktop road behind them, proceeding much faster than the speed limit. Ahead, a fifth vehicle bore down directly toward them. Within minutes, they were surrounded.

Clark dutifully used his turn signal and pulled off onto the dirt shoulder. As the military Jeeps converged, he saw that each vehicle carried at least two soldiers in full uniform, plus sidearms. Three men even carried machine guns. They looked like they meant business.

The military police were stone-faced and clean shaven, their

eyes hidden behind sunglasses. A no-nonsense corporal walked up
to them. "You are trespassing on U.S. government property. Turn
around and get out right now, or you'll find yourselves in a world
of trouble."

Jimmy had pulled out his camera and pressed the button to
expose the lens. He waved his press card and nudged Clark to do
the same. "We're from the Metropolis *Daily Planet*. We're here to
do a story."

"Not on this base, you aren't. No press allowed."

"There's a base here?" Clark said. "I don't see anything."

"There's no base."

"But you just said there was a base."

Two other soldiers closed in, hefting their rifles. The corporal
rested a hand on his sidearm. "I told you, sir—turn around." He
pointed meaningfully at a metal sign dangling from a strand of
barbed wire: WARNING! BEYOND THIS POINT TRESPASSERS WILL BE
MET WITH LETHAL FORCE!

Lois would never have allowed herself to be so quickly evicted
once she smelled a story. Clark pressed, "Could you please give
us the name of someone we could talk to? We'd like to arrange a
meeting—"

"No interviews." The corporal was angry now. "Are you
deaf?"

Clark had never faced so many drawn weapons before, except
as Superman. Now even Jimmy was nervous. "Maybe, um, we
should do as they say, Mr. Kent."

"Okay, we're stymied." Clark took off his hat and absently ran
the brim through his fingers. Keeping his eye on the Jeeps that had
pulled up to block them, he shifted the car into reverse and backed
up slowly, then turned around.

Jimmy looked over his shoulder as they rolled back down the

lonely highway in the direction they had come from. None of the soldiers had so much as moved. "That's the end of the story, I guess, Mr. Kent. We're never going to get inside that base."

Clark nodded grimly. "These soldiers are just doing their jobs. We have to respect that and leave them alone."

Jimmy sagged into his seat. He packed his Graflex back up and put it into its leather case.

Clark hid his smile, though, as the clutch of soldiers diminished in his rearview mirror. With his super-vision he had scanned the area, and he had seen enough. He was already making plans for just how to get into Area 51—using his own means, later . . . after dark.

CHAPTER 30
THE *DAILY PLANET*

AT ANY OTHER TIME, LOIS WOULD HAVE SNICKERED AT Clark's assignment to chase little green men, but she had already taken a lot of flak for believing Superman's claim that he wasn't from Earth, and Lois did not like to be ridiculed. If Clark did get definitive proof of a real alien spacecraft, then no one would doubt Superman's statement.

Besides, this particular UFO was much more interesting to her because LuthorCorp planes had been chasing it. Since Clark was on the scene in Podunk, Arizona, Lois decided to approach the story from an entirely different angle.

And that angle had to be Lex Luthor.

After learning of Blanche Rosen's tragic and way too convenient death, Lois had gathered her scraps of evidence about what a snake Luthor was, and she had no intention of stopping now. She needed to do this for Blanche and for all those unfortunate employees who had been fired or had mysteriously died of "natural causes." Those men and women had just been doing their jobs, trying to make a living.

At her desk, Lois withdrew into her thoughts. She glanced at the framed photo of herself and her kid sister, Lucy, standing next to their father, the general. Lucy had always been Daddy's little girl, and her career as a stewardess was considered an "appropriate" job for a young, attractive woman. But what about women like Blanche Rosen?

Fighting back her anger, Lois walked into Perry White's office, dropped a stack of her notes on his desk, and explained what she had found. "I started digging like you told me to, Chief—and this story goes far beyond Luthor simply firing all his female employees and some older, disposable men. Even *I'm* surprised at how deep and how insidious this is. I turned over a rock and uncovered a whole nest of squirming, slimy things." She explained about her source and how she had been brutally silenced. "Murdered, Chief. No doubt about it."

Perry looked down at the obituary. "Says here 'hit and run.'"

"*Murdered.*" Lois showed him the death notices of all the former LuthorCorp employees who had died in LuthorCorp-funded medical centers without being allowed to speak a word in public. "Poor people who were exposed to deadly levels of radiation during the construction of an atomic power reactor on a secret island base."

"Says here 'natural causes.'"

"*Murdered.*" She showed him her sketches and photographs of Luthor's base, which she had surreptitiously taken in his munitions factory. "These plans are further proof. Luthor is setting up an entire control center outside the boundaries of the United States. Why would he do that if he's conducting legitimate government work?"

Perry looked skeptically at the blurry photo of the blueprints from the wall of Luthor's sealed factory office. "I see a map that doesn't mean anything and sketches that you did yourself."

"It's proof!"

"Not proof that I can publish in the newspaper, Lois—and you know it. Coincidences, yes. Suspicions, yes. But if I go ahead with this story, Luthor's attorneys will have a field day with us in court. Great Caesar's ghost, I'm not saying I don't believe you. I don't need to tell you your job. I'm saying that I can't publish this exposé until you have something concrete."

Lois felt her face burning. "Then send me down there. I'll make my way to that island and come back with all the proof you need."

Perry put his cigar in his mouth but didn't light it. "You want the *Daily Planet* to send you on an all-expenses-paid Caribbean vacation? I've already got Kent and Olsen out in Las Vegas chasing little green men."

"This could be the biggest story the *Planet* has ever run!"

He raised his hand when he could see she would continue to protest. "Keep digging, Lois. Get me something tangible. Prove me wrong."

She headed toward the door, barely keeping her temper in check. "I will, Chief!"

CHAPTER 31
LAS VEGAS STRIP

FORTUNATELY FOR CLARK, JIMMY OLSEN WAS A SOUND sleeper. After the young photographer began to snore softly in his bed, Clark left a note on Atomic Age Motel stationery stating that he had gone for a walk, just in case Jimmy woke to find him gone.

In a blur, he donned his blue and red suit, slipped outside, ducked behind the motel unseen, and took off. No flashy public show, no oohs or aahs. The cape hem fluttered about him in an uneven ripple, and gravity fell away. This was *his* time to fly.

As he rose above the glittering expanse of the Las Vegas Strip, Kal-El looked at the kaleidoscope of casinos and hotels. Despite the late hour, countless people were gambling, attending shows, losing fortunes, or making a small profit, which only enticed them to gamble more. From high above the tallest buildings, he could hear the faint jingling of slot machines paying off, roulette wheels spinning and clicking, chips clattering together, nightclub bands playing, people talking and laughing, cars honking their horns.

And police sirens. Then fire engines.

Though his curiosity about the flying saucer tugged him toward

Nellis Air Force Base, his sense of duty made him concentrate on the emergency instead. He could not follow his own interests if somebody was in trouble. He circled around and raced toward the source of the sirens, sure that the Las Vegas police and firefighters wouldn't mind a little extra help.

In addition to the usual searchlights skating across the sky to commemorate some new Las Vegas extravaganza, dazzling beams painted the Champagne Tower of the Fabulous Flamingo, billed as the world's most luxurious hotel. Kal-El wondered if a fire had occurred inside, but he saw no smoke. The flurry of activity centered on one penthouse room, one open balcony—and one man standing on the edge, threatening to jump.

Suddenly the emergency took on a different character. Kal-El focused his super-vision until he could see the man, still dressed in a gray business suit with a long, thin black tie that had been loosened, his collar unbuttoned. His face was florid; tears streamed down his cheeks. His expression flickered between grief and terror. He had taken off his shoes to leave his feet bare, perhaps for a better grip on the ledge.

This wasn't a fire, a robbery, or an attempted assault. This man wanted to take his own life.

"I've lost everything!" the man shouted in a rough voice. "I can't pay my markers. They'll kill me anyway!"

Hotel patrons thrust their heads out of nearby windows, beseeching the man not to jump. From inside the penthouse room, Kal-El picked up the earnest voice of a manager. "We can sort this out, sir. Come back inside. The casino will work out a payment plan for now."

Far down in the streets below, fire trucks pulled up, sirens wailing, lights flashing. More police cars joined them. Firemen left their trucks and pulled out a circular frame with a broad stretcher, which would never be able to catch a man after he fell thirty stories.

From inside the penthouse, a burly security man whose body did not seem designed for the tuxedo he wore stepped out onto the balcony. "You don't want to jump—you know you don't. Come off that ledge." He abruptly extended a hand to grab the jumper by force, but his move only startled the man. He sprang from the ledge and dove out into the air, closing his eyes as if in prayer.

Absorbing everything in a second, Kal-El streaked toward the Flamingo.

A chorus of gasps rang out, breaths drawn in unison. Crowds on the streets below stared upward.

The falling man seemed to be imagining he was flying. He had his arms outstretched, his jacket fluttering—in total silence, apparently convinced he wanted to die.

But Kal-El actually *could* fly. He swooped down, matched the speed of the falling man, and caught him. "I've got you, sir," he said in a comforting voice. "You're safe." Smiling, he descended toward the waiting crowds of wide-eyed onlookers, police, and firemen in front of the Fabulous Flamingo.

Kal-El couldn't guess what psychological complexities had driven the jumper to take such drastic measures. Gambling debts, no matter how bad, did not seem to be reason enough to end one's life. Why would this person want to throw everything away?

The suicidal man began pounding on his shoulder, struggling to break free, but Kal-El tightened his grip, careful not to let the man slip out of his grasp before they landed on solid ground. "Please don't struggle." His red boots touched down on the sidewalk as applauding people backed out into a circle to give them room. Kal-El spoke in a deep and reassuring voice, but he didn't know if the man could even hear him. "You'll be all right now, sir. These people will take care of you." Two firemen rushed forward to take the sobbing jumper.

Kal-El felt a strange wrenching sensation in his chest. Even superhuman strength and speed could not touch the panic and despair over finances that had gripped this man. Now that he was safely in the hands of the authorities, he would not be allowed to hurt himself.

But was that enough?

Kal-El stood, hands on hips, his cape rippling behind him in a night breeze. Ever since he had willingly donned the hero's mantle, he had been learning just how much he could do for the people of Earth. He hadn't revealed his real Kryptonian name to anyone, but he was happy with what they chose to call him—the name Lois Lane had coined. *Superman*. It had a nice ring to it.

Still, he couldn't stay. Soon reporters would crowd around and bombard him with questions. Kal-El had questions of his own elsewhere, and he could not miss this opportunity. It was his chance to learn if the U.S. military had found an alien spacecraft . . . whether another ship from Krypton or from some other world entirely. What if the crashed object contained another young refugee from his destroyed planet? His father, Jor-El, could not have been the only one to see the disaster coming.

Kal-El had to know.

Waving to the gathered awestruck spectators, he raised his fist again, looked up to the open slice of starry sky between the Flamingo towers, and soared into the night.

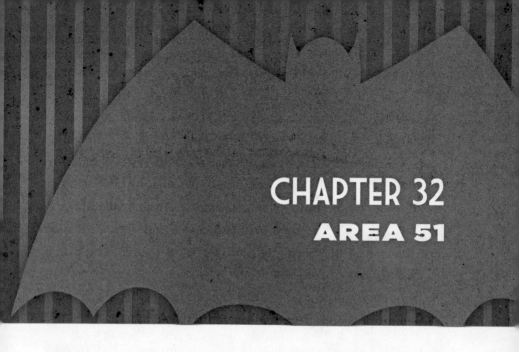

CHAPTER 32
AREA 51

FOR A MAN WITH BRUCE WAYNE'S CONNECTIONS AND Batman's technology, finding a secret facility inside the Groom Lake restricted area proved to be no great challenge.

He had his own private Wayne Enterprises jet and a pilot's license to fly it, and his plane had been modified to land on even the most minimal airstrips. After dark, most of the rural landing areas in the Nevada desert were shut down and unattended. A small ranch strip west of Crystal Springs looked to be ideal for his purposes.

Leaving his plane unattended on the empty airstrip, he donned his mask and armor to better blend into the darkness. Bats like swift, jagged shadows flitted about in the clear, moonless night.

He crossed the many miles of painfully open terrain on a newly designed high-powered motorcycle, which had been developed as a military all-terrain prototype by Wayne Enterprises. The cycle's wide tires and rugged suspension were housed in black aerodynamic armor, and—most important out here—its engine was virtually silent, thanks to a superior muffled stealth mode. Like a loping coyote, the cycle glided along the sand, scrub, and rocks.

He'd overcome the problems of distance and inaccessibility; now he had to deal with security. Judging by Luthor's insistent memos, even the bald industrialist knew very little about the place. Fortunately, the base's primary line of defense was its secrecy and miles of exposed, empty buffer zone. He needed to avoid all roads, and he could use no lights.

The first barrier was a simple barbed-wire fence strung with warning signs: RESTRICTED AREA. ACCESS BEYOND THIS POINT PROHIBITED. The wires were easily cut, and after idling the cycle through, he gripped the throttle with his dark glove and raced toward his destination.

A mile farther, he encountered more daunting fences—barbed wire and increasingly strenuous warnings: LETHAL FORCE IS AUTHORIZED BEYOND THIS POINT. The fence was electrified with enough voltage to give any intruder a severe jolt, but his insulated gloves protected him. He cut the wire and made his way through.

The barrier line immediately beyond this fence carried a much more powerful charge, deadly voltage. He unclipped leads from his utility belt, attached them to the wires with alligator clips, and grounded them, making the fence safe for him to get through.

As the cycle carried him onward with barely audible purring, he used front-mounted metal detectors to scope out buried land mines and other pitfalls. He activated the cycle's "trail of bread crumbs" system, which spat regularly spaced dots of pigment visible only in infrared. He placed filtered goggles over his mask and rode across the now greenish-hued desert landscape.

Finally, he spied the diaphanous glow of a complex ahead, nestled at the base of barren mountains. The Jeep roads met at a cluster of standard military buildings, Quonset huts, long rectangular barracks, hangars, warehouses, igloo-shaped storage domes, a tank farm. Guard towers sported brilliant searchlights.

Military police patrolled the inner perimeter, rifles shouldered, while growling Jeeps circled the outer roads.

He ditched the cycle behind a pile of boulders, then activated a sounder on his utility belt that would emit a locator ping so he could find the vehicle again. He made his way closer on foot.

Hidden by his dark cape, he moved forward in a low crouch to take advantage of the minimal cover. He extended his palm and, listening for feedback from the sensitive metal detector in the gauntlet, avoided several buried booby traps. Following established military procedure, the soldiers had placed land mines on a precisely spaced grid that made them easy to get around.

He sat in perfect stillness for several long minutes, watching carefully.

The base soldiers were alert, but not alert enough. They had been drilled repeatedly—so frequently, in fact, that he could use that to his advantage. Even a genuine breach of security would seem to be just another exercise at first. He was certain no intruder had ever penetrated this deeply into the restricted area.

The main research hangar was unmistakable, and that was where he had to go. He would need to use his grappling hook to get over the barricade, and from there he'd resort to metal-eating acid, diamond-edged cutters, even smoke bombs or tranquilizer darts if the smoke alone didn't create a sufficient diversion. In his utility belt he had everything he needed.

Piece of cake.

IT TOOK HIM FORTY-FIVE MINUTES TO GET INSIDE THE secure hangar, fifteen minutes longer than he had anticipated. Now he had to move quickly. Judging by all the military security in this forsaken place, the U.S. government considered the mysterious object to be as important as Luthor seemed to think it was.

All of the base research activities had shut down for the night, and now the exotic object sat in the middle of the hangar under security lights, surrounded by complex instruments; adjacent tables were piled with notes and black and white photographs.

He stepped forward, feeling a clear sense of awe. Without a doubt, the sleek, silvery vessel looked like an alien spacecraft, a flying saucer with aerodynamic lines and propulsion curves unlike anything he had seen in his own research and development for the aircraft industry.

As a rational man, he had never believed in stories of alien visitors or Martians spying on Earth. As he studied the object more carefully and began to guess exactly what it was, he found himself even more surprised by the truth.

He hadn't expected this at all.

CHAPTER 33
AREA 51

KAL-EL FLEW OFF, LEAVING LAS VEGAS BEHIND. HE WAS glad to have saved a life, but he still felt unsettled and uncertain about what lay in store for the poor man. The complexities of the human psyche, the twisted burdens that forced everyday people to make extremely bad decisions—those were not problems Kal-El could solve with a burst of super-speed or strength. He was reminded of all those difficult and disturbing letters written to "Lorna for the Lovelorn."

He flew silently away from the neon glow and out across the empty landscape. Radiant heat still wafted up from the desert sands, and thermal currents swirled around him like invisible smoke. Accelerating, he flew northeast, keeping himself just under Mach 1 so as not to create a prominent sonic boom. In minutes, he had passed the hurdles that military security had thrown up against him and Jimmy the previous day, when they'd approached via more conventional means.

He found the large dry lake bed, its smooth alkaline surface sparkling in the starlight; a military landing strip marred the otherwise pristine-looking flat. Long, straight roads cut across the desert, running from the Tikaboo Valley to the east and over the mountains and mesas from Yucca Flat and the atomic testing grounds. All of the roads converged like a targeting cross on the secret installation.

With his sharp vision, Kal-El spotted the central research hangar amid the barracks, warehouses, storage tanks, and blocky buildings. Decreasing speed, he landed gently atop the corrugated roof, dodging searchlights from the guard tower.

Kal-El was not accustomed to lurking in shadows like some prowler, but this mission was a personal one. He didn't want to be seen. Though it made him uneasy, he would have to bend the rules. The demanding pull to learn who he was, to see if he was truly alone on Earth, trumped his other concerns.

As quietly as he could, causing as little damage as possible, Kal-El popped the rivets on a sheet of the research hangar's roof. He pried the zinc-coated steel upward, opening a way for him to get inside. He scanned the skeleton crew of base security, and when he was satisfied that he had tripped no alarms, he dropped down inside the hangar. With barely a whisper of noise, he settled onto the swept concrete floor and looked around.

The cavernous bay was dim and quiet, lit only by a few emergency lights around the edges and a set of bright utility spotlights in the center. His blue eyes immediately locked onto the object he sought: a silver spaceship.

Kal-El wished he knew more about Kryptonian science, more about the small craft that Jor-El had built to send him away moments before their planet exploded. Up in his Fortress of Solitude, Kal-El still had the crystalline data-storage units along with recorded messages that his parents had placed in his ship, but even those were not enough to answer all his burning questions.

The flying saucer on display was of a completely different

design, a technology that had not originated on Krypton. Had another alien race created it? The vessel was much too small to carry a human-sized adult. Could it have been designed to hold a baby, like the ship that had saved him from his doomed planet? Or was this craft simply used by a more diminutive species?

If the alien occupant had survived the crash in Arizona, the soldiers and scientists in Area 51 would have taken him or her captive. Maybe the precious passenger was even now in a military holding area on the base.

Taking a step forward, Kal-El scanned the craft with his X-ray vision to penetrate its inner workings—and to his surprise he found no passenger compartment. No room, in fact, for any living creature. This strange vessel was nothing more than a case to hold exotic propulsion systems and automated controls. The whole machine was a drone of some kind. A scout ship from another world?

"It's a LuthorCorp prototype." The deep voice came out of the shadows behind him. "As you well know."

Kal-El spun, saw the dark-suited figure, the black cape, mask, and cowl. *Batman.*

Batman stepped into the glow of the utility lights. "Luthor sent you to get the craft back for him, didn't he? His other efforts failed."

At first Kal-El didn't understand what the other man was implying. He scanned with his X-ray vision to determine if Batman carried a piece of the devastatingly powerful green mineral. He saw numerous tools, cables, vials, darts, and other devices he could not identify but no sign of the debilitating emerald rock.

Kal-El countered, "It's more likely that *you* came to steal the ship—just like you stole from Luthor before." He realized that several pieces of the analytical gear connected to the strange object had come from Batman's belt rather than the Area 51 scientific teams.

Batman clearly took offense. "I'm not a common thief."

They faced off, tense, ready for battle. At any other time, Kal-El would have assumed that his powers could subdue any opponent, but the green rock Batman had carried . . . what else did he have up his sleeve?

"Then what were you doing to the craft?" Kal-El persisted. "Trying to sabotage it?"

Batman pressed with his own questions. "What does Luthor have over you, Superman? Why do you do his dirty work?"

Kal-El drew an exasperated breath. "I *don't* work for Luthor!"

"The evidence suggests otherwise." Batman's voice was brittle. "You were there to protect Luthor's mansion. Now you've breached military security to get his precious test craft back."

"*I don't work for Luthor!*" Kal-El raised his voice, not accustomed to having his word doubted by anyone—especially by a shadowy cat burglar in a dark mask. "Haven't you read the newspapers? Luthor claims that I helped *you* escape, that we're partners in crime." The very idea offended him.

"It wouldn't be the first time someone's given a false story to the press," Batman answered coolly. "Luthor would do anything to retrieve this prototype. And here you are."

"I came seeking answers. I intend no harm." Kal-El squared his shoulders, keeping himself between Batman and the silvery craft. It was time to turn the tables, keep his opponent off balance. "And I'm not the *only* one who broke into a high-security government installation."

After a long, tense pause, Batman added, "I'm here for answers, too." He took a step closer, not intimidated by Superman or his reputation. "Maybe you should ask yourself what Lex Luthor is doing with a prototype spaceship. Look for yourself; study the design." He held up a scanner in one dark-gloved hand. "The propulsion system, the metal-fabrication technique—they're identical to notes and blueprints contained in secret LuthorCorp documents."

Batman walked past him and applied a sort of electronic stethoscope to the skin of the "alien spaceship," then attached another set of leads to create a sonic-echo map of the sealed interior, verifying what Kal-El could see with his X-ray vision. Now that he knew what to look for, he did detect the hints of machining and subtle design commonalities that could have come from a cutting-edge arms manufacturer.

And that would explain why unmarked LuthorCorp planes had tried to stop the Air Force jets from intercepting the UFO, why they had been willing to use some kind of energy scrambler to make the F-100Ds malfunction when the pursuit got too close.

Even though it wasn't the answer Kal-El wanted to hear, Batman's assessment was correct. This was not an extraterrestrial vessel. This craft had been constructed on Earth, in secret. *A LuthorCorp prototype.*

He slowly came to an uncomfortable conclusion. Perhaps Batman hadn't just been burglarizing Lex Luthor's mansion. Maybe he'd been uncovering information for his own reasons, just as Kal-El had come here to do.

Suddenly sirens shattered the peaceful night, cutting through the tension. Rotating magenta lights flashed on inside the hangar, and a klaxon blared. A strained voice bellowed from loudspeakers in the ceiling, calling for a full-fledged response to an internal security breach.

"We can't be seen here," Batman said. "Neither of us."

Kal-El glanced upward. Someone might have noticed the open

sheet on the hangar roof, or some sign of Batman's break-in . . . a hole in a fence or a cut lock.

Kal-El turned to launch himself toward the ceiling. Though he had meant no harm, he knew his presence would raise too many questions. He could haul Batman out of here just as he had carried him away from Luthor's mansion—and they could continue this conversation elsewhere.

But Batman had vanished without a sound. The shadowy figure was simply *gone*, along with his equipment.

Kal-El shot a final glance at the fake spacecraft, thinking of all his lost hopes, then flew through the hole in the corrugated roof. He paused just long enough to bend the metal sheet back into place and weld it securely with a quick burst of his heat vision before soaring off into the night, just as the Area 51 military police surrounded the hangar.

They would find nothing inside.

CHAPTER 34
LUTHOR'S ISLAND

A WEEK AFTER GENERAL CERIDOV RETURNED TO SIBERIA, ALL of Luthor's systems were in place, all components assembled to his exacting personal specifications. The array of energy-beam transmitters stood ready, their dishes and antennae pointed toward the Caribbean sky, startlingly modern next to the abandoned Spanish fort.

Lex Luthor was about to change the world.

Inside the computer-filled control room, large screens displayed images of important cities, *calm* cities, soon to be filled with terrified citizens wailing for rescue. Soviet nuclear missiles would shortly be on their way to Metropolis, and Luthor alone would save the human race. He had everything firmly in hand.

Wearing hooded cleansuits, his technicians stood around the humming computer banks, while others used compasses and grease pencils to plot trajectories on glass maps. The radar screens remained blank for now, but that would all change as soon as General Ceridov initiated the launch from silos in the USSR.

Though Luthor had little need for a bodyguard on his own island, Bertram stood at his side nevertheless. "We will push both superpowers to the brink, Bertram. The world's greatest leaders will hide under their beds. They'll pray, they'll whimper, and when they see that only *I* can possibly save them, I'll have them in the palm of my hand."

Bertram rarely made comments and never asked questions. Luthor had no evidence that the man was particularly intelligent, yet he earned his master's respect simply because he didn't talk all the time or make stupid rejoinders. If only more men could be so wise. . . .

At his command desk, Luthor picked up a red phone, listened to clicks and static as he was connected by a secure transatlantic cable (which LuthorCorp had privately laid). His call passed through the Soviet network, bypassed the usual monitoring substations and listening devices, and after an interminable wait, was finally connected with Ceridov.

"We are prepared and waiting, General. Have you taken care of all the details on your end?"

The other man's voice was scratchy from the distance, but his words were clear enough even through the popping static. "I am ready, comrade Luthor. Generals Dubrov and Endovik are like rabid dogs anxious to be loosed. They have already been to see the premier twice, demanding permission to launch a preemptive strike. I have a way to send a counterfeit message to them, and they will believe they have the necessary permission. I am confident they will not hesitate, nor will they doubt what they are doing."

"And your name is completely absent from all records?"

"I am a black-star KGB general! My name never appears on any records."

Soon, though, Ceridov would control the entire Soviet military. In their preliminary discussions, he and Luthor had proposed dividing the world in half, each with his own to control, but the KGB general probably dreamed of expanding his sphere of influence deeper into Southeast Asia, China, and more of Europe. Luthor was certain his counterpart would never be completely satisfied with half the world.

And neither would he. In fact, he was already making plans to deal with that very problem. First, though, the next step. "Your missiles are reliable?"

The general's voice exuded a gruff pride. "Our R-7 rocket successfully placed Sputnik into orbit, which is more than your American space program could manage! We have loaded three R-7s with nuclear warheads. They will devastate Metropolis—unless your weapons stop them. You are positive you can stop these missiles? Much as I hate you capitalists, I do not truly intend to destroy America. Too many parts of it will be useful."

Luthor didn't have to consider his answer. "I designed the entire system personally, and I supervised the installation of the Wayne Enterprises components. There will be *no* errors."

He hung up the red phone and turned to face the screens again, silently waiting.

LESS THAN AN HOUR LATER, SEVERAL OF HIS TYPICALLY quiet technicians gasped when sweeping arcs on the radar scopes revealed a trio of bogeys: the missiles launched from the Soviet Union. Without warning, the Russian R-7 rockets cruised toward America on a polar trajectory that would bring them down over the Distant Early Warning line along the edge of the Arctic Circle.

Luthor smiled, knowing that red phones would be jangling on the desks of the world's leaders. The U.S. military must have been scrambling to launch a counterattack with fighter jets and bombers, which could do nothing against these intercontinental missiles.

To prevent a full-scale war, the Soviet premier would insist, quite stridently, that the launch was "accidental." People might even believe his claims, because right now the premier himself was giving an important speech at the United Nations in Metropolis: ground zero for all three nuclear missiles. No one could evacuate in time.

With each sweep of the radar, the traces showed the inbound warheads getting closer. . . .

CHAPTER 35
METROPOLIS

SINCE HE COULD NOT REVEAL WHAT HE HAD DISCOVERED inside Area 51, Clark's trip had not yielded much of a story. After he and Jimmy returned to Metropolis, Clark had tried to cobble together a background piece using the old rancher's tale, as well as anecdotes of previous UFO sightings and Project Blue Book, but Perry filed Clark's draft article directly in the wastebasket, saying, "If there's no little green men, there's no story, Kent."

Instead he dispatched Clark and Jimmy to cover that week's UN General Assembly meeting. "The Soviet premier is scheduled to give another one of his blowhard speeches, and there's some funeral for the king of a country I've never heard of. Squeeze something interesting out of it. Nothing much else going on in the world today."

"It's the *United Nations,* Mr. White. It's got to be interesting." For Clark, the UN was a symbol of hope that all nations could find common ground and cooperate, much as he imagined the lands and peoples of Krypton had done.

When he found himself staring up at the tall UN building, Clark realized that in his relatively short time in Metropolis, he had never actually gone inside. He and Jimmy flashed their press passes and hurried to the hushed observation gallery. Clark took out his notebook, sure that he was about to see a compelling example of diplomacy in action.

Instead, he found that the routine activities of diplomats were neither particularly exciting nor newsworthy. The ambassadors were mostly sedate old men barely interested in their own goings-on. The speakers droned on in a babel of languages while interpreters translated in real time; the spectacle played largely to an audience of empty chairs.

The opening session consisted of a forty-five-minute parade of diplomats expressing their condolences that the king of Timacu had died (at the age of eighty-seven, and after fourteen wives). Each member nation expressed its official sorrow before the next ambassador expressed an even more extravagant amount of grief, and so on, until it seemed that the whole world considered the king of Timacu to have been a statesman of such profound influence that civilization itself was unlikely to continue without him. Clark decided to search the *Daily Planet*'s archives to find out what the king of Timacu had actually done during his reign.

Jimmy took several uninspired photographs of the sparsely populated rows of seated men. Clark leaned over and whispered in his ear. "This is slower than the town hall meetings in Smallville."

Presently the General Assembly came to life when the bombastic Soviet premier took the podium and began his speech by shouting. The blustery head of the Communist Party attempted to change the opinions of his rival diplomats through sheer vehemence rather than refined oratorical skills and convincing rhetoric. To emphasize a point, the premier actually removed a shoe and began hammering the podium before him, vowing to bury any other nation that did not agree with his ideology.

Frowning, Clark took notes. "He's not winning any friends, that's for sure."

Back in Kansas, he and his father had often listened to radio news broadcasts together. Though Jonathan Kent hadn't taken a lot of interest in world politics, he certainly hadn't trusted the Communists. "Son, I hope I've raised you to admire our core values. America's not perfect, far from it, but even with our faults, this is the best darned country in the world. Don't ever stop believing in truth, justice, and the American way."

"I won't, Pa," Clark had promised.

And he never had.

The Soviet premier had just reached the crescendo of his speech when blaring air-raid sirens drowned out his sound and fury. Uniformed UN security guards rushed in, calling for an immediate evacuation of the building.

INSIDE PERRY WHITE'S OFFICE, LOIS LANE LOCKED HER ARMS across her chest. "I can catch the next flight to Havana, hire a boat, and go find that island of Luthor's. Clark and Jimmy's trip was a bust. Now give *me* a chance."

He shook his head, holding the cigar in his right hand. "Don't remind me how much money I just spent on a wild goose chase after flying saucers."

"You have to go where the story takes you," Lois insisted. "You taught me that yourself."

"Go find a big story right here in Metropolis, preferably one that doesn't require an expense account. Something might just fall in your lap."

Scowling, she was about to make a flippant comment when Perry's radio blasted the piercing emergency broadcast signal.

Out in the bullpen, the other reporters flocked toward the shortwave.

"—emergency bulletin. The Soviets have just launched three nuclear missiles toward the United States of America. Soviet officials at first insisted this was an accidental launch, but now they are silent. The missiles are on their way. Likely targets are Metropolis and Washington, D.C. Proceed immediately to your nearest civil defense shelter. This is not a drill."

"There's a fallout shelter in the basement—" someone began, and in shock, people began to run for the door, leaving their personal items behind.

"Great Caesar's ghost!" Perry said. "Lois, there's your story—if anybody survives to read it."

JIMMY WAS SO ASTONISHED THAT HE NEARLY DROPPED HIS camera. "What do we do now, Mr. Kent?"

The UN security guards urgently ushered the diplomats out of the General Assembly hall down to the civil defense shelter. The corridors of the UN were sheer pandemonium, overlain with a tapestry of languages.

"Get to the shelter, Jimmy—quick." Already Clark's mind was racing ahead to how he could slip away. Ambassadors of free countries and dictatorships alike elbowed each other aside, crowding into stairwells, rushing downward alongside custodians, secretaries, and cafeteria workers. Clark urged Jimmy into the throng, then managed to lose his friend in the jostling, frantic crowd.

He ducked into an empty office, glad for the confusion. If Soviet missiles were inbound, he didn't have much time. But if anyone could stop them, *he* could.

CHAPTER 36
LUTHOR'S ISLAND

AS HE WATCHED THE MISSILE TRACES ON THE RADAR SCREEN come over the North Pole, Luthor's smile broadened. Closer . . . closer . . .

It wouldn't do to take care of them *too* quickly, *too* easily. He had to let the rockets cross into American airspace, at least. Unless the world's leaders were absolutely convinced they were about to die, they wouldn't show enough gratitude. First, they had to bite their nails, fall to their knees sobbing, make promises to God or confessions to loved ones (which they would regret later). Luthor was glad to be far away on his little island, where he didn't have to hear all that sniveling.

On the large polar-projection map mounted to the control center wall, a cluster of blinking dots marked the three missiles as they crossed the DEW line, headed down over northern Canada and the mid-Canada warning line, then crossed the Pinetree Line at the fiftieth parallel. The graceful arcs looked so beautiful as the R-7 rockets pushed relentlessly toward the United States, toward Metropolis.

For years, U.S. rocketry scientists led by Wernher von Braun had been developing and perfecting such weapons, but they had never managed to test a long-range warhead-carrying missile. The American Atlas-A rocket was not yet ready for launch, but Luthor was both surprised and unsettled to see how well Soviet technology functioned.

First Sputnik, now this. The United States had certainly fallen behind in the space race.

But here was Luthor's perfect window of opportunity. His death-ray transmitters were aligned and powered up. The wall screens displayed shaded zones of "guaranteed kill" for the beams, and the first missile had almost come into range. His targeting computers whirred and clicked, lights blinked, and magnetic tape wheels spun.

Not trusting such an important step to mere minions, he personally aligned the targeting vectors, then counted down the seconds to when he would avert a nuclear holocaust.

His energy-beam dishes, pointed to the sky, would project lightning bolts superior to any Zeus had ever thrown. Luthor activated the systems, and the control bank's indicator lights glowed green. Now to save the world, just in the nick of time.

He turned the operation key and, with a thin smile, hit the large firing button.

Nothing happened.

His smile faltered. He reset the system and punched the firing button again. The beam generators failed to shoot out powerful blasts of energy. The newly installed components simply froze. The Wayne Enterprises technology refused to work!

The missiles kept coming.

Once the detonations occurred in Metropolis, the United States would mount a nuclear launch of its own, using squadrons of long-range bombers on desperate missions carrying hydrogen bombs.

By then, it would all be much too late, completely out of control. The whole planet would be swallowed up in a nuclear holocaust.

At his side, the normally silent Bertram said simply, "Do you have a backup plan, sir?"

Luthor hammered his fist impotently on the firing button. "No, I don't have a backup plan! When the first plan is perfect, who needs a backup?"

Bertram did not state the obvious flaw in that reasoning.

Suddenly the radar screen showed another blip, a small object racing at supersonic speed on a direct intercept path with the missiles.

FASTER THAN A BULLET, HIGHER THAN A JET, KAL-EL FLEW for his life—for everyone's lives. Even the rarefied air created enough drag to slow him, and the heat of his passage surrounded him with a faint, warm glow.

With hyperacute hearing, he could detect the constant rumble of rocket engines. The missiles with their deadly payloads reached apogee and now plunged like high-tech javelins toward their programmed target.

But Kal-El was America's own super-weapon.

He slowed enough so that he could intercept the first missile without annihilating its nose on impact, which would have scattered the radioactive payload across the sky. Exerting himself against the R-7 rocket's momentum, he pushed the nose cone, tilting the missile upward, altering its trajectory. Kal-El pushed against gravity, against the very air, and finally the missile flew toward space. The Soviet R-7 had neither the power nor the fuel to reach escape velocity, so Kal-El gave it an extra shove.

The missile climbed higher and higher, beyond even Sputnik's orbit. Eventually it would explode in empty space, where it would cause no damage.

With no time to rest or celebrate this triumph, Kal-El streaked back down toward the remaining two missiles.

Now that he knew how to divert them, he easily damaged the rocket engines with his heat vision, sent the missiles sputtering, and then intercepted their long cylindrical bodies one at a time.

As he bore the second R-7 out of Earth's atmosphere on his shoulders like Atlas and heaved it into space, Kal-El was reminded of how he had carried the sinking *Star City Queen* to safety in Metropolis Bay. This time, though, he was saving all of Metropolis, perhaps the whole world.

After he hurled the third and last nuclear missile away to where it could cause no damage, he let himself drift in the sky, looking down at the beautiful world below—the coastlines, the clouds, the geometric patterns of the cities, roads, and croplands.

His world . . . safe.

CHAPTER 37
THE WHITE HOUSE, WASHINGTON, D.C.

AT ANY OTHER TIME, LOIS WOULD HAVE ROLLED HER EYES if asked to report on an awards ceremony, even a presidential presentation, but since Superman was involved, she definitely wanted to cover the story. He had, after all, prevented an all-out atomic war.

All of the aspersions Lex Luthor had cast on Superman were instantly forgotten (not that the reporters had dug up any dirt on him anyway). Lois wished she could have seen Luthor's face, but the bald industrialist hadn't appeared in public for weeks. Probably sulking, she thought.

With the missiles miraculously diverted and destroyed, the people of Metropolis had celebrated in the streets, throwing confetti and cheering. Taxi drivers honked their horns. Restaurant owners gave out free food. Flower sellers threw blossoms up in the air. Old women and curmudgeonly men hugged each other. Even the Soviet premier was said to have collapsed into a chair, weeping with relief.

Judging by the number of reporters packed into the press corral on the White House lawn, Lois wasn't the only one who recognized the significance of the story. For the official occasion, she wore a formal lavender dress and new gloves, and she was determined to portray Superman exactly the way he deserved: as a hero.

Superman stood there, handsome and muscular but clearly out of his element before the excited crowd. She thought it was charming. His bright blue and red outfit did not show a smudge, despite the fact he had recently wrestled with three Soviet nuclear missiles. Even the black curl on his brow was perfectly in place. But though he could bend steel in his bare hands and stop a bullet with his chest, he seemed endearingly . . . *shy*.

Lois thought about how he had so easily swept her up in his strong arms as her car plunged off the Twelfth Street Bridge, saving her—if she could have, she would have found a way to save *him* now. However, accepting the adulation of an appreciative nation was an ordeal Superman would just have to endure. . . .

Though he was the president of the United States, Dwight Eisenhower looked very small in his gray suit next to Superman. Eisenhower was himself a hero, having led armies in World War II, and had been reelected by a landslide along with his running mate Richard M. Nixon. Now, though, even the president looked intimidated in the presence of Superman.

To resounding applause, Eisenhower extended his hand, and Superman vigorously pumped it. The president tried to cover his flinch, obviously concerned that the other man might crush his hand, but the hero was perfectly restrained. A hundred flashbulbs went off to capture the moment.

Eisenhower stepped up to the podium, from which sprouted a bouquet of large microphones. "Today, Superman, America gives you our sincerest gratitude. As president, I want to thank you from the bottom of my heart, and also from the heart of every U.S. citizen, and every citizen of the world. You saved us all."

Lois was a bit starry-eyed herself, but that had more to do with Superman than the presidential honor he was about to receive. She found herself moved by his humility and sincerity; Lois realized she was even blushing, and she quickly lifted a white-gloved hand to cover her cheek.

Eisenhower continued. "Because of clashing political ideologies, the human race has been pushed to the brink of extinction. Such a thing must never happen again."

Lois had heard the Communist leader speak virtually the same words after he had emerged from the UN fallout shelter, pale and shaking. Once the crisis had passed, his rhetoric was less vitriolic. He protested that the launch of the nuclear missiles had been neither intentional nor authorized. Why would he do such a thing, he demanded, when he himself was at ground zero at the time?

Two traitorous rogue generals had been identified and branded as criminals—Endovik and Dubrov. Both men, having disobeyed direct orders, had been removed from their positions and summarily executed. The premier insisted that there was no need for continued international tensions. He seemed to think the world should just forget about the whole affair. Lois didn't believe it for an instant, nor did she entirely swallow his explanation.

Continuing the ceremony, President Eisenhower opened a velvet-lined wooden box and withdrew a finely worked medal suspended from a red, white, and blue ribbon. "For all you have done, Superman, this is the highest accolade our country can bestow—the Presidential Medal of Freedom."

Superman's chest swelled with pride. He raised his square chin and met the president's gaze with his clear blue eyes. "I accept it gladly, Mr. President."

Eisenhower reached forward with the medal, fumbled with the pin, and attempted to attach it to Superman's chest. He frowned.

In an awkward moment, he tried again, to no avail. The pin could not penetrate the tough blue fabric.

Many more camera bulbs flashed. The onlookers waited anxiously.

Finally, Eisenhower took a step back, nonplussed. The pin was bent.

With self-effacing humor, Superman extended a hand. "Why don't I just hold that, Mr. President?"

Eisenhower quickly handed it to him and returned to the microphone, eager to move on. "Superman, we are proud to have you as one of our foremost citizens. You are the defender of truth, justice, and the American way."

Though her applause was muffled by the formal white gloves, Lois clapped more vigorously than her fellow reporters. She felt inspired, possibly more from her own heart than from the actual speech. She even had tears in her eyes. If only her father could see her now—tough little Lois turning into a girly, emotional mess!

From the podium, Superman caught her stare and returned Lois's smile, blushing a bit himself. For a long moment, he didn't seem to be seeing any other face than hers.

CHAPTER 38
WAYNE ENTERPRISES

IN THE MONTHS AFTER THE DISASTROUS SOVIET MISSILE launch, the U.S. military-industrial complex went into high gear, devoting resources, manpower, manufacturing capabilities, and vast sums of money to the nation's defense. Though President Eisenhower and the Soviet premier publicly reaffirmed their mutual commitment to peace, no one believed that the Cold War had thawed.

Since the unofficial shakeup of its board of directors, Wayne Enterprises had quietly become a new company, entering a veritable renaissance. Accompanied by a very pleased-looking Richard Drayling, who had been reinstated as a board member, Bruce Wayne toured the expanded production line at a Wayne Enterprises aircraft assembly plant.

With Alfred acting as go-between again, Bruce had invited Drayling to the manor for a private luncheon and a heart-to-heart conversation, during which he showed the older man the incriminating files he was holding over the heads of the other nine directors. He also explained how he had hamstrung the guilty men, how he was using them to get back at Luthor, and how he had effectively removed them from any real power in Wayne Enterprises. Drayling was quite gratified at how Bruce had handled the situation, and the old man now appeared to be much younger than his years. "You have more of your father in you than I thought, Mr. Wayne," he said. "Perhaps I misjudged you."

By now, several former directors had been reassigned to probationary positions, where Bruce knew they could cause no further harm; the others held jobs that carried no responsibilities at all. LuthorCorp would get nothing more from them. The new board members—drawn from the most successful project managers in each research division—were entirely loyal to Bruce's vision for the company, now that he had begun acting like a real administrator.

Many eyebrows had been raised at Bruce's seemingly abrupt transition from lightweight playboy to responsible businessman, and some people had expressed open skepticism about his abilities in the corporate world. Analysts, however, made the assumption (which Bruce did not correct) that he simply surrounded himself with "good people."

Now the fabrication lines had begun producing a new series of state-of-the-art fighter jets for the USAF. These exotic designs had been in development at Wayne Enterprises for more than a year, but Bruce had accelerated the production timeline. The first deliveries were well ahead of schedule.

Surrounded by the clamor of the assembly line, the rolling belts, clanging tools, and hammering rivets, the two men strolled along on their inspection tour. Bruce's expensive business suit seemed incongruous with the bright yellow hard hat he wore. Smiling, he greeted supervisors and line foremen, then shook the hands of several workers who had been busily welding fuselage skins together.

Bruce raised his voice to the jumpsuited work crews. "Things have changed around here. I've been taking a more direct role in this company."

Drayling nodded, adding his support. "And I intend to be seeing you all more often, in person."

Thanks to several major new defense contracts, the price of Wayne Enterprises stock had soared, improving the profitability of his company. Again and again, Wayne Enterprises successfully outbid LuthorCorp for new government contracts, and Bruce knew the real reason. Without his spies copying the best Wayne Enterprises work, Luthor no longer had the edge he'd once taken for granted.

In the last two months, given full creative freedom, Bruce's research teams had developed amazing designs, innovative weapons, and vehicles that were not just refinements of tried-and-true existing technology but genuinely new approaches. Every breakthrough, every report, every prototype was channeled directly through him.

Naturally, he made a point of keeping the most daring advances for his "personal testing."

INSIDE THE CAVE, BRUCE DIDN'T MIND GETTING HIS HANDS dirty. Engine grease covered his knuckles, darkened his fingernails. He slid beneath the black automobile, inspecting the axles, the transmission. Its lines were predatory, its paint coat polished to such a high gleam that it looked like a clear midnight sky.

Straightening, Alfred raised his welding helmet and extinguished the blowtorch. "I neglected to install the minibar and magazine rack, sir, but you'll find everything else quite in order."

Lying on his back, Bruce rolled out from beneath the chassis, wiping his hands on a rag. He hauled himself to his feet. "And the entire body is bulletproof?"

"Doubly armored, sir. Would you like me to take a few potshots in order to demonstrate?"

"We'll test it soon enough, Alfred. And the windshield glass?"

"Triple-sandwiched transparent polymer, along with a strong, virtually invisible wire grid to help maintain integrity. This is the best vehicle that money can buy—as you well know."

Bruce raised the hood and inspected the high-powered engine, which made the largest American V8 look like a windup toy by comparison. A rocket nozzle above the rear exhaust ports could provide emergency thrust.

He had made most of the modifications himself, diverting R&D developments from Wayne Enterprises before they could be released to government contractors. Naturally, such extraordinary breakthroughs had to be demonstrated in the field, and he looked forward to doing the testing himself.

Though the car's design was functional, it also displayed a flair for the dramatic—swooping fins, armored tires, gadgets to respond to any conceivable situation . . . something James Bond would have envied. Anyone who glanced at the vehicle would immediately know that it belonged to the mysterious Batman.

However, Bruce still found it maddening that he could not reproduce Superman's powers. Their encounters at the Luthor mansion and in the Area 51 hangar had only heightened his interest. He knew how challenging it had been to penetrate the incredible security at Groom Lake, but Superman had gotten in without even breaking a sweat. And later the other man had flown high enough and fast enough to stop all three Soviet missiles, hurling them away from Earth. That was no parlor trick, and it could not be explained by the technology Luthor had stolen to design his bulky battlesuits.

Even so, this new rocket-powered car was quite impressive.

Opening the door of the vehicle, Bruce slid into the biodynamically designed seat. Alfred, with his perennial dry wit, had taped a note to the front control panel: BATMOBILE.

"Stand clear, Alfred. I'm going to fire her up. Are the tires secure on the rollers?"

"Indeed they are, sir. I wouldn't want your first test drive to terminate prematurely against the cave wall."

Alfred primly inserted earplugs and stood against the rock wall, waiting as Bruce started the ignition process—atomic batteries to power, turbines to speed. The engine purred, hummed, then roared to full power. And he hadn't even engaged the rocket booster yet.

The vehicle shuddered, tires screaming on the rollers like fractious thoroughbreds in the starting gate. The dashboard gauges inched toward red fields as he increased power. Bruce ran diagnostics that continually monitored the vehicle's systems. Thus far he was very pleased. *Batmobile* indeed!

When he finished his tests, Bruce climbed reluctantly out of the black vehicle. A smile showed beneath Alfred's pencil-thin mustache as he removed his earplugs. "It seems adequate, Master Bruce. The Wayne Enterprises scientists have produced another miracle."

Bruce drew a deep breath and let it out slowly. In spite of the car's armor, engine power, built-in weaponry, and evasive devices, Superman trumped all of it. "Yes, miracles, Alfred . . . but they're not yet miraculous *enough.*"

CHAPTER 39
LUTHORCORP

NSIDE HIS CORPORATE HEADQUARTERS IN METROPOLIS, Lex Luthor's office was a well-defended island in a sea of covertly armed receptionists whose primary job was to prevent him from being interrupted: At any moment, Luthor's great mind might be on the verge of an important breakthrough.

He sat in intense silence, studying the plans for the production model of his advanced armored battlesuit. Enhanced shoulder and neck protection, impenetrable casing over vulnerable areas, a jetpack for short flights, magnetic boots, built-in projectile weapons, protective gauntlets. The wearer of such a suit would become the world's most powerful soldier . . . perhaps even powerful enough to defeat Superman.

Luthor had always been annoyed by the grandstanding hero. That blue suit and red cape—where had he gotten such an outlandish costume? And since he had helped the cowled burglar to escape from his mansion, Superman was clearly more than an attention-seeking gadfly. Granted, after the incomprehensible failure of Luthor's energy-beam defense system, he admitted that a superpowerful alien freak might have his uses. Even so, Superman would have been much more tolerable if he'd been controlled by LuthorCorp.

Fortunately, because his death-beam system had been a carefully kept secret on his island, nobody was aware that the energy rays had failed at the most crucial moment. Luthor's disgrace, his shame, his *error* was entirely a private matter. But that didn't make it any less maddening.

After the debacle, he had received a cryptic telegram from behind the Iron Curtain—a message from General Ceridov informing him that the military traitors Endovik and Dubrov had not, in fact, been executed but, better still, had been sent to the Ariguska gulag. Ceridov seemed to believe that the stunt with Superman was one of Luthor's ploys.

Good; let him keep his delusions, Luthor thought.

The KGB general had kept his fingerprints off the entire incident, as had Luthor. Even so, Luthor was more than annoyed by Superman's continued intervention. Yes, he had saved the world, which almost—*almost*—balanced out the fact that he had made a fool out of Lex Luthor. Nobody made a fool out of Lex Luthor.

As a result, he had decided to investigate the mystery of Superman with even greater vigor. How could the brute be stopped if he happened to get out of control? Luthor didn't like any aspect of his plans to be out of control. Superman had to be taken out of the picture, or at least thoroughly leashed.

An hour earlier, he had received a formal letter from the secretary of defense, regretfully turning down Luthor's appeal to submit new bids for several contracts that had been awarded to Wayne Enterprises. Just yesterday, a major bid for helicopters had been awarded to Northrop Aircraft. Queen Industries had just won out on the contract for the new Arrow short-range missile. LuthorCorp's medical division had lost a lucrative contract for a radiation treatment to be used in the case of heavy fallout exposures; Tyler Pharmaceuticals had come up with an equivalent—and cheaper—system.

Wayne Enterprises was, however, his only true competitor. Luthor now realized he'd made a mistake—a *mistake!*—in underestimating Bruce Wayne, believing him to be an insipid hedonistic playboy, all money and no brains. Since Luthor's insiders at Wayne Enterprises had been so useful for so long, he hadn't worried about the handsome goof-off. Now, astonishingly, Wayne actually seemed to know what he was doing, and his paid-off board members had been rendered impotent. Obviously Wayne knew, or at least suspected, their treachery. And none of them had bothered to inform *him*! Idiots.

When the intercom on his desk buzzed, he stabbed at it irritably. "What?"

"A man to see you, Mr. Luthor. He insists you'll want to talk with him, though he's not on the calendar."

"Who is it? Senator McCarthy will be here soon."

"His last name is Buchheim. He claims you knew him from Wayne Enterprises."

Luthor stiffened. "Send him in—and don't let anyone else see him. Is Bertram here?"

"I'll call for him, Mr. Luthor."

Larry Buchheim walked in, looking sheepish, red-eyed, broken. Luthor had always considered the man weak. Anyone who left incriminating evidence lying around was a sloppy fool, beneath contempt—except when he could be put to good use. Unfortunately, this man's usefulness had ended the moment that Bruce Wayne had transferred him out of active management.

Buchheim approached his desk, hat in hand, squeezing the brim nervously; his suit was rumpled. Luthor had heard that the man's wife had left him—a fact that should have given the idiot more time to concentrate on the job at hand, become a useful member of society.

Buchheim stood in front of the single chair across from the desk, careful not to take a seat without being invited. "I have information for you, Mr. Luthor. Good information."

"That'll be a refreshing change. Your last offerings proved useless."

"It wasn't my fault. We were ordered to do it, all of us. Wayne knows about our connections with you. He uncovered the dirt you have on each of us."

Since Luthor had already suspected this, he was unimpressed by Buchheim's news. "How did he do that?"

"He must have hired the world's greatest detective. He had photos, documents, records of my bank account. He knows everything, Mr. Luthor."

"Poor you." His thoughts raced ahead to determine how he could remove all evidence from his end.

"Some of the others are bound to be coming to you as well, but I wanted to get here first. He's going to dismiss us all—I know it. I need a job at LuthorCorp. You owe it to me, after what I did for you all those years."

"I *owe* you?" Luthor actually barked a laugh, unable to believe this man's gall. "I seem to recall that you were paid—well paid, in fact, for technology that proved *faulty*!"

"That was Wayne's doing, too, sir. Once he discovered our connection to LuthorCorp, he ordered us to continue providing components and blueprints to you, but I've since learned that he altered them somehow, modified the designs in subtle ways. The pieces we supplied, Mr. Luthor, weren't *supposed* to work. He sabotaged them, just to spite you."

Buchheim reached inside his suit jacket and pulled out a folded piece of paper. He leaned forward to place a small sketch on Luthor's desk. The drawing showed the diodes and transistors that had been cleverly, but improperly, connected in the control circuits that Luthor had co-opted for his energy-beam system. Without a careful and meticulous inspection, no one would ever have noticed the flaw.

The last piece fell into place in Luthor's mind. The components he had so carefully obtained from Wayne Enterprises and installed in his flawless energy-beam system were duds, *designed* to fail? He had used technology stolen from Wayne Enterprises so he could put the system online faster, test it sooner, pit it against the Soviet missiles. There had been no fault in his design—no *error*. Luthor's only real mistake had been in trusting the competence of others.

"Buchheim, do you have any idea what you've done?"

"That's why I came here. I know what Wayne Enterprises is working on now, and I can help you develop it before they do. New technology!"

"New technology…I'm a fan of new technology, Mr. Buchheim. Give me something new over something old any day. That's one major difference between myself and Bruce Wayne: He surrounds himself with relics from fallen empires, museum-quality garbage. I, on the other hand, see how things can be improved, and I figure out how to profit from that." Luthor opened a desk drawer and reached inside. "However, sometimes the old ways are reliable and effective. You just can't improve on certain ideas."

He withdrew a Luger P08 pistol, for which he had paid a great deal. The gun had supposedly been carried by Dr. Mengele himself, and Luthor's labs had authenticated one partial fingerprint.

"This type of pistol has been in service for decades. The

Germans began using it at the turn of the century." He pointed it directly at Buchheim's chest and fired without another word. The bullet ripped through the man's sternum, knocking him backward into the chair. He slumped like a scarecrow in the seat.

The gunshot was loud, but the office was soundproofed. This was by no means the first time Luthor had needed to keep his activities here absolutely private. The former Wayne Enterprises employee twitched and bled, then lay still. Luthor waved away the bitter smell of cordite about him. He hit the intercom again, much more relaxed now. "Is Bertram here yet?"

"Yes, sir, he's just arrived."

"Send him in."

When the burly bodyguard stepped through the door, he regarded the body in the seat without comment.

"Clean up the mess before Senator McCarthy arrives for our luncheon. And bring in a new chair. That one is stained."

Bertram grabbed the dead man's arms and dragged him away. Already on to other business of the day, Luthor took a sheet of paper from his desk blotter and put aside the battlesuit plans. With neat, precise handwriting, he jotted down the names of the other eight directors who had been under his thumb.

When Bertram finished the cleaning chores, Luthor handed him the paper. "These men are liabilities. Take care of them. I want it done quickly."

"Yes, sir. Quickly."

Luthor raised a finger. "Quietly, if possible. But if not . . . well, *quickly* will be good enough."

HE POURED SCOTCHES FOR BOTH HIMSELF AND JOSEPH McCarthy while they waited for lunch to be served. The senator from Wisconsin, firebrand of the House Un-American Activities Commission, settled himself comfortably in a brand-new chair across from the desk.

The meek and silent kitchen staff delivered a tray for each man: thick rare steaks, baked potatoes, and an iceberg lettuce salad smothered with thousand island dressing. As he cut into his own fillet, Luthor enjoyed the smooth glide of the steak knife's serrated edge through the tender flesh. The bloody juices oozed out with an appetizing aroma. "Good American heartland beef, Senator."

The senator also attacked the meal. His round eyes were intense, his face set in a perpetual scowl that made him appear as though he ate only mustard and pickles. After the recent missile launch, McCarthy had gone on the warpath against the evil Communists with renewed fervor. In years past, the senator had been a great ally in helping to promote the Cold War tensions that led to the arms buildup. "Let's talk business while we dine, Mr. Luthor. I'm due back on Capitol Hill later today for more HUAC hearings."

"We're both busy men, Senator. We can both accomplish a great deal."

McCarthy crunched into his salad, wiping a smear of dressing from the corner of his mouth. "And there's still much to do. It wasn't so long ago, Mr. Luthor, that you yourself made me see the danger posed by the Communist menace. I only hope we've responded in time and with enough vehemence." He launched into his typical diatribe against the Commies, as if he were sitting in front of a TV camera instead of in a private meeting.

Luthor grew bored with the man's limited scope of thinking and brought him up short with a single comment. "Senator, there's something even worse than Communists."

McCarthy blinked at the astonishing comment, a bite of steak poised in front of his mouth.

Now that he had his guest's undivided attention, Luthor laid the groundwork for the next step in his plan. After being terrified by the near-holocaust, all of America was starry-eyed over that fool Superman, and even McCarthy didn't see the flaw in their misplaced faith. Not yet. Luthor would lead him down the next path.

The mutual fear that he and General Ceridov had managed to engender between the U.S. and USSR was a resounding and lucrative success, and it had led him to consider larger possibilities. Luthor did not think small and did not like to share—not with Ceridov, not with anyone. Therefore, he had to create a titanic enemy that would dwarf even the Soviet Union.

"Communists may be opposed to all that we fundamentally hold dear, Senator. They enslave their own people. They threaten the American way. They want to deny us life, liberty, and the pursuit of happiness. However, while we disagree on basic ideals, even Communists are still human. *Aliens,* on the other hand, are a far more dangerous menace."

"Aliens!" McCarthy laughed and took another drink of his Scotch. "You can't be serious, Luthor."

"Deadly serious. An alien already walks among us wearing a blue suit and bright red cape, pretending to do good deeds and lulling us into a false sense of security."

"You're referring to Superman?" McCarthy chuckled again. "But he's a hero. He saved America."

"But for what purpose? Who knows where he's really from or what he wants? He told Lois Lane that he comes from a dead planet called Krypton. *Krypton?* It sounds made up. Is it beyond Mars? Past Alpha Centauri? In the Andromeda Galaxy?

"He won't reveal his true name. How long has he lived among us? Does he pay taxes? Is he even an American citizen, or is he here illegally? Can we really take him at face value? Is that how the House Un-American Activities Commission treats the hidden Communists among us? Do you presume they are fine human beings who can't mean us harm?"

McCarthy's thick brows drew together. "I've never considered that. We don't actually have an immigration policy for . . . extraterrestrial visitors. Even so, you can't deny that Superman's done great work."

"He took care of those Russian missiles too easily, if you ask me, Senator. And the whole launch scenario—two Soviet generals disobeying orders, both men now conveniently executed? Don't you think that sounds suspicious?"

"But the Soviet premier was in Metropolis at the time. He would have died in the blast. He couldn't have known anything about it."

"Unless he knew there was no real threat after all. Can we be sure the entire event wasn't some put-up job staged by Superman, or maybe one of his alien comrades? Think about it! *How do we know there were even warheads on those missiles at all?* He could be a Communist agent, living among us in plain sight. Maybe the Soviet Union is breeding 'supermen' of their own."

McCarthy gasped at the idea.

Luthor continued. "Even worse, maybe Superman has his own plans and means to pit us against the Russians. After we've nearly annihilated each other, then he and his alien conquerors can simply come in to pick up the pieces. What if there's an entire invasion coming?" He pushed aside his plate and leaned close. The other man now appeared very concerned by these new and deeply disturbing ideas. With his paranoid nature, McCarthy seemed to believe that everything made perfect sense.

"Senator, you've seen Superman's powers yourself. What if he decides to turn *against* us? Then where will we be?" He sat back and started to eat his salad. "I promise you, when the aliens do come—and I'm convinced they will—we'd better be ready for them."

Luthor measured his satisfaction by the level of alarm that showed on Joseph McCarthy's ashen face.

PRESIDENT EISENHOWER HAD ENTRUSTED HIM WITH THE protection of America, and Kal-El took his job seriously. He needed to do more. Clark Kent asked for a few days off from the *Daily Planet,* ostensibly to visit his mother in Kansas. But he had other plans.

Stopping in Smallville before he got down to his real work, he handed the Presidential Medal of Freedom to Martha Kent for safekeeping. She had tears in her eyes. "I wish your father could have been alive to see this. Oh, I was so proud when I watched you on TV, though the reception was a little spotty. What was the president like in person?"

Martha had baked a cherry pie this time, her best ever, and he chatted with her as he tucked away a second piece along with a tall glass of milk. "I'm going to need the energy, Ma, since I've got a lot of work ahead of me."

Then—as Kal-El instead of Clark Kent—he sprang into the sky, became part of the wind, and soared above the Earth to undertake a thorough surveillance behind the Iron Curtain. He flew across Europe to East Germany, then continued north and east toward Leningrad, passing over restricted Soviet airspace. He crisscrossed the sky, not caring who saw his red and blue blur. In fact, he *wanted* to let the Communists know he was keeping an eye on them with his super-vision.

He studied the activities of the Soviet military, noting the movement of their troops, flying over the missile silos, all prominently marked with red stars. With Sputnik circling Earth, Kal-El was certain their scientists were already working on a much more sophisticated satellite that would carry high-resolution cameras to photograph secret installations like Area 51. Fortunately, the U.S. also had new jet aircraft in development, including high-altitude spy planes. But no camera—no matter how sophisticated—could match Kal-El's vision. It was his duty to keep an eye on whatever mischief the enemy might be planning.

As he raced over a Soviet industrial city adjacent to a military base, he saw the open scars of mines, smelters, smokestacks belching black clouds into the sky. A squadron of MiG-19 fighters chased after him, their engines hurling the aircraft forward at incredible speeds, breaking the sound barrier, pursuing him at Mach 1.2. But he was too fast for them. Kal-El laughed as he streaked ahead across the steppes, leaving them far behind.

Finally, when he reached the Siberian wilderness, he discovered one isolated complex that worried him greatly. Hundreds of acres of thick forest had been blown down, knocked flat as though a titanic shock wave had spread out in a circle like ripples in a pond. The only thing he could imagine capable of unleashing so much destruction was a hydrogen bomb.

Naturally, the Soviets would test their most powerful nuclear weapons in isolated Siberia, while the U.S. detonated their bombs in the empty Nevada desert or on vacant South Pacific atolls.

Focusing his vision, he saw a large circular crater surrounded by fences, barracks buildings, a camp, even the containment building and cooling tower of a small nuclear reactor. People were tiny moving dots, and he discerned armed guards watching groups of enslaved workers. One of the infamous Soviet gulags! The labor crews had turned the crater into some kind of quarry, removing residue from the explosion or impact, excavating . . . what? A large metal dome covered the bottom of the quarry, its thick plates reflecting the hazy sunlight, hiding the real secret from prying eyes.

Suspecting sinister activities, Kal-El squinted his eyes to use his penetrating X-ray vision, but his glance reflected back. He could not see through the metal, no matter how hard he pushed. *The entire dome must be lined with lead,* he thought. *Radiation shielding?* For the Soviets to go to such great lengths to hide their activities, he had no doubt that the dome must contain something threatening.

He needed to find out what it was.

Kal-El swooped down to land on top of the dome that covered the bottom of the pit. The gulag guards spied him immediately, and shots rang out from their AK-47s. Several shots struck Kal-El in the back and shoulder, but he brushed them aside as though they were gnats. Bullets ricocheted, leaving silver impact stars on the metallic dome. He knifed his hand into the hemispherical shell, broke the seam of the metal plates, ripped the sheeting, and cracked open the dome like an Easter egg to expose what was inside.

Suddenly an emerald glow bathed his face, a sickly luminescence that seeped upward like a plague. Excavated and exposed at the base of the crater lay a jagged boulder of green mineral half-buried in the dirt. A strange form of radiation streamed upward.

Back at Luthor's mansion, a much smaller fragment of this green rock had been enough to bring him to his knees. What lay beneath him now was thousands of times larger and more powerful.

Kal-El tried to cling to the edge of the dome, but his muscles had turned to water. His vision swam before him, then went black. With limp hands, he tried to keep his balance, tried to crawl away, but he slipped into the gap that he himself had made in the lead-lined dome. He couldn't breathe, couldn't think.

Totally drained, he slid down through the hole.

The Soviet guards continued to shoot, but he no longer cared. Unconscious, Kal-El fell to the bottom of the meteorite quarry, but he felt nothing when he struck the ground.

CHAPTER 41
WAYNE MANOR

WHILE CLARK KENT WAS AWAY IN KANSAS, LOIS WENT TO Gotham City to interview Bruce Wayne. One question was foremost in her mind: Would Bruce help her dig up dirt on Lex Luthor, or was the playboy millionaire just as corrupt and narcissistic as his fellow industrialist? She intended to hit him with some tough questions.

Bruce received her graciously in the imposing manor house. He offered her a choice of beverages, suggesting trendy new cocktails, the names of which he must surely have made up himself; he was already sipping a martini-like drink he called a Vesper.

When she merely asked for coffee, the attendant butler seemed at first surprised, then pleased. "As you wish, Miss Lane." Before long, he returned carrying a heavy silver coffee service that wafted a rich aroma. The coffee was so full-bodied she could almost believe Alfred had rushed down to Colombia himself, picked the beans, roasted them, and hurried back in time to make her this pot. It was the sort of thing Bruce Wayne was expected to do for his guests.

In the meantime, the millionaire suavely entertained her, not the least embarrassed when she rebuffed his charm and asked to get down to business. Lois wasn't impressed by wealth or the airs of the rich and powerful. This man might fancy himself to be like James Bond from those books he read, but she could tell it was all an act. He wasn't a real hero, like Superman.

"Mr. Wayne, I have been researching a story on LuthorCorp and its CEO, and I'm convinced something shifty is going on. Lex Luthor's got a lot of disgruntled employees and a lot of questionable business dealings."

He raised his dark eyebrows at her candor. "Disgruntled employees aren't the most reliable of sources, Miss Lane."

"My source was murdered shortly after she spoke with me. That tells me that Luthor must not have wanted her talking."

"Wouldn't it have made more sense if he'd silenced her *before* she spilled the beans?" He took another sip of his drink. "You'll need solid proof if you're going to accuse Lex Luthor."

"That's where you can help me." She took a long sip of coffee, which tasted as delicious as it smelled.

"Believe me, since Lex Luthor is my primary rival, if dirt were to be found, I would already have it."

"And would you give it to me for my story?"

He just looked at her.

She pressed on. "In recent years, Luthor secured far more than his share of lucrative defense contracts. But you just turned the tables on him, didn't you? Luthor can't be terribly pleased with Wayne Enterprises these days."

"The contract-bidding business is a competition among giants of industry. Surely you don't mean to imply that Wayne Enterprises was underhanded in getting those contracts?" He displayed a hint of a wry smile, and for that she liked him a little better.

"I think it's more likely that LuthorCorp used dirty tricks to win the earlier bids. It's Luthor I'm interested in, Mr. Wayne, but let's look at your own company. You appear to be taking much more personal responsibility recently for the day-to-day affairs of Wayne Enterprises. What's changed?"

"My father built this company from the ground up. When I discovered that some of my directors didn't quite share the same vision as he had, it was necessary to make a few changes to the organizational chart." He casually drained his martini glass, got up, and poured himself a second drink from a silver shaker.

"That's a quite a lot of housecleaning. Those men were entrusted to run Wayne Enterprises for years while you were out sowing your wild oats."

Pacing, he gave her another mysterious smile, which raised all sorts of questions in Lois's mind. She wasn't sure she wanted to know what this dashing young man had been up to during the years he'd been gone from Gotham City.

She continued, holding up her reporter's notepad and scribbling shorthand with her metal pen. Now to get to the meat of the story. "Four of your former board members have been found dead, and the other five men have disappeared. Rather suspicious, wouldn't you say? The readers of the *Daily Planet* want to know your thoughts on this. Any comment?"

Showing great consternation, Bruce took a seat in a club chair and set his martini glass aside, no longer interested in the drink. "All right, Miss Lane, I'll give you a juicy story for your paper. As it turns out, I discovered that most of my board of directors had been bribed, blackmailed, or otherwise coerced— by Lex Luthor. Over the years, they've been conducting corporate espionage, providing LuthorCorp with unfair advantages on the technological front, slipping him details about contract bids we were about to submit.

"Once I caught them red-handed, I had to replace them with men I trusted." He regarded her intently. "And as soon as Luthor no longer had his spies at Wayne Enterprises, he began losing contracts. We won because we're a better company, Miss Lane, with better people. And we produce a better product. On a fair playing field, Wayne Enterprises not only competes, we win."

Amazed that he'd revealed so much to her, Lois was writing as fast as she could. "Haven't you just admitted a personal motive for murder? People could assume this was a revenge killing. And the five men still missing—"

"On the contrary; I had already taken care of the problem, and I am shocked and outraged by these deaths. When I transferred those men, my actions were entirely aboveboard, and I had them where I could prevent them from doing any further damage to my company. I had nothing further to gain by their deaths. I can only hope the missing ones are safe and unharmed. Maybe they've gone into hiding for their own safety?"

Bruce did not seem unduly alarmed. "I should point out that I've already turned over my evidence of their malfeasance to Captain James Gordon at the Gotham City Police Department. You are welcome to interview Captain Gordon as well. I have nothing to hide."

Lois wasn't sure she believed the glib statement. "I'll check it out. Thank you."

He looked closely at her. "You might ask yourself whether *Luthor* didn't have more to gain by keeping those men silent. Extortion is a serious crime. Falling victim to it is not. If one of those men had pointed fingers back at LuthorCorp . . ."

The butler appeared so silently that he startled Lois. He made the quietest throat-clearing sound, a polite interruption, but Bruce reacted as though a fire alarm had gone off. "Yes, Alfred, what is it?"

"A rather dramatic story on the television set, Master Bruce." The butler looked dutifully over to where a round-tubed set was built into the wood-paneled wall. He flicked a switch, turned a knob, and stepped back as the tubes began to hum and warm up. "Miss Lane will find it of interest as well."

Bruce turned to the gray screen, and Lois waited impatiently for an image to appear out of the shadows of the cathode ray tubes. Of course, Bruce Wayne had one of the new color televisions—rich boys and their extravagances. She had seen a color TV only once before; considering how expensive they were, she doubted the gadget would ever catch on.

Finally the image sharpened, and she saw a gruff Russian spokesman wearing a fur-lined uniform. The picture was grainy and color shifted as though the red, green, and blue hues were not adjusted properly. The man spoke in Russian, raising a fist. His face was red with anger.

The disembodied voice of a translator came over the track. ". . . for all the world to see the illegal activities of the United States of America. We have captured a blatant American spy. We have footage of this man as he flew over restricted Soviet airspace, as he made a threatening approach to Leningrad and then attempted to attack our defensive bases."

Lois gasped when the camera shifted to show a battered dark-haired man being dragged forward. In spite of the TV set's poorly adjusted color, there was no mistaking the blue uniform, the red cape, or the bold yellow S emblazoned on his chest.

"Now all the countries of the world can see the illegal aggression of the United States. This prisoner will be dealt with by Soviet justice. We have captured your Superman—and, frankly, we are not impressed."

Superman could barely stand, shackled by wrist and ankle

manacles. More lengths of thick chains were draped over his shoulders. The Man of Steel looked on the verge of collapse. His face was grayish, weary, completely defeated.

Lois was stunned and sickened to see him like that, and her heart began pounding. Her mind raced, and she was desperate to think of some way to help. Her knuckles were white as she clutched her notepad. It took her a moment to realize that Bruce Wayne was staring just as intently, just as full of disbelief.

A news commentator broke in, Edward R. Murrow himself. "The White House has issued an immediate statement. President Eisenhower denies that Superman was on any official mission for the U.S. government. Whether diplomatic efforts will free this greatest American hero, or whether he will be left in Communist clutches, remains to be seen. Stay tuned to this channel for breaking news."

A test pattern briefly came onto the screen; then the original footage of a chained Superman being dragged before the cameras was repeated. Lois turned away, tears stinging her eyes.

Bruce said crisply, "That will do, Alfred. Turn it off."

Looking extremely agitated, he couldn't seem to get Lois out of Wayne Manor quickly enough. She was only too happy to oblige. "Thanks for the interview, Mr. Wayne. I . . . I have to be going, anyway." She rushed out faster than Alfred could show her the door.

CHAPTER 42
LUTHOR'S ISLAND

AFTER THE HAPLESS OAF BUCHHEIM HAD REVEALED WHY the death ray failed to fire, Luthor immediately returned to the Caribbean island base. His technicians had studied the malfunctioning systems, but since those men did not possess his genius, they couldn't see or fix such an esoteric problem. Minions could be counted on only to a certain extent, after all. Luthor would repair the damage personally and get the beams working again.

Redesigning the Wayne Enterprises components took only an hour, and he easily completed the work during the flight in his private jet from Metropolis to the island. He gave the hand-drawn blueprints to the technicians, and they modified the devices as instructed, then tested them to verify that each component performed to its proper specifications.

Now it was time for another test firing, and this one would nourish the seeds of paranoia he had planted in Senator McCarthy's mind. Even General Ceridov wouldn't know what was happening.

After giving instructions to his control-room operators, Luthor stood outside in the tropical sunshine next to the gridwork towers, his back to the hodgepodge of modern buildings and ancient fort structures. The swiveling dish generators and antenna beam projectors pointed toward the sky at a new, and unseen, target in space.

As the moment approached, he felt the thrumming energy, sensed the crackle of static in the air. He imagined the power levels rising inside the island's reactor, ramping up to peak energy output. Hurled toward the sky, that destructive power would carve a tunnel through the atmosphere all the way to orbit, toward one tiny blip no larger than a basketball with long antennae.

He hit the transmit button on his Handie-Talkie and said, "Commence firing." He shaded his brow and watched, squinting his eyes in the bright sun.

When the projectors discharged, the gout of energy sounded like a bull elephant stampeding into the air. Serenely passing overhead, Sputnik continued alone in orbit—until Luthor's beam vaporized the satellite in an instant. Its monotonous bleeping fell silent.

Neither Soviets nor Americans could have seen exactly what happened, but they would soon note that the signal had abruptly vanished. Now that the suggestion had been planted in his mind, McCarthy would do the rest of the work for him. *Sputnik must have been destroyed by aliens!*

Satisfied that his energy weapons did function as expected, Luthor was ready to ratchet the world's fears to a fever pitch. The Cold War was no longer the only threat that mankind faced. Yes, this was a very good day.

INSIDE THE CONTROL CENTER, HIS TECHNICIANS CHEERED with wild abandon—a refreshing change from their previous test, after which they'd all believed civilization itself was going to end.

The red telephone on his desk rang like an alarm bell. Only Ceridov could reach him here, and Luthor was surprised the KGB general would respond so quickly. How could he already know Sputnik had been destroyed? How had he put the pieces together and known to call here? But Luthor couldn't imagine any other reason why the Soviet officer would contact him now. Nevertheless, still pleased with himself, he picked up the receiver with a smile.

Instead of bellowing in anger, though, Ceridov sounded immensely smug—an unexpected turn. "Ah, comrade Luthor! You are a difficult man to track down."

"Intentionally so."

"But you will be glad I found you. I have obtained a fine specimen that will interest you. I can solve our mutual problem. He has been, how do you call it, quite a 'pain in the shoulder' for us both."

"What are you talking about?" Luthor was in no mood for riddles during what should have been his moment of triumph.

"Are you unable to receive television broadcasts on your island? Can you not listen to the radio news?"

Luthor snapped his fingers for one of the techs to turn on a large wall screen, adjusting the channel to pick up a television broadcast originating from Miami. Within moments, he was viewing the footage of Superman beaten and in chains.

Astounded, Luthor stared at the laughably impotent super hero. Ceridov had captured Superman! To analyze, even dissect the self-proclaimed alien—here was a chance Luthor could not afford to pass up. "What have you found out so far? Does he wear a jetpack beneath his cape? Is his suit made of some impenetrable material?"

"He carries no obvious technological enhancements in his uniform or on his person. Your 'hero' is as weak as a kitten." The general snorted. "I used to drown useless kittens when I was a boy."

"Well, don't drown this one until I've had a chance to put my medical researchers on the problem." Luthor couldn't control the eagerness in his voice.

"Our Soviet eugenics program can learn much from studying him, too. However, because you are my comrade and partner, we can perhaps share this information—for a price."

"Money is no object if you give me access to Superman."

"Oh, not money, comrade. Now that I have seen your island, I want a small nuclear reactor like your own."

Luthor frowned. "You have your own reactor in Ariguska."

"Soviet scientists claim this modified model is the best we can produce. Yours is better. With efficient atomic power, I can run my entire gulag without constant delays and equipment failures. After you send your men to build me new reactor, I will let you interrogate and torment Superman."

Luthor didn't have to think about his answer. "I agree to the terms." When he hung up the red phone, he couldn't stop smiling. Yes indeed, this was a very good day.

CHAPTER 43
THE CAVE

EVEN WITH THE ADDITIONAL LIGHTS AND CATHODE-RAY tubes, shadows always lingered in the Cave. Bruce hunched over the monitor screens, watching several news reports at the same time. All of them replayed the same footage of Superman, barely able to stand, weighted down by chains, his Communist captors pushing him along like a whipped dog.

He muttered to himself, "He's really gotten himself into a mess, hasn't he?"

Alfred had unrolled charts on the large map table so that Bruce could try to pinpoint the source of the damning Soviet news broadcast. "I am familiar with that preoccupied look on your face, Master Bruce. Superman needs your help."

Bruce glanced at another screen. President Eisenhower had called an immediate news conference, demanding that the USSR release their captive American citizen . . . but no one could actually prove Superman *was* an American citizen, since he claimed to be an alien from a planet called Krypton.

"I haven't decided whether or not to rescue him." His voice was distant.

The butler was surprised. "What are your concerns about him, sir?"

Bruce looked up. "I'm not sure I know where his loyalties lie. At first I thought Superman worked for LuthorCorp, but I can't convince myself of that. Even the circumstantial evidence I've seen is contradictory. I don't know why he was in the Area Fifty-one hangar. He may just be an amateur doing these heroics for his own reasons, saving people because it makes him feel good."

Alfred made a noncommittal sound. "Hmm, an amateur vigilante—that reminds me of someone else I know."

"I know why *I* do it, Alfred. I made a promise on the grave of my parents that I would rid this city of the evil that took their lives. It's personal for me."

"Then perhaps you should ask him the next time you see him, sir—if there is a next time." The butler turned his attention back to a monitor screen.

Bruce had chosen to fight crime on a personal level, secretly and in the dark, not grandstanding as Superman did. He had vowed to save people by squashing the petty criminals who caused real harm, like termites chewing away at the foundation of a stable society.

When he learned they were in danger, he had even quietly protected the remaining members of his board of directors, those men who had been threatened and blackmailed into cooperating with Luthor. He had suspected—correctly—that Luthor would try to eliminate them after they no longer proved to be useful. But Bruce did not want to have any part—however tangential—in their deaths. The five surviving members who had "vanished" were, in fact, hiding under assumed identities, all arranged by Bruce himself. He had saved them from Luthor's assassins, whether or not they deserved that mercy. And he would find some way to make Luthor pay for the others.

His own parents had been killed by a small-time thief, one weak and desperate man who, for whatever reason, felt entitled to take someone else's money rather than earn his own. That thief, that gunman, that *murderer* had left a six-year-old orphan there in the alley.

Superman, though, rescued sinking passenger ships, prevented aircraft from crashing, saved dozens of people at a time from burning buildings . . . even prevented an all-out nuclear war. Those Soviet missiles would have killed millions of parents, not just two in an alley behind a theater in Park Row. Perhaps, Bruce thought, he should look through both ends of the telescope to see the micro- and the macrocosm.

Superman had shown his potential, his dedication. He could certainly be an ally in the war against crime. But how did he *do* the things he did? One way to find out.

Bruce squared his shoulders. "Obviously I have to rescue him, Alfred. Is the plane ready?"

Unruffled, the butler walked to an expanded grotto and, with a melodramatic flourish, yanked off the tarp that covered a sleek, angular object crouched in its parking circle like a black-armored pterodactyl. "All fueled up and ready to go. Fluids topped off, engines calibrated." The butler smiled. "I managed to take care of that before bringing you your dinner last night."

"That was a good dinner, Alfred. Please give my compliments to the kitchen staff."

The batlike plane was an exceptional thing, breathtaking in its modern configuration, unlike any other aircraft that had ever flown. The texture of its hull would confuse standard radar tracers, making the fast-flying plane seem to be a cloud, a flock of birds, or some other atmospheric disturbance. This design was so cutting-edge that nobody at Wayne Enterprises guessed it had ever gone beyond the concept stage. This aircraft was far more advanced than even the new-design jets now rolling off the Wayne Enterprises production lines.

Alfred raised the tinted glass canopy. "Very spacious, Master Bruce. You will be able to accommodate a certain passenger."

"He should be able to fly himself—he's done it enough times."

"Judging by the images on the television, sir, he doesn't seem capable of walking across the street."

"Good point, Alfred. Is the cycle loaded aboard?"

"I wouldn't let you leave home without it, sir. I had hoped you would take the Batplane out on at least one test flight before putting it into service."

"'Batplane'?"

The butler simply raised his eyebrows.

Bruce climbed into the cockpit. "This *is* the test flight."

Alfred walked around the dark aircraft, performing a preflight inspection. "I presume you'll also be requiring your suit? It's freshly cleaned, pressed, and on board."

Bruce could never tell when the acerbic butler was truly joking. He flicked on the control switches, warming up the systems.

"One last thing, Master Bruce. Now that Superman is in chains and on the other side of the world, do you intend to become the country's new hero?"

Bruce frowned. "No, Alfred. If I wanted the spotlight, I'd wear a bright blue and red outfit. That's not my style."

CHAPTER 44
ARIGUSKA GULAG

WEAK. KAL-EL HAD NEVER FELT SO WEAK, SO CLOSE TO death, or so confused about what was happening to him. Gravity itself seemed to drag him down. Every breath required a laborious effort. He thought he might be dying.

Chained to the steep rock wall near the bottom of the Siberian quarry, he hung like a rag doll in the late afternoon shadows. The smashed-open lead dome no longer hid the central meteorite mass, and the green light emanating from the mineral debris at the crater's base offered no warmth whatsoever. It felt like acid on his skin. The sunlight was only a watery yellow glow through unyielding high gray clouds. He was so cold. Constant shivers racked his body.

General Ceridov stood before Kal-El, black obsidian stars prominent on his epaulets, his knuckles braced on his hips. His grin displayed square teeth stained by the expensive American cigarettes he bought on the black market. "American news media has made a hero out of you, but I see another propagandist lie. I am so disappointed—you are no *Superman*!" He slapped Kal-El with a vicious blow that knocked his head to the side. A trickle of blood ran from his lip.

Blood! He had never bled before.

Around him in the quarry, the pathetic gulag prisoners slaved away with pickaxes, shovels, and metal carts, chipping fragments of the green mineral from the main mass. The unprotected gulag workers filled metal carts that were emptied into a storehouse of meteor fragments. For what purpose? Kal-El pitied them, even in the face of his own disaster.

The eerie emerald radiation continued to debilitate him. General Ceridov seemed to have figured out that Kal-El could not recover so long as he remained here in the quarry. He strained against the chains but could barely pull them taut, let alone rip the bolts from the stone wall.

The KGB general punched Kal-El in the stomach with the force of a cannonball. "Great American icon! My weakest slave here could beat you to a pulp."

Ceridov strode along the gravel path to where two gaunt workers huddled in tattered Soviet military uniforms. Still playing the bully, he grabbed them both by their collars, one in each hand, and yanked them to their feet. "Do you see these men, Superman? These are great military leaders of Soviet Union: generals Endovik and Dubrov. *They* are the ones who launched missiles at your country, and now they pay the price for it."

The two beaten men glowered at Ceridov, but having been directly exposed to the intense meteorite radiation for many weeks, they both looked withered, their skin bruised, their bones beginning to warp and twist. As he tormented them, a flash of green light shone in their eyes, which drew a puzzled frown from Ceridov. The fallen generals looked as sick as Kal-El felt, yet he saw something else at work here, an alteration of their body's chemistry even worse than what was happening to him.

Though he knew what Endovik and Dubrov had done, Kal-El would have broken his chains and protected the two pathetic men. This was truly inhuman treatment. At the moment, though, he could hardly lift his head. He couldn't even save himself.

As guards came forward to whip the two scapegoats, one of the defeated generals, Endovik, collapsed to the rocky ground, writhing. Veins stood out in his arms and neck—veins that pulsed a decidedly greenish hue. His companion, Dubrov, whose face also twisted and contorted with the pain of transformation, began to snarl, flexing his fingers.

Ceridov shouted in alarm, obviously trying to cover his fear with a veneer of anger. "Guards! Drag them to the holding bunker. Lock them up with the rest of the monsters."

Swiping a hand over his oiled reddish hair, Ceridov turned back to Kal-El, struggling to regain his composure. "I expected those men to last longer before succumbing to the contamination, but the concentration is very powerful here. Perhaps it will happen to you, too."

As the struggling, writhing prisoners were hauled off, Kal-El watched them, unable to comprehend what was happening.

"Once transformation begins, they survive for only a few days," Ceridov assured him. "After we isolate the factors that make them into such brutes, we can adapt that knowledge to our own eugenics program. Soon we will have Soviet Superman."

Ceridov hefted a chunk of the glowing green mineral and waved it in front of Kal-El's face. The green light burned him, and the rough surface of the quarry wall at his back seemed to bite through his cape, his uniform, into his skin.

"I do not know why meteorite takes away your powers." The

general frowned at the mineral specimen in his palm. "Your countryman Lex Luthor has medical research laboratories and scientists eager to dissect you—but only when I am finished." Holding the emerald rock, he swung his fist, smashing Kal-El on the chin with it. "And I am nowhere close to finished."

LOIS HAD A PERSONAL STAKE IN PROTECTING SUPERMAN. After all, he had saved *her,* and she owed him. No, there was more to it than that, she realized, more than simply canceling debts and evening the score. As much as she had been fighting the idea, Lois realized she loved Superman. Though they had met only a few times in person, it was enough for her to know how she felt. *Really* felt.

And now . . . if only she could figure out how to help him.

While the world listened to the provocative accusations made by the Soviet premier, Lois concentrated on the idea that Lex Luthor had always carried a personal grudge against Superman, and she had uncovered hints of the man's secret trips to the USSR. To her, there were many nagging, unexplained questions about the launch of the Soviet missiles, not to mention Luthor's covert Caribbean island base.

No doubt in her mind. She was convinced that Luthor had something to do with the crisis.

Since she couldn't go to Siberia, she decided to approach the problem in a roundabout way that no other reporter was investigating: the LuthorCorp angle again. Maybe she could pull a few surprises out of her hat. Maybe she could help Superman after all.

She was willing to bet her career on it. She couldn't think of anything more important. And there was no time to waste.

Nevertheless, Perry didn't want to hear her theory. "Everyone's chasing that story, Lois—which is exactly why I'm giving you a different assignment."

"Chief, Superman *is* my story! I did the first interview. I should be—"

"While the whole world was in a panic about Superman, *something* blasted Sputnik out of orbit. No earthbound technology could have accomplished that: The Soviets wouldn't know how to do it, and the U.S. doesn't have a weapon with that range. Normally the Russians would have blamed Superman . . . but thanks to them, he's got a perfect alibi. I want you to find out what did it."

"Why not send Clark? When will he be back from visiting his mother?"

"Kent hasn't checked in for days, which is yet another worry. I need someone on this story *now*, Lois." He cut her off before she could suggest another reporter. "Since the attack on the satellite, Senator McCarthy is raving about the alien menace more than ever. Now, I'm no fan of McCarthy." Perry looked as though he wanted to spit. "However, if we're being watched by aliens— Martians or Venusians or whatever creatures come out of those pulps Olsen reads—what would be a better target than our first orbiting satellite? We can't bury this story, Lois."

Lois automatically assumed Luthor was involved with the destruction of Sputnik, too. There was little he *wouldn't* do to achieve his aims, but even he couldn't blast a satellite out of orbit . . . could he? She feigned interest in the hopes that she could use this assignment to get to Superman in some way. "So that's my angle, Chief?"

"The *Daily Planet* is sending you down to Redstone Arsenal in Huntsville, Alabama. I've arranged for you to have direct access to our rocket boys. I want an interview and a feature on von Braun himself. Get them to show you around. Wear a short skirt if you have to, show a little leg."

Scowling, Lois leaned across Perry's desk and thrust a finger in his face. "I don't need pointers from you on how to get a story. *Any* pointers."

Perry toyed with the chewed end of his cigar, twirling it in his fingertips. "No, you don't, but I do need to keep you on track about *which* story you're covering. Have von Braun speculate on what could possibly have blown up Sputnik. Cover America's efforts to build a Redstone version of those R-7 missiles the Commies launched against us. We're Americans, and we have American know-how. We built the atomic bomb—we can do anything. When are we going to have the capability to launch a comparable strike against the USSR? Get down to Metropolis airport and board the next flight to Huntsville, or wherever the closest airport is. I'm sure you can talk somebody into putting you on a plane."

Lois was about to rebel against Perry's unexpected fervor, but another plan was already forming in her mind. "Fine. I'm on it, Chief."

Interviewing Wernher von Braun sounded like an interesting assignment; however, there were so many other important things to deal with. Superman captured and held prisoner by the Communists, the loss of Sputnik, Senator McCarthy's railing about an alien threat. . . . And Lex Luthor had a secret island base. How could he *not* be at the bottom of it all?

At last she had the opportunity to sneak off to the Caribbean, make a little side trip from Huntsville to Havana. Like the good reporter she was, Lois Lane would find her story—and rescue the man she loved.

CHAPTER 46
SIBERIA

THE BATPLANE SCYTHED THROUGH THE NIGHT SKY, theoretically undetectable by Soviet radar. The glowing red lights of multiple gauges illuminated the cockpit, his dark suit, and his reinforced cowl.

Heading north at top speed but mindful of the fuel reserves, he crossed over Canada and Greenland, and took a short polar arc before dropping down into Siberia. He was confident of his destination.

The only time he had glimpsed weakness in Superman was on the shore across the lake from Luthor's mansion, when the Man of Steel had been exposed to the glowing green mineral. Luthor had obviously been running tests on the sample, intrigued by its properties and potential. The meteorite display had been labeled "Ariguska."

In the USSR.

In Siberia.

That had to be where the Soviets were holding Superman.

He threw the plane into a steep dive, streaking barely above the tops of the dense Siberian forest. It was vastly different from his little Wayne Enterprises private jet. He was sure he hadn't been detected, and he doubted anyone in the Ariguska gulag would be watching for a solo raider to free their captive. Due to the complicated politics, even the U.S. Special Forces would never have received such swift orders to mount a rescue mission.

He, on the other hand, was just one person with one goal. And a great arsenal of weapons and technology. He could make his own decisions and do what large governments couldn't, in much the same way as he tackled criminals the Gotham City Police Department couldn't catch by conventional means.

When the Batplane's navigation systems informed him that he was within a few miles of his destination, he began to search for a place to land. He found a clear ridgetop and circled to survey the area with the craft's nose-cone spotlights.

With takeoff-and-landing technology that was similar—but generations superior—to what was used on an aircraft carrier, without the capture tether, the sleek plane needed very little cleared area on which to set down. As he approached Ariguska, the forested lands gave way to desolation. Whole swaths of primeval forest had been flattened by the impact decades ago, and the regrowth was comprised of stunted and unnatural foliage. Interesting.

He returned to the ridgetop for his final approach, deployed the engine scoops, and blasted with reverse jets and undercarriage thrusters. The Batplane slewed on the loose rocks, tore up fallen and bent tree trunks, and finally skidded to a stop. A perfect landing, except for a few scratches and scrapes on the fuselage. Flipping toggles on the control panel, he raised the canopy and extended a ramp from the undercarriage to deploy his motorcycle, which was all fueled up and ready to go.

He climbed onto the cycle, started the engine, and put it into silent stealth mode. Forgoing headlights, he powered up the night scope and raced off down the ridge, dodging downed trees and rough terrain. His dark cape flapped behind him in the wind.

As Batman, he used his cape for protection, disguise, and operatic intimidation. Superman, on the other hand, wore his bright red cape for . . . what? Just to show off? Color coordination?

The cycle's thick tires grabbed the barren ground, making maneuvering easy and acceleration smooth as he dodged dirty patches of snow. He saw only shadows as he raced along, keeping his head down and protected by the windscreen. He didn't have far to go.

The forest encircling the camp and the crater was more than just stunted; it was mutated, horrific. The trees were appallingly twisted and distorted, their monstrous branches knotted and gnarled like some alien plant creature from a sci-fi pulp magazine cover. The pines themselves seemed to be screaming in agony, branches extended like clawing fingers, roots anchored in soil filled with poisonous residue that had seeped into the ground.

But he wasn't afraid of trees. The Soviet guards would give him enough trouble. Olive-uniformed men walked brisk patrols around the camp perimeter in the cold night. Their heads were covered with fur *ushanka*s, and they rested Kalashnikovs on the shoulders of their thick jackets.

As he approached, slinking forward in the darkness, he pulled out two of the small drug-tipped Bat-shuriken. His aim had to be perfect, since he saw only a small area of exposed skin that could be nicked by the sharp points. The tiny finger-sized throwing bat sliced through the air and struck the first guard at the base of his jaw. He cursed, slapping at his neck, no doubt complaining about Siberian blackflies that could attack even in the cold of night. The other guard chuckled—as a second shuriken whizzed past his face. The first guard crumpled from the paralytic-anesthetic, and his comrade ran toward him, shouting. Two more throwing bats scythed the air, and one struck home. Shortly, the second guard sprawled unconscious on the cold ground as well.

He dragged the two limp forms away from the searchlight beams and relieved the unconscious men of their rifles and holstered pistols, tossing the guns far into the twisted forest. He trussed and gagged the men, then moved on.

The large work camp had ranks of barracks, a headquarters building, and a concrete containment dome over a nuclear power reactor, from which white coolant steam rose. Harsh lights shone down, giving him few shadows for cover.

He took a mental inventory of his useful devices, which would have made even James Bond proud. Moving cautiously, he slipped around the site, peering into buildings to search for Superman. He saw brutishly secure, thick-walled blockhouses with no windows and heavily armored doors. Angry growls and pounding sounds came from inside, and he noticed that even the armed guards avoided those buildings. In the prisoners' quarters he found only stacked bunks that harbored gaunt workers asleep from exhaustion. The soldiers' barracks were marginally more humane.

He didn't see Superman anywhere.

The quarry itself was well lit with bright floodlights. Down in the pit he spotted a small work crew toiling around the perimeter of a half-dismantled dome, barely able to lift their heavy picks and shovels. Only a few guards watched over them. At first, it was hard to understand why the Soviets would man a round-the-clock excavation effort, but then it became clear that these particular prisoners were being punished, forced to give up sleep, probably forced to work until they dropped dead.

Scattered at the bottom of the crater lay chunks of the glowing green rock—the same substance that had weakened Superman.

The dome must have been put in place to block the green radiation, but now it was smashed.

Then he spotted the telltale blue and red costume, Superman chained to the quarry wall like Prometheus, exposed to the emerald glow. The conclusion was obvious: If the glowing mineral deprived Superman of his powers, then holding him down in the quarry was a perfect way to keep him incapacitated . . . maybe even kill him.

Fortunately, Batman did not have the same vulnerabilities.

Staying low, he raced along the shadowed paths, descending into the steep-walled pit. He switchbacked his way down the quarry ledges, but there was altogether too much light for his comfort.

He slid down a steep gravel chute, making more noise than he intended, and emerged with his suit covered with dust. He abruptly ducked his cowled head as a bright spotlight glided over him, but the darkness and dirt gave him enough cover. He had to stun two more guards before he reached the bottom, where Superman was chained.

Along the way, he primed and dropped a handful of tiny flash mines, small concussive devices that he could activate to confuse pursuit. Though he hoped for the best, he didn't expect to just stroll out of here.

Finally, he reached Superman, who looked weary unto death. "Wake up. Time to get out of here."

Superman lifted his head heavily. The blue eyes soon focused, and instant realization sprang into them. "What are you doing here?" he said in a small, weak voice.

"What's the matter—not used to having someone rescue *you*?" He unsnapped one of the containers in his utility belt. "I've decided to take a chance that you really are playing for the right team."

He didn't have time to break the chains or pick the locks, so he used a tiny insulated bottle, applied a line of potent fluid more devastating than hydrofluoric acid. Smoking and sizzling, the metal acid burned through the manacles—and Superman was free. He collapsed, slumping against the dark figure.

Draping one of Superman's limp, blue-clad arms over his shoulder, he propped up the other man and propelled them both along as best he could. They had to keep out of sight of the guards.

The downtrodden night crew of gulag slaves noticed them first. They let out wild cries, pointing, shouting incoherently. "They want us to rescue them as well," Superman said, still groggy.

Alerted by the shouting prisoners, the guards sounded the alarm. Seeing the two costumed figures, they opened fire. The commotion drew the attention of the sentries in the towers, and bright searchlights immediately swung down, freezing the two men in a blinding glare.

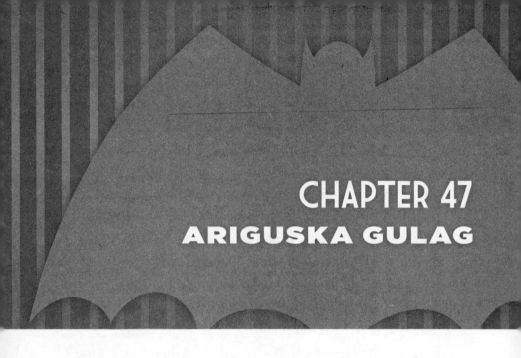

CHAPTER 47
ARIGUSKA GULAG

THOUGH FREED FROM THE CHAINS AND SHACKLES, KAL-EL still felt a crushing weight dragging him down. He could barely stand, let alone fly. And now the Soviet guards were shooting at them.

As he staggered along, his cape dragging behind him like a wet rag, Kal-El had to lean on Batman just to keep himself upright and moving. His vision, which should have been able to project heat beams or penetrating X-rays, now left him with only a blur.

Guards rushed out of the barracks, hastily grabbing their Kalashnikovs. Deafening sirens pounded his skull. Batman ducked from a renewed spray of gunfire and pulled Kal-El into the meager shelter of some large rocks that had slid down the quarry bank. Bullets stitched the ground around them, pockmarking the wide gravel path. Several ricocheted loudly from the boulders.

"I hope . . . you've got a better plan than this," Kal-El managed to croak.

"I'll improvise." Batman grabbed at his utility belt and hurled a handful of small spheres that exploded on impact, releasing clouds of noxious purple smoke. The Soviet soldiers opened fire, and bullets punched through the curling wisps of gas.

"Get away from . . . green rock," Kal-El said. "If my strength returns, I can help."

"I wasn't counting on your powers. I've got it under control."

From the quarry's edge, another group of riflemen shot down at them. Kal-El tried to shelter his unexpected rescuer with his own body, but now that he was without his powers, he didn't know if he was bulletproof. Nevertheless, his uniform was made of fabric from Krypton; perhaps that would be good enough. He felt—yes, felt!—three shots hit him in the back. It was as though he'd been punched hard, but the bullets didn't penetrate the suit or his skin.

Bullets also struck Batman, and though he staggered from the impacts, his suit seemed nearly as impervious as Kal-El's. "We need to get out of this camp," Batman said.

The guards assigned to the work crew in the crater turned to help their fellow soldiers above. The hollow-eyed prisoners, already poisoned from exposure to meteorite radiation, knew they had no chance of survival. Condemned to work themselves to death, with nothing to lose, and seeing Superman and Batman as their only chance, they attacked the surprised guards with pickaxes and shovels. One guard went down as a shovel blade split his head open, his *ushanka* tumbling onto the cold, muddy ground. His rifle discharged, and the bullet spanged off a boulder.

A pickax struck a uniformed man in the chest, and the maddened workers managed to murder a third guard before a hail of bullets cut them down.

It was all over in a few seconds, before Batman could make a move to save them. Kal-El's heart ached as he said, "They were dead . . . when they got here."

Batman pulled him along toward the top of the quarry. "And it's my job to make sure you're not. I have a way out."

When they encountered more guards at the edge of the pit, Batman detonated his flash mines, and bursts of blinding light sent the Soviets reeling. Extending one gauntlet, Batman activated a nozzle, and a thin, high-pressure stream of instant-set epoxy squirted out, splattering the guards and their guns, tangling them in a sticky, rubbery mass, like a silkworm's cocoon.

During this brief reprieve, he dragged Kal-El past the struggling guards tangled in the epoxy web. "Now all we have to do is get past the rest of the camp's defenses, and we're home free."

THE ALARMS BROUGHT GENERAL CERIDOV OUT FROM HIS warm quarters. As he ran outside, still pulling on his fur coat and shielding his eyes against the glare of spotlights, he saw not only the red and blue figure of Superman but another man in a more sinister outfit helping to rescue him. The dark-cowled man looked like a devil—no, a bat. He kept pulling strange things from his belt, throwing-darts, incapacitating gas bombs, small explosives.

Two *super heroes? Where do the Americans get them?* he wondered.

He heard gunfire, saw the searchlights, but somehow the two ridiculously costumed men evaded capture, always one step ahead of the gulag guards. Superman was still barely able to stand, but since his weakness was brought on by the green meteorite, Ceridov supposed the effects would likely diminish as the two got farther away from the quarry. He figured he had only a limited time to stop them from getting away.

The Soviet Union had its own supermen . . . less refined, perhaps, but almost certainly more powerful. As the two escaping figures raced toward the stunted forest, the general smashed open the locks of the thick-walled blockhouse. Inside, the restless monsters continued to rumble and pound. As soon as the locks fell away, the heavy doors exploded outward, and Ceridov sprang back, calling his own guards to stand close, rifles aimed and ready.

Endovik and Dubrov—or rather, what they had become— were the first to emerge. Their bodies were swollen, muscles not so much bulging as bloated, visible beneath their torn garments. Cords of sinew twisted at their necks. Tufts of spiky hair as sharp as porcupine quills protruded from random spots on their bodies. Their lips were curled back in a rictus of constant agony, and their eyes glowed an emerald green.

Only five of the mutated creatures remained alive. Three more had been torn to bloody pulp within the bunker, but nobody had dared to go in and clean up the cells. The maddened mutants had fed upon the flesh of their dead comrades, and the stench was appalling. The five creatures lunged out into the open, coiled with pent-up energy as though their blood had become boiling nitroglycerin. The five glared at Ceridov, but he saw a dim remnant of intelligence and awareness on their faces.

He raised his voice. "I know your minds are still there—I know you can understand me!" He could not let them doubt the bald-faced lie he was about to tell them. "I have the cure you need. I have the antidote to the meteorite radiation—but first you must earn it!"

The furious creatures flexed their arms, simmering, staring. Ceridov could not give them time to think. He pointed toward the two costumed figures disappearing into the forest. "Them—capture them! Bring them back here, and then you shall be free!"

With uncontrollable bloodlust, the mutated creatures raced into the night.

CHAPTER 48
LUTHOR'S ISLAND

WERNHER VON BRAUN WOULD HAVE PROVIDED AN INTER-esting interview, and under other circumstances, Lois might have been eager to press the former Nazi scientist about the American rocketry program and the mysterious destruction of Sputnik. But she had to do *something* to save Superman, whether or not Perry White approved. That was her top priority.

She would not stand by and let her beloved hero hang in chains, crippled and paralyzed, while diplomats and ambassadors squabbled. She knew what a great man he was, with such a large heart and all the devotion any woman could ask for. She could not just leave him to rot in a Communist prison camp.

Over the past several months, she'd built up quite a case against Lex Luthor, but she'd been unable to grab the brass ring of "proof" that Perry White demanded. She knew Luthor hated Superman because the hero had upstaged him at every turn, and Luthor was enough of a genius that he *could* have set this up. It reeked of him, all of it.

Lois was a good enough reporter that she intended to catch Luthor in the act.

Rather than going to Huntsville to talk with the rocket scientists, she took a connecting flight to Miami, then another to Havana. Cuba was filled with enough unrest to inspire a dozen newspaper stories—Batista battling Castro's rebels in the jungles, and all those pasty-white Russian visitors who clearly weren't there to soak up the Caribbean sun—but Lois was fixated on a tiny island that appeared on no map. She was going to catch Luthor and get him to tell her where Superman was being held. Then she would help rescue Superman, even if it killed her, though she hoped it wouldn't come to that.

She went down to the docks in Havana Bay and talked to the fishermen using broken Spanish and a pocket dictionary. She looked for a volunteer to take her to a place she had sketched in her notebook, a close approximation of what she remembered seeing in Luthor's headquarters and the somewhat blurry photo she had taken of the map.

The grizzled men spoke in a mixture of Spanish and English. Some thought they recognized her sketch as Crab Key, but others denied it. Three of the men clearly knew the place she was talking about, but they were frightened. They shook their heads. "The dragon lives there," one man insisted in broken English. "We have seen smoke from his lair and fire shooting into the sky."

Lois smiled. "Yes, that sounds exactly like the place."

She had to bribe and flirt and beg, but she finally found a cocky young Cuban man who agreed to take her out there. He remained shirtless, possibly for Lois's benefit, but she was focused only on finding Luthor's hideout so that she could help Superman.

They left the dock at sunset with beautiful romantic splashes of color across the western horizon. Lois remained at the bow, listening to the hum of the engine and the slosh of the waves as the young man steered his boat out to sea in the deepening darkness. It was the only way they could arrive unseen.

She wore deck shoes, khaki trousers, and a short-sleeved blouse. She had her own camera, a model much smaller than Jimmy Olsen's, but it would be enough to get pictures, to get proof.

Since it would take hours to reach the small island, she forced herself to catch a nap on the way. When her young captain finally shook her awake, Lois glanced at her watch—4:00 A.M., an hour before dawn. She had to get ashore and situated for cautious surveillance. Also, her boat captain friend needed time to get far enough away that Luthor's observers wouldn't spot him.

He had turned off the engines, and the boat made no noise as it approached. The island was a silhouette outlined by stars and the Milky Way, but it also shone with constellations of its own—industrial towers, brightly lit buildings, and factory structures built up in the hulking ruins of an old Spanish fort. She turned to the young fisherman. "Meet me here this time tomorrow for the other half of your money. *Comprende?*"

"*Sí, señorita.*" He smiled at her, but she couldn't be sure how much enthusiasm he really had about coming back. Though he'd been blustering and confident when setting out from Havana, he seemed much more anxious now as they drew closer.

She stepped off the boat and waded the rest of the way to the beach as quietly as she could. When a jet of flame belched up from one of the industrial centers—perhaps exhaust gas burning off or a rocket test firing—the young man turned the boat around and, keeping the engine at low power, crept out to deeper water beyond the cove, then sped away. The foaming, glistening wake settled quickly.

Lois splashed onto the sand, where she found shelter in a cluster of leaning palm trees at the edge of the beach. She kept to the cover of the trees as she approached the complex. Dawn had begun to brighten the sky.

After sunrise, when she saw the secret base that Luthor had built, Lois allowed her curiosity to get the best of her. She snapped photographs of the ruined old fort connected to the modern control building. Most curious was a set of giant towers topped with suspicious-looking dish-projectors pointed toward the sky, rocket launchpads, industrial hangars, a sprawling construction yard along the coast, a shipbuilding dry dock. Though many of the high-tech installations baffled her, she took photographs anyway.

She could not determine just what the bald genius was up to. Did Luthor think he was in a spy novel or something?

Suddenly Lois heard a hissing hum and a strange throbbing noise, and several large shadows fell upon her. Three flying men loomed overhead: guards wearing thick green armored suits, like the shells of iridescent beetles. A large crest or collar protected their heads, and they had absurdly thick gauntlets and boots made of an unknown purple metal; jetpacks kept the men suspended in the air.

She recognized the square head and blond crew cut of Lex Luthor's ever-present bodyguard Bertram. Lenses telescoped out of the smooth purple gauntlets, and thin heat beams strafed the ground at her feet, turning the sand into a line of smoking glass.

Bertram's voice boomed from a speaker set in the armored breastplate. "Surrender, or we'll tear you to pieces." He moved forward, intimidating. "You don't belong here."

"A little full of yourself, aren't you?" Lois said flippantly. "I was just looking for a nice beach for sunbathing."

Maneuvering with the backpack jets, spreading the thick purple boots in an imposing stance, Bertram landed in front of her. His two cohorts dropped on either side of her, hemming her in. She was tempted to take a photograph but decided it would just provoke them.

She swallowed hard but tried to remain aloof. Lois was very annoyed to have been caught so quickly, and she didn't want to show any weakness in front of these goons. "I'd like to see your boss—I've got another interview request."

Bertram clomped forward, seized her camera, crushed it into a handful of jagged fragments, and unspooled the exposed film. He placed his hands under her armpits with powered metal gloves and roughly picked her up off the ground. "Believe me, we'll take you right to Mr. Luthor."

Together, the three guards accelerated into the air with their jetpacks. As she dangled uncomfortably in Bertram's grasp, Lois suppressed a grimace of pain and decided that she much preferred to fly with Superman, cradled safely in his arms.

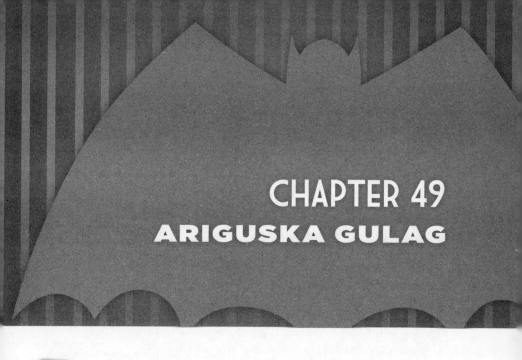

CHAPTER 49
ARIGUSKA GULAG

THE TWISTED FOREST OUTSIDE THE GULAG PROVIDED plenty of places to hide as they made their way back to the Batplane.

Dragging Superman in a fireman's carry away from the gulag's perimeter fences, Batman plunged into the sharp-edged shadows, seeking refuge among the twisted trunks and black branches. The searchlights couldn't find them here.

Darkness, shadows, and fear had always been his advantages. Now he had to call upon his skills more than ever.

Gunshots and sirens rang out behind them. He had hoped some of Superman's strength would return as they put more distance between themselves and the quarry, but the meteorite's taint also permeated the forest. Now it seemed to ooze up from the ground wherever they stepped.

Get to the cycle . . . to the plane—away from here and out of Siberia.

"How much farther?" Superman sounded a little stronger. "We aren't going to . . . walk home?"

"Leave it to me. I have it all planned."

"You . . . said that before."

"I meant it."

Taking advantage of the tumult they had left behind, the rest of the sleeping gulag prisoners seized their chance to break out of their barracks and run loose, tearing down fences. All those diversions would keep the guards busy, but the casualties would be horrific. Given all the gunfire behind them, dozens, if not hundreds, of slaves must already have been dead.

More worrisome, though, were the crashing, ferocious noises that came from the stunted forest behind them. Something else was pursuing them, something large. Something *hunting* them.

Superman raised his head and forced himself to stand on his own. "I'll try to walk."

"Right now we need to run."

They both saw movement between the skeletal branches—huge forms, each one swollen to twice the size of an average man, with pulsing veins standing out against translucent skin. These twisted beings might once have been gulag slaves . . . humans succumbing to prolonged exposure to meteorite radiation. Seeing their targets, the beasts lunged forward.

Time to fight. He wasn't sure he had enough large-scale and small-scale weapons, diversions, and tricks left in his utility belt. He would have to be resourceful. As always.

Three of the five horrific mutants wore grayish gulag outfits; the other two clung to tattered Soviet military uniforms. One of the mutant officers, like a territorial animal howling in rage, grasped the twisted trunk of the nearest withered pine, snapping it in two; the broken tree's sap bled green.

"Keep . . . running," Superman said.

Focus on the mission. Escape. No need to battle these monsters.

Batman snatched a flash grenade from his utility built and threw it toward the five beast-men. He shielded his eyes with a dark gauntlet, and a supernova-bright flash seared the night air. In the dancing afterimage, the trees looked like a Gothic woodcut of horrors. Unnatural knots and burls in the trunks looked like screaming faces. The branches thrashed and writhed in agony, as if burned by the flash.

He and Superman kept running, picking up speed. The mutants followed.

It seemed unlikely that the tools and weapons remaining in his utility belt could take care of these beasts. He had a new grappling hook, a large Batarang, and seven of the tiny Bat-shuriken, though considering the mass and bulk of the monsters, he doubted the paralytic sedative would be strong enough. There were several more items, but he would have to improvise. He might need to use everything in their effort to get away. Withdrawing elastic wires and tiny weighted bolos, he quickly devised trip cords between trees. One of the lumbering beast-men smashed into them, tangled himself, and uprooted a tree, unable to snap the high-tensile-strength cord.

Growing gradually stronger, Superman pushed himself forward, sweat running down his brow. Another chemical grenade dispersed burning pepper smoke that curled outward to sting their pursuers' eyes.

Guessing that they must be close, Batman activated a gauntlet switch—a remote operation system that could summon the cycle. Out there, the engine would be turning over, powering up, the guidance system homing in on his signal.

But the creatures were upon them now. He and Superman would have to fight them hand-to-hand.

The two former Soviet officers were the first to attack. Superman pounded his fists against the monsters, but their bodies were impregnated with the very contamination that had weakened him in the first place, rendering his blows ineffectual. With one desperate punch, he drew blood—emerald blood—the exposure to which nearly drove him to his knees.

But he wasn't the only one who could fight. Batman called upon jujitsu, tae kwon do, karate, and techniques from a dozen other schools of combat so obscure that few Westerners had ever heard of them. He struck and struck again, hand blows, full kicks, flying body slams.

These monsters, not trained in subtlety, relied on sheer brute force. A hammer-blow to his cowl sent him reeling, and he could barely see straight. Despite the armor and bulletproof fibers of his suit, he felt his ribs crack when one of their opponents landed another locomotive punch. He staggered backward.

From a packet inside his left armored glove he released a cloud of potent anesthetic mist . . . which did nothing more than surprise his attacker.

He spun about on a boot toe and went after the nearest monster with a leaping kick, driving a hard heel into its jaw and causing it to stagger back. His reinforced gauntlets added power to each punch as he struck and struck once more. He easily ducked a sluggish roundhouse punch, then pounded the beast's hairy solar plexus. His skills were the only close-range weapons he had left. His full attack was barely enough to make the monsters pause.

But a pause was all he needed.

The automated cycle roared in from among the trees, following the locator device in his armor. Calling to Superman, he dove for the cycle and threw himself on top of it. "Here! Behind me!"

The barely stunned mutant creatures loped toward them, but Batman had the controls now and could see through the night scope. After Superman collapsed onto the cycle behind him, he accelerated hard, increasing his available engine power by switching off the stealth mode. They roared away, the heightened sound of the engine louder than the mutants as they rapidly left the creatures behind.

CHAPTER 50
ARIGUSKA GULAG

AFTER RETRIEVING HIS WHIP, GENERAL CERIDOV STOOD surveying the massacre. The fences were torn down, and the prisoners had run amok. Seventeen of his incompetent guards were dead—killed not by Superman or that other costumed intruder but by the pathetic gulag slaves themselves! He would not be reporting that detail to Moscow.

In frustration, Ceridov cracked his whip in the air, but not many prisoners remained alive for him to strike. Under the harsh searchlights, the general did not like what he saw. He had a lot of cleaning up to do, and he would need to request an entirely new complement of political prisoners from Party headquarters. Much had to be accounted for.

And unless he recaptured Superman, he would never convince Lex Luthor to provide a superior power reactor to replace the faulty one that had served the Ariguska gulag for years.

When the five lumbering mutants returned empty-handed but still demanded the mythical cure he had promised, that was the last straw. Though their bodies were enlarged and their muscles had grown into lumpish tumors, their brains seemed to have atrophied. The disgraced Soviet generals glowered at him; the three former gulag slaves, now stronger than motorized construction machines, carried a confused violence about them. Apparently in some dim corner of their primitive brains, they expected that Ceridov would still take care of them.

Seeing the monsters approach, Ceridov called for his surviving guards to stand with him, holding their Kalashnikovs ready. The mutants might have been stupid and ugly, but he doubted they would try anything. "I told you to capture two people! Where are they?"

The five creatures clenched their fists and stirred, looking uneasily at the armed guards. An unmistakable glint of vicious hunger shone from behind their eerily green eyes.

Ceridov doubted they'd be articulate enough to explain what had happened, but he didn't want to hear their excuses anyway. He lashed out with his whip, specifically targeting Endovik. The whip's end sliced a deep cut that oozed green blood.

The second lash failed to touch any skin. Endovik caught the end of the whip in his massive fist and yanked so hard that he nearly dislocated Ceridov's shoulder. The monster seized the braided whip in both hands and shredded it. Dubrov lunged, and the other mutants roared as they attacked.

The gulag guards had already seen many of their comrades slain by rebellious prisoners, and they did not hesitate to open fire now, peppering the mutants with bullets. But the five creatures brushed the gunfire aside as though the bullets were no more than biting blackflies.

Leaving the guards, Ceridov ran. He blocked out the screaming and yelling behind him, as well as the sickening ripping sounds that followed.

He ran into his headquarters building and threw the wooden

door shut, slamming the bolts home. Inside the fenced and isolated gulag, he had never needed a particularly sturdy lock, but within moments the creatures began pounding on not only the door but the thick log walls themselves. The tongue-and-groove paneling with its unsettling wood-grain patterns rattled loose from the walls.

The door splintered and flew inward like a hailstorm of kindling. One of the thick walls was literally torn apart as huge hands ripped the logs away. Part of the building collapsed, crushing the potbellied stove in the corner.

Ceridov dove for the lone window on the opposite side as the mutants pushed in after him. Tarred rags had been stuffed around the sill to prevent drafts. Now the general used his broad shoulder to smash the glass. The window was barely large enough for him to squeeze through, but he did, and he fell onto the dirt and a patch of hard snow outside.

Behind him, a roaring Dubrov jammed his massive head and shoulder through the window, but his body was too large to fit. Jagged shards of glass tore his flesh as he squirmed, finally splintering the logs and smashing the window opening wider.

Ceridov was already running across the compound. The soldiers' barracks and the prisoners' quarters were even flimsier constructions than his headquarters, offering no viable shelter. The reactor control room and the containment building, on the other hand . . . he would find shelter there. Those were the sturdiest structures in the gulag.

When he heard the growling snarls behind him—and no further gunshots because all the guards were dead—Ceridov put on additional speed. His right arm was numb from when the monster had torn the whip out of his hand, and he couldn't tell if any bones were broken. At the moment, shock and adrenaline kept him from feeling pain. He flung open the steel door of the reactor building and slammed it behind him. He hoped the lock would hold.

The control room held a set of gray metal stations, each with a cathode-ray tube displaying black and white images from the adjacent reactor room. A constellation of dials, gauges, and black Bakelite knobs covered the walls. The needles showed that the reactor was operating at maximum level, but so far nothing had edged into the red.

The Soviets had once been so proud of this program. In June 1954, the "Peaceful Atom" facility in Omsk had been the world's first nuclear plant to generate electricity—another example of Soviet technological superiority. Many more of the graphite-moderated power reactors had been built across the Soviet Union. This one was much smaller, an experimental design that not only powered the gulag but provided many radioactive isotopes for Soviet nuclear research.

Now he hoped it would offer him the protection he needed.

The blows against the steel door were like artillery shells fired from a destroyer. The massively overgrown fists continued to pound, and the door started to buckle.

Ceridov began to wonder whether the control room might be a trap rather than a shelter. He had no way out other than through the large bulkhead door into the reactor chamber itself. And with the reactor running so high, the radiation levels inside would be lethal.

Bolts popped from the steel door's hinges, and a huge blunt-fingered hand pushed its way through, bending the door further.

At the control bank, he tried to shut down the reactor but quickly realized that it would take too long. The fuel rods were all in place. It was a water-cooled reactor, filled with boiling liquid that pumped out high-pressure steam. Graphite moderators surrounded the rods, and thick, hot pipes circulated the steam through turbines. Even the heavy lead shielding would not be sufficient to protect him.

With sick fatalism, Ceridov decided that the mutants would be more immediately lethal than the radiation. He ran to the hatch and activated the emergency releases. His throat was dry. He was panting too hard to think. Fortunately, the gulag's engineers had not bothered to install safety systems or protective interlocks.

The monsters smashed through the main door just as Ceridov opened the bulkhead. Shoulder to massive shoulder, Endovik and Dubrov charged into the control room, their bestial lips drawn back to expose teeth ready to rip out Ceridov's throat. Very little remained of their once proudly worn military uniforms.

Ceridov stumbled into the reactor chamber and swung the heavy bulkhead door shut behind him. Barely a second after the deep clang, he heard the creatures pounding at the thick barrier.

The air inside the reactor chamber had a sizzling humidity filled with crackling steam. Ceridov staggered backward, trying desperately to recall if there was a second exit. He knew the radiation was all around him, ripping into his cells, poisoning him. But if he could move quickly enough . . .

With a concerted effort, the mutated creatures tore the bulkhead door off its hinges and hurled it into the reactor chamber. The thick metal rectangle smashed into the nest of coolant pipes, shattering them. Geysers of steam erupted from pipe breaches, and reactor fluid levels began to drop as boiling water rushed out of the containment vessel.

Dubrov and Endovik reveled in the chaos, splashing through the water that swirled furiously around their ankles, not even feeling the heat. The mutated gulag slaves threw themselves into the destruction with primeval relish.

Automatic warning alarms began to sound, along with evacuation sirens. In the control room, all the gauges must have been well into the red, but the five mutants didn't seem to care. They knocked loose pressure control wheels, smashed lights, waded forward into the thickening radioactive steam.

"Cer-i-dovvvvv!" one of the disgraced generals yelled.

Fleeing deeper into the deadly maze, the Soviet general burned his hand on a hot metal surface. Inside the containment tubes, coolant fuel bubbled and churned until the transparent observation windows blew out, spraying contaminated water everywhere.

A lattice of pipes was uprooted and thrown aside, and Endovik stood there, his glowing green eyes rolling and crazed. Seeing his prey, he yowled, and the other mutants came running. Their skin seemed to be rotting now, burned and scabbed, beginning to fall off.

General Ceridov scrambled for a way to get back out. The monsters had torn off the vault door. If he could just retreat outside, he could run past the fences, hide in the twisted forest.

Bathed in radiation, he knew he was already dead, being cooked from the inside out. But letting these mutants tear him limb from limb seemed the worst possible way to die.

Ceridov could barely see through the steam and flashing red lights as the monsters advanced toward him. Dubrov approached from the other side.

Spitting curses and shouting, Ceridov ran toward them. Dubrov and Endovik, grinning horribly, closed in to intercept him.

CHAPTER 51
LUTHOR'S ISLAND

THE CARIBBEAN HUMIDITY MADE LUTHOR'S ISLAND HEAD-quarters a sweltering hot box, but Lois had plenty of other reasons to sweat.

When the battlesuited henchmen dragged her into the control center, Lex Luthor was staring at a wall full of screens like a businessman analyzing the stock market. Projected images showed the Kremlin, Big Ben and the Houses of Parliament in London, the Eiffel Tower in Paris, the United Nations headquarters in Metropolis. He had his eye on the whole world.

Luthor frowned at the interruption. "What have you found now, Bertram?"

Lois pulled her arm free. The armored gauntlets were powerful enough to crush granite, but they weren't particularly nimble. She shook herself and stood defiantly. "So, is this a new subsidiary of LuthorCorp? I must have missed the ribbon-cutting ceremony."

Luthor's face darkened. "You like to trespass, don't you, Miss Lane? Unfortunately, this is a bit more serious than your transgression at my munitions factory. You really must learn to respect personal boundaries."

"I don't respect *you*, if that's what you mean. The whole world has seen Superman in chains, but what they don't know is how *you* orchestrated it. He's a hero. He's saved countless lives." Sure enough, mentioning Superman was like jabbing Luthor with a cattle prod. She could see it in his reaction. A thought occurred to her, and she smiled. "You're *jealous* of him, aren't you?"

He chuckled. "Jealousy is an emotion for children, or at least for those who have no self-confidence. Why on earth would I be jealous now that Superman has gotten himself caught?"

"Are you denying your involvement?"

Luthor's smile was bland. "Of course not. I just wanted to know how you made the connection."

"I'm not going to make it easier for you to cover your tracks." She crossed her arms and fell stubbornly silent.

Luthor shook his head with irritated disgust. "Superman, Superman; he's like a movie star for young girls to swoon over— James Dean, Jeffrey Hunter, Marlon Brando. It's . . . undignified. All flash and no substance. People forget who's really helped them the most." His voice had begun to rise, but he controlled himself again by taking two deep, calming breaths. "Trust me, Miss Lane, I haven't even gotten started with Superman, but I am pleased that General Ceridov has removed this pest."

"Ceridov? How do you spell that, so I can get his name correct in my article?"

Luthor met her gaze with his cold, soulless eyes. "There won't be any story about that freak Superman."

"Freak? Says a man as bald as a cue ball!"

Bertram stiffened in the armored suit that made him look like some absurd beetle. He clearly wanted to defend his boss's honor, but Luthor was quite capable of watching out for himself. "Now that Superman has been incapacitated by exposure to the green mineral, we can study him. Dissection should prove that he is in fact an alien, different from anyone else on Earth."

Alarmed, Lois said, "He already admitted that—and he's come to *help* us. The world *needs* Superman."

"Can't you see it's a trick? How can an investigative reporter be so gullible?" He made a sound of disgust. "Maybe being a woman makes it impossible for you to be objective. Wake up, Miss Lane! Don't just take him at face value—no one rescues people and saves the world *as a hobby*! It's inconceivable."

"Not to someone with a soul," Lois quipped. "Is unconditional compassion such a foreign concept to you?"

He looked as if he had taken a large bite out of a particularly sour pickle. "He is powerful, and he is mysterious, and that makes him dangerous."

"You're far more dangerous than he is, Lex Luthor. And far less human."

Luthor suddenly realized something. "You really care about him, don't you, Miss Lane? Like a little lovesick schoolgirl." His expression took on a more calculating look. She refused to answer, which was itself an answer.

Luthor continued, "We have an arrangement, Ceridov and I. Soon Superman will be turned over to my researchers. Think of the medical and pharmaceutical breakthroughs I could discover by peeling him apart—not to mention the wealth it'll bring in."

Lois was outraged. "Didn't he more than prove his worth by saving our country from the Soviet missile launch?"

"You can't count on Superman, Miss Lane. How can the United States place itself in his debt? It would be the greatest folly to rely on a man who might change his mind on a whim. Luthor-Corp, on the other hand, is creating reliable technology that won't be swayed by emotions. You've seen these new battlesuits—

powerful defenses that can be used by anyone duly placed in command."

"Someone like yourself?" Lois said.

Luthor shrugged. "There are more pressing threats than you realize, Miss Lane. Your own newspaper has failed to report on the most important danger to the people of Earth. The Communists are a red herring, as you will soon see. I intend to prove to the world that *I* am their real protector, not Superman."

Lois glanced at the stony-faced Bertram, then back to Luthor. "What could possibly be a bigger threat than the Communists in the middle of the Cold War? They've already launched three nuclear missiles at us!"

"Such a disappointing lack of imagination." Luthor regarded his fingertips, then turned to his bodyguard. "Bertram, keep Miss Lane in one of our guest cells for the time being. It would be easier, and certainly more efficient, if we simply disposed of her, but I don't waste any possible resource. Superman has already demonstrated an affection for her, and she obviously loves him. Once General Ceridov sends his prisoner here, perhaps Miss Lane's presence will convince him not to resist our investigations."

"I won't do it, Luthor. I refuse to cooperate!"

"Why, Miss Lane, who said your *cooperation* was required?"

As the battlesuited guards grabbed a shouting Lois and dragged her out of the control room, Luthor folded his hands and turned to stare at the screens. "With Superman out of the picture, it's the perfect time for my next little surprise."

CHAPTER 52
SIBERIA

THE BLACK CYCLE RACED ACROSS THE UNEVEN TERRAIN like a predator giving chase. Kal-El slumped on the back, still wondering about the mysterious yet strangely honorable Batman. What sort of true hero hid his features behind a dark cowl? And yet, of all the citizens in the USA, only Batman had taken direct action, had risked his own life to save him from General Ceridov and the deadly meteorite radiation.

As they put more distance between themselves and the quarry, Kal-El felt his crippling weakness begin to subside. The invisible chains that dragged him down were dissolving, and with each breath he felt more of his strength return. His vision became sharper. Closer to normal.

Batman guided the cycle expertly through the dark forest, seeing his way with an infrared night-vision visor. He passed through the last of the stunted trees, then out to an open, windswept ridgetop where a dark plane waited like a massive metal condor, ready to take them to safety. Kal-El had never seen such an exotic aircraft design, and he wondered whether Batman himself might have

access to certain alien technology. Kryptonian, perhaps? Maybe
he was even an alien himself . . . but that was too much to hope
for.

Batman stopped the cycle and remotely opened the plane's
canopy. "It'll be crowded, but there's room inside for two. You're
not in any shape to fly yet, and I've got to get you out of here."

As Kal-El climbed into the sleek aircraft, Batman stowed the
cycle in the fuselage undercarriage, then swung into the cockpit.
Sealing the canopy, he activated the controls, and the engines
roared to life, causing the whole plane to throb. "We'll be gone
before the Soviets know what hit them."

With a burst from the vertical launch boosters, the plane lifted
straight into the air, then leaped forward with a screaming thrust
of afterburners, climbing steeply.

Pushed deep into his seat by the acceleration, Kal-El looked
down as the plane soared into the night, away from the gulag.
There was no way he could have saved all those helpless political
prisoners thrown into the camp by the Communist government.
He vowed to come back—

Then a blinding flash occurred, followed by a searing, rolling
shock wave that carried a burst of light, radiation, and heat toward
them. A nuclear flash. He strained to see through the dancing
black spots in his vision.

Batman clenched his gauntleted hands around the controls,
holding the plane against the sudden buffeting of turbulence.
Dials and gauges spun, blinking in the blackness. The sleek plane
shuddered as it tried to outrace the shock front that tossed them
about. Batman took the plane into a near vertical climb, not
leveling off until they had finally escaped the spreading storm.

Kal-El focused again, concentrating as he pushed his eyesight, discerning more details through the blazing aftermath. "It's gone. The quarry, the gulag, the barracks buildings. Everything, wiped out."

"Including the meteor."

"Including any prisoners that were left alive," Kal-El said sadly.

"There was nothing we could have done." They flew onward in silence, both lost in thought. Kal-El knew the other man was right, but he was simply not accustomed to failure, to being so helpless.

Though the debilitating weakness was dissipating, Kal-El could still feel his vulnerability, his weakness, and he needed to heal as much as he needed to understand what had happened to him. He didn't wish to return to Metropolis until his powers were restored, not until he had a better grasp of this strange material that had crippled him. Luthor had possessed one sample of the green Ariguska mineral; how many more hunks of the glowing rock were out there for evil-hearted men to use against him?

"Let me guide you," Kal-El said. "There's a special place up in the arctic. We can stop there to rest."

Batman turned, his dark cowl making him look inhuman in the red lights from the cockpit displays. "You have a secret base?"

"A fortress . . . my Fortress of Solitude. I usually fly there on my own, but I will show it to you. I . . . trust you."

"Now you've piqued my curiosity."

The black plane soared into the uncharted polar wilderness, cruising over white wastelands of unconquered terrain and twisting frozen rivers. Kal-El was uneasy, yet he had made up his mind. This was a private place where he could ponder his Kryptonian heritage, where he could contemplate both his existence and his destiny. He had never taken anyone here before.

But he sensed something different about Batman. He had an

unusual philosophy about fighting crime, to be sure, as well as a certain darkness to his personality, and perhaps he held even more secrets than Kal-El himself. But behind the steely resolve was also a kind of altruism.

Maybe they both fought on the same side after all.

Dawn had painted eerie blood-orange light across the rough ice fields by the time Kal-El guided them to the isolated range of glacier-covered mountains. Even from a great distance, he spotted the latticework of interlaced white crystal shafts. The gigantic angled spires formed an incredible alien palace at the base of a sheer icy cliff.

As new daylight reflected through the crystal faces, Batman found a place to land on the broad ice field. The plane dropped on its vertical thrusters, surrounded by spiraling whirls of ice and snow kicked up by the engine blasts. Batman had proven himself a man of few words, but he was utterly silent now. Kal-El pretended not to notice that he marked the plane's position on his cockpit log.

When they emerged, the air was intensely cold. Kal-El was impervious to temperature, but he could see that Batman, even with his incredible suit and imaginative devices, was still just a man. Kal-El would take him inside the shelter quickly.

But Batman stood with his dark boots planted, his cape rippling around him in the arctic wind. He did not seem to be in any hurry as he stared at the amazing facade of the Fortress of Solitude. "I am not a person easily impressed, Superman. But this will do it."

CHAPTER 53
THE FORTRESS OF SOLITUDE

OUT IN THE ARCTIC WILDERNESS, WHERE NO SPY PLANES or prying eyes would find it, Superman had erected a structure that surpassed anything millionaire playboy Bruce Wayne had ever seen: an incomparably alien cathedral built from clear crystal shards and white pillars.

Though the polar air seemed cold enough to break stone, the glowing light emanating from the fortress's crystals made the interior crackle with life and heat. In the center of the primary chamber, where the prismatic spires focused the wan sunlight, Superman seemed to be in his element, drawing power from the sun itself.

"This is what remains of my home planet, Krypton," he said. "This is how I learned what little I know of my origin, my past, and my real parents."

Behind his cowl, Batman frowned. How could any person not be skeptical about comments like that? "I read Lois Lane's interview with you in the *Daily Planet*. I know what you claimed to be. I just . . . never believed it."

Yet as he stared about him, how could he doubt the evidence of his own eyes? Even the brightest minds at Wayne Enterprises were not capable of building something like this fortress. Lex Luthor, on his best day, could not have conceived it.

Superman touched a green crystal. A misty cloud of turbulent air formed in the vaulted chamber, and the image of a white-haired head appeared within it. A somber yet noble visage spoke in an incomprehensible language.

"That's my father, Jor-El. He predicted the end of our planet, warned the Kryptonian Council, but my father—Krypton's greatest scientist—was defeated by politics, incompetence, and *complacency*. A dictator named Zod was his downfall, but the people of Krypton were responsible for the end of their own world."

He touched another crystal, an amber one this time. A beautiful woman appeared, and Superman gazed at her wistfully. "My mother, Lara. I was just a baby when they placed me in a small ship and launched me into space, daring to believe that I might reach Earth and find a home here. As far as I know, I am the last survivor of Krypton."

A child all alone . . .

A memory shuddered through him: *How could the reflection of blue steel be so bright in such a dim alley? "He just wants the pearls, Martha. Just the pearls."*

Another set of lost parents, blood in an alley.

Surely that single gunshot must have been as loud as a whole planet exploding. . . .

In other crystal-lined alcoves, humming mirrors vibrated and displayed scenes from an amazing planet: racing chariots drawn by ugly iguana-like creatures, volcanoes spewing red lava tinged with green, incredible tidal waves, a magnificent city protected by a shimmering dome.

Superman's voice was barely audible. "My real name—my Kryptonian name—is Kal-El."

Shunting aside the memory of Thomas and Martha Wayne, locking those images away for safekeeping, Batman considered his questions, put the pieces together. "So when you were an infant, your ship landed here on Earth . . . somewhere in America? Where—and more important, *when*?"

Kal-El hesitated. "You want me to tell you everything? Are you willing to give up your own secrets, Batman?"

He bent his cowled head down, focused on the problem. "I'm trying to add up the time frame. The Ariguska meteor impact occurred in June 1938, and it just so happens that you are incredibly vulnerable to that green meteorite material. If my guess is correct, your spaceship landed on Earth at approximately the same time."

Superman pondered this. "Yes . . . yes, it did. Are you suggesting that the Ariguska meteor, and those green rocks, are radioactive fragments of Krypton?"

"It's a possibility."

Superman looked both intrigued and disturbed by the revelation. "But why would a rock from my home planet have such a profound effect on me? Why—and how—could it drain my power?"

"I didn't say I could offer an explanation, just a clue." Shaking his cowled head, he said, "It is impossible for me to believe, yet impossible to deny. You aren't from Earth. You *are* an alien. Have you heard Senator McCarthy's accusations?"

"I'm here to *help*," Superman insisted. "The United States is my country, my home. Being an adopted son does not make me any less loyal. I will defend our way of life and protect people from man-made dangers and natural disasters alike. I use my strength and skills to benefit mankind." He looked up. "As you seem to do, Batman. I was suspicious of you at first, because of your tactics, but I now believe you do fight on the side of the law."

"I fight on the side of *justice*," he corrected. "Justice and the law are not always the same. I do what is necessary to prevent crime, to stop criminals, to save the innocent."

Superman seemed troubled. "But without the law we have no civilization, and without civilization there is anarchy. People can't just write their own laws according to how they feel."

Superman's naiveté and seemingly unquestioning adherence to the law began to rankle. "Zero tolerance is a hallmark of people who refuse to *think*. When you're dealing with human psychology, the answers aren't always black and white . . . Kal-El." The name felt strange as he said it. "Isn't there a difference between a psychopath who steals purely out of greed and a desperate father who steals a loaf of bread for his family?"

Superman frowned. "That would depend on if the father hurt or killed someone. Does it give any consolation to a grieving widow that the murderer had a 'good reason' for committing his crime?"

Batman wrestled with the question in his own mind, remembering one desperate thief with a gun hiding in the alley by Park Row. Had that man been desperate for money to feed his family, or maybe to buy medicine for a sick baby? Doubtful. But even if the mugger had had understandable motives, that would not bring Thomas and Martha Wayne back from the dead.

The fingers of a black gauntlet clenched, forming a fist, but he forced himself to relax. "I watched President Eisenhower give you the Medal of Freedom. I know that was a great moment for you, but leaders aren't perfect. Political power and wealth can corrupt any man, no matter where he's born. A man like Lex Luthor can steal more money with the stroke of a pen than a hundred petty criminals can with their guns." He looked up at Superman. "Which is more important—stopping a small-time thief or battling corrupt leaders?"

Superman answered with remarkable ease. "The world looks to us as heroes. We have to do *both*."

J IMMY OLSEN DIDN'T KNOW WHAT TO DO, AND HE HAD nobody to talk to.

Clark Kent had chosen a particularly bad time for an extended visit to his hometown back in Kansas. Lois Lane had flown off to interview Wernher von Braun and his team of rocket scientists (though Mr. White was furious that she hadn't called to check in). The other reporters in the *Planet*'s bullpen were in a feeding frenzy with so many major stories to choose from.

But Jimmy was most worried about Superman. Tensions remained high between the U.S. and the Soviet Union, and no new footage had been shown of the captive hero in more than a day. He was afraid something even worse had happened to Superman. He had looked sick, defeated. . . . Jimmy had never felt so upset and helpless. He didn't think the situation could get any worse.

Until a huge alien battleship appeared in the skies above Metropolis.

He bounded down the stairs rather than wait for the slow elevator. Thirty floors. He was out of breath by the time he reached street level and pushed through the revolving doors to join the astounded throng. He stared up into the sky, transfixed, his mouth open in shock.

A black shadow crossed over the street, like the edge of an eclipse. The interstellar engines did not so much hum as growl as the craft cruised overhead.

The angular battleship was studded with sharp spikes and gun barrels; jagged, unearthly lettering marked its hull plates in garish copper red. Arcs of blue-white electricity sparked from the spearlike prongs, traveling upward like a Jacob's ladder from Dr. Frankenstein's laboratory. Balls of static lightning bounced off the polished hull, shattering windows on the highest skyscrapers of Metropolis, blowing out power lines.

Jimmy stared. "Oh, my gosh!" Then he remembered his camera. He adjusted the focusing bed, pointed the lens upward, and took photograph after photograph until he ran out of film.

Police cars with wailing sirens wound their way through the stalled traffic. One squad car smashed the bumper of a Chevrolet and kept driving along; nobody seemed to notice, because both the policeman and the Chevy's driver were too busy staring into the sky.

Overhead, like sentries taking position, four more incredible alien craft joined the primary battleship, looming above the Metropolis skyline.

Jimmy had seen enough movies to know exactly what was happening. This was a full-scale invasion—from Mars, or maybe even someplace worse! He had always known flying saucers were real! Despite his disappointments at Mercy Draw and Area 51, Jimmy had remained convinced that visitors were coming to Earth. Maybe they had been here all along in human disguise, gathering information, spying, like in *Invasion of the Body Snatchers.*

When the alien commander transmitted his message, however, these extraterrestrial visitors did not remotely resemble human beings. Nor did they come in peace.

The space invaders had found a way to break into all television and radio signals. People gathered around a display model of a new color television in an appliance store to watch, shuddering in horror. Car radios all boomed the same message on every channel.

The alien leader's face was a mass of rotting tentacles that surrounded a clacking beak. It looked even worse than the master Martian in *Invaders from Mars,* more hideous than the creature in *It Conquered the World,* more disgusting than the mutant in *This Island Earth.* In fact, this guy would have given nightmares to *The Thing.* It had a single glowing gelatinous eye in the middle of its warty forehead, baleful and eerily reminiscent of the haunting orb in *It Came from Outer Space.*

Jimmy realized that he watched far too many sci-fi movies.

The inhuman commander's demand was implacable and terrifying. "The planet you call Earth is now under our dominion. Surrender, or be destroyed."

The alien voice bubbled and gurgled as though its vocal cords were composed entirely of phlegm. "We have monitored your radio broadcasts in order to learn your language. We have no interest in dialogue—you will hear only our demands. All inhabitants of Earth are now our slaves. Cooperate, and we may allow some of you to live. Your females may be useful for breeding purposes, since our males find them pleasing." The alien paused ominously. "If we do not receive your unconditional surrender within one hour, we will level your cities, one by one."

Jimmy heard terrified wails from the listeners; some people had actually fainted on the street. Staring at the immensely powerful ships overhead and their crackling weapons, he guessed that all governments would be helpless. He swallowed hard.

With Superman captured, who could possibly save Earth now?

CHAPTER 55
LUTHOR'S ISLAND

THIS WAS HIS MOMENT OF GLORY.

Luthor sat in a swiveling executive chair inside the broadcast chamber on his island. Due to shielding and scrambling, no one would be able to pinpoint the origin of his signal. He smiled, drew a deep breath, and felt his chest swell with confidence. Yes, this time it would be Lex Luthor to the rescue. All humanity would cheer him. Finally, they would see who was truly important and who wasn't.

Before giving the go-ahead, he studied himself in a hand mirror, not to primp and preen but to practice his expressions. He intended to show confidence and righteous indignation, the better to focus the anger that every human would be feeling. Anger and revenge had always been easy for him. Empathy, however, was a lot harder to manage.

His private makeup specialist spent a great deal of time applying pancake and special creams, using fine brushes to highlight his strong, stern features (and also to keep his bald pate from glistening under the spotlight). The cameras could not capture so much as a hint of perspiration on his brow.

He swiveled the chair, placed his elbows on the mahogany desktop, and folded his hands together. Indeed, he looked very presidential, although his aspirations went well beyond that. A large microphone stood directly in front of him; he gazed sternly into the camera lens and said, "Begin the broadcast." The red light glowed atop the camera. He began speaking.

"Fellow citizens of Earth, this is Lex Luthor. I am broadcasting from an undisclosed location so that I can complete my vital task without interruption from these . . . horrific alien invaders." He had already installed the systems he needed and planted the appropriate equipment. His broadcast, like that of the bogus alien commander's, would appear on every television channel, every radio station.

"Many of you know my achievements. I am a man who does what is necessary, and I must do so again. President Eisenhower—do not fear, sir. America is safe. The world is safe." He leaned closer. "LuthorCorp is on your side."

He made his eyes blaze, intensified his expression, and raised his voice. "Know this, alien commander: The human race will never bow to invaders! Earth is *our* planet, and we are its proud people—*free* people who will never be your slaves. You will wish you had never come here!"

He had assumed Eisenhower would stall for time or, worse, make a pathetic call to Superman for help, even though he was still being held prisoner in the Ariguska gulag. General Ceridov had been silent since the previous day, but the KGB general had no further part in Luthor's plan anyway. The American president was equally irrelevant. Lex Luthor would preempt everything else.

The loathsome alien commander responded to the bold challenge with outrage, tentacles thrashing around its face. The single eye pulsated. Static discharge prongs on the invading battleships crackled, preparing to unleash bursts of intense disintegrator beams.

Luthor continued his fiery speech. "Behold what LuthorCorp can do—what a *human* genius can do." He raised a fist and called to his technicians, who were out of camera range. "Open fire!"

The giant alien craft loomed over Metropolis, where one of the tallest buildings was the main headquarters of LuthorCorp. Now rooftop panels slid aside, and towering dish transmitters rose up on hydraulic platforms—directed-energy cannons of the same type that should have vaporized the Soviet missiles, that *had* destroyed Sputnik once the sabotaged components were repaired. Their generators had already built up a full charge.

Before the alien commander could fire, Luthor's directed-energy projectors targeted the primary battleship. Lancing rays blasted the huge interstellar engines, ripped a gaping wound along the armored hull, and blackened the bizarre alien inscriptions. Several explosions occurred on board. The invaders' static weapons did not discharge but instead pulsed backward into the interior of the battleship and blew up the alien bridge.

Secondary explosions ripped sequentially through the interior. Concussions blew out bulkheads and spewed white-hot flame through the split hull. Like a wounded animal, the invaders' command ship lumbered across the sky, trailing plumes of black smoke as it tried to flee. Reeling out of control, the vessel roared over Metropolis, sinking lower and lower.

It traveled just far enough to clear the center of the city. With a final gasp, it plunged with an enormous splash into the bay. Before the wreck had settled into the shallow water, before the first round of cheering from the humans on the street subsided, the battleship self-destructed in a white-hot flash that blew all components to pieces. Windows in warehouse buildings shattered for many blocks along the bayside, and a pillar of fire and steam shot high into the air.

Luthor didn't think President Eisenhower would complain about what he had done.

But the rest of the ships wouldn't be quite so easy. After all, Luthor couldn't let this invasion look like a simple problem. The giant alien ships, obviously vengeful now, swooped down upon the city.

CHAPTER 56
METROPOLIS

THE AIR IN HIS LUNGS FELT BRACING AS HE STREAKED ALONG at top speed, and Kal-El's muscles sang with renewed energy. Now that his powers had returned, his vision was filled with details seen across the entire spectrum in an intensity that made the whole world seem new.

He was Kal-El. He was *Superman*.

And he was back.

Racing behind him like a night-camouflaged predator, the Batplane nearly kept up with him. Kal-El slowed just enough so that the two could fly in parallel. The dark aircraft's powerful engines, no longer silenced, roared like Soviet R-7 rockets. Metropolis lay just ahead.

Superman listened in on the radio band, picking up panicked transmissions from around the world; Batman had his own receivers inside the cockpit. Both men were suddenly aware of the astonishing alien invasion fleet that had appeared over Metropolis. With Earth threatened by giant interstellar battleships, Kal-El's inclination was to charge in and rescue humanity from the fearsome extraterrestrial enemies.

Batman, though, wanted to *understand* the threat first. He opened the frequency that connected him to Superman, who wore a compact listening device Batman had produced from his remarkable utility belt. "I've seen your fortress, Kal-El, and I am convinced that *you* aren't from Earth . . . but forgive me if I remain skeptical about this alien invasion. Something isn't right. . . ."

They shot forward and got a look at the gigantic alien battleships that hovered over the city, preparing to fire their exotic weapons. The largest ship had just crashed and exploded in Metropolis Bay, but the remainder of the invasion fleet had powered up ominous weapons to commence their retaliatory attack.

A crackling discharge spat out of the pronged weapons and blew the roof off a skyscraper, showering rubble down on the people below. A flaming ovoid cannon set a second tall building on fire, blasting out windows and filling the interior offices with a poisonous black smoke. As the first three ships continued to strike, another group of five huge flying saucers arrived to join the remaining invader, strengthening the attacking force.

Streaking closer, Kal-El focused his intense gaze into the infrared band, and heat beams lashed out, strafing the underbelly of the lowest-flying alien craft. Immediately adjacent to him, the Batplane launched a brace of small rockets that streaked in and exploded, knocking out the weapons clusters on the jagged noses of two other alien craft.

"They're not as powerful as they appear to be," Batman said.

When the first incapacitated great ship began to plummet toward the crowded buildings, Kal-El saw that he had to catch the monstrosity before it caused more casualties. As he dove in to grab the reeling, out-of-control vessel, Kal-El focused his penetrating vision, shifted to the X-ray band of the spectrum, and peered inside the gigantic craft to see how many weapons the ships carried, how many alien crew members were aboard.

To his surprise, the extraterrestrial battleship was completely *empty*—nothing more than an exotically decorated metallic shell, borne on a sophisticated propulsion system.

A larger-scale version of the LuthorCorp prototype he had seen in Area 51.

"They're not real!" Kal-El shouted at Batman. "There are no aliens aboard!"

"I thought that might be the case," Batman replied. "These aren't spacecraft. They're *props*, empty constructs."

Kal-El felt anger surge within him, mixed with confusion. "This is a scam—Lex Luthor's scam?" He caught the hollow ship, hefted it like an empty wrapper, then hurled the hulk far out into the swampy and uninhabited barrens outside the city, where it couldn't cause any damage.

"But why?" Kal-El shouted. "What could Luthor possibly want?"

"It's a ploy to create fear. And fear creates lucrative defense contracts. Senator McCarthy has been raising the spectre of an alien attack, and now Luthor's built these ridiculous artificial ships to create a planet-wide panic."

Kal-El understood all too clearly. "He'll demand new weapons to be used against the imminent threat, and he'll promise to save us all—for a price. You were right about him."

"You just aren't cynical enough, my friend. I'll break into the broadcasts just like Luthor did and send a signal to inform the world of what's actually happening. This alien danger is not real. None of it is."

A greater anger built within Kal-El. He had struggled against the public's unreasonable fear of his own alien heritage. He had been accused of having a secret and sinister agenda. But alien visitors weren't the real evil here. Lex Luthor was.

And now that Luthor's involvement was exposed, he wondered what the man would do next.

Arms extended, flying swift and hard like a living projectile, Kal-El punched his way through the hull of another alien ship. Inside the core framework, he grasped a structural girder and ascended high into the sky.

Glad to find a satisfying outlet for his anger, he drove the fake alien ship as far and as fast as he could. Within seconds he had reached the edge of the atmosphere, and, pushing with all his strength, he shoved the false invader out into space to drift harmlessly . . . where it belonged.

CHAPTER 57
LUTHOR'S ISLAND

ON THE SECRET ISLAND BASE, LUTHOR HAD SEEN FIT TO create a secure holding cell inside the tower of the old Spanish fort connected to his headquarters. The stone-walled chamber had a thick double-locked door and bars on a window that overlooked the ocean.

However, since the cell appeared to be rarely—if ever—used, Lois hoped to find a way out. Luthor's arrogance was his greatest vulnerability, and he wouldn't dream that a woman could outwit him.

Moments after Luthor's guards had locked the study door, a noise and a loud eruption of water came from the edge of the island, but tall palm trees blocked her view of the source. From the small cell window, she was astonished to see an enormous alien-looking battleship rise from the construction yards on the far side of the island. Another ship rose, then another, then their engines flared with a dazzling array of bright lights. The "alien invasion fleet" accelerated across the ocean. Within minutes, another group of ships streaked off to follow the first.

Knowing Jimmy Olsen's interest in flying saucers, Lois was

sure the young photographer would fall for the deception, hook, line, and sinker. So would most of the people of the world. But the "spaceships" were decoys. Lex Luthor was nothing more than a con man with expensive toys.

She had to tell the world about it before the great leaders were duped into accepting whatever terms Luthor imposed. She also had to help Superman.

She needed to get out. Now.

But Luthor was never going to let Lois out of this alive; she could see that. Worse, he intended to use her as bait, forcing Superman to submit to all the tests he wanted to perform. And Lois knew the big handsome guy would do practically anything to save her. He was predictable like that. She could not let him sacrifice himself for her.

As if she needed more incentive to get out of here . . .

She pounded on the thick door, but no sound carried through, and apparently no guards waited outside. Luthor probably didn't have henchmen to spare at the moment, since he was too busy planning world domination. Even so, she could see no way to pick the heavy locks or pry loose the old iron hinges. She was stuck.

It was going to have to be the window. The bars were slightly above her eye level, but the mortar looked old and crumbling. Maybe she could tug and twist them free. When she reached up to touch the iron bars, though, a powerful electric jolt threw her across the room. She skidded unceremoniously backward on the floor, her nerves jangling and yelling, her whole body twitching. Lois slowly picked herself up, her pride more injured than her body. Now she saw the naked contact wires connected to each iron bar. Time to figure out a plan B.

Lois had no superpowers, of course, but she did have her experience and skills as a reporter. Before meeting Superman, she'd extricated herself from plenty of desperate circumstances, and she could do it again.

Superman needed *her* help now. She had to find some way to circumvent the electrified bars. Luthor had left her nothing but a Paper Mate pen and her notepad. Did he expect her to write a last message? A will?

Standing on a small wooden bench so she could peer through the barred window, Lois considered her options, racking her brain for a solution. She stared once again at the electrified bars, the wires that made them live contacts. All she had was her pen and a notepad.

A metal pen.

Clipping the pen's shaft to the spiral binding of the notepad, now she had enough metal to stretch from one naked wire on the electrified bars to the next, enough to blow out the circuit—she hoped. The pad of paper should provide adequate insulation for her fingers . . . maybe.

She had to take the risk. She loved Superman and everything he represented. Unlike many people Lois had met as a reporter, he was a genuinely good and decent person. Though she was somewhat reluctant to dig so deeply into her feelings, she realized that she was willing to do just about anything for him. For once, in so many ways, she had met her match.

Squeezing her eyes shut, Lois jammed the metal pen across the contact wires at the base of two bars. Sparks showered out, accompanied by an oily smell of electrical burning. She jerked her head away but held the metal contact in place. The circuit blew, then nothing—no more sparks, no more sound.

Gingerly, she tapped the cell bars with a fingertip, expecting to flinch from another shock, but she received none. Her notepad was scorched and curling. She used the flat pad to protect her palm as she smashed at the bars, trying to break the mortar loose. The iron rods weren't overly thick or well anchored; apparently the electricity was supposed to be the primary deterrent. She twisted the bars, then tugged backward, throwing her whole weight into the effort.

Finally, the first bar worked free as gray mortar flaked away. When the end was loose, she bent the short bar upward and worked double time on the adjacent bars. Within minutes, she had created a gap large enough to worm through. Breathing hard and sweating, she pulled herself up to the thick stone sill, then wriggled her head and shoulders out of the gap.

She was at least fifty feet above the ground.

The stone blocks of the headquarters tower had been stacked roughly atop one another, mortared together centuries ago. She would have to work her way around to a ledge, lower herself to the next floor, and hope to find another foothold. Her deck shoes should give her enough traction.

No matter what, it was better than remaining a guest of Lex Luthor.

Now that she had climbed free of her cell, she could see the island's small harbor and two modern speedboats tied up at the dock. If she reached the ground, she could run out to the dock, power up one of the boats, and race westward into the ocean. She would eventually be rescued, she was sure.

But she couldn't let Luthor continue with his plans. If the Soviets were still holding Superman prisoner, then *she* had to do something.

Luthor's main control room was two levels down in the modern portion of the building. With fingertips and toes, she could work her way along the stone blocks of the outer wall and reach one of the lower windows. She would figure out what to do once she got inside.

She had already seen Luthor's radio transmitters and microphones. If she managed to gain access, she could send a message, broadcast a warning to the world—even call for help. During the supposed alien invasion, her father would certainly be monitoring the airwaves. She hated to rely on General Lane, but even Lois couldn't do everything herself.

Not looking down, she worked her way precariously along the ledge, ignoring the seagulls that swooped around her. Mountain climbers did this sort of thing every day. Sir Edmund Hillary could have done it with his eyes closed while singing an aria, she told herself.

Lois reached the open window to one of the rooms adjacent to the control center and swung herself inside. By now her calves burned, her arms ached, and her fingertips were raw, but she was very glad to be on a solid floor again, even if it was inside the lair of Lex Luthor. Down the corridor, she could hear the hum of activity, transmitted words from numerous screens and radio speakers. She heard Luthor cursing and drew particular pleasure from the fact that he did not sound happy at all.

Several slithery white cleansuits with hoods hung on wall pegs, and Lois slipped into one as an idea rapidly took shape in her mind. She covered most of her head with the hood, tucking her dark hair out of sight, and obscured her face with a set of lab goggles; a clipboard completed her disguise. Looking intent on her duties, she strode brazenly into the buzzing control room.

Luthor sat in the middle of the controls and screens, watching it all. She had to force herself to keep from staring at the images on the video screens: huge "alien" ships hovering over Metropolis.

And Superman! He flew alongside a sleek black plane, hurtling forward to engage the invading ships directly above Metropolis. Lois drew a quick breath, so overjoyed to see that Superman was free from the Soviet prison camp that she nearly called his name out loud. The weakness that had afflicted him seemed to be gone! No wonder Luthor was cursing.

The radio bands were filled with chatter and outraged transmissions. Luthor's ploy had been discovered, and the game was up!

"Acquire new targets," Luthor growled. "Forget the alien ships—there's a new enemy to destroy."

A SQUADRON OF NEW-MODEL WAYNE ENTERPRISES ATTACK craft came roaring up behind the Batplane, flying in perfect formation over Metropolis. The newly commissioned jets swooped in with amazing maneuverability and opened fire with a suite of targeted rockets.

"The Air Force has been itching to try out these production models," he transmitted to Superman.

Without revealing his identity, he used the Batplane's communication system to spread a warning throughout the squadron. "The alien ships are fakes. There is no real attack from outer space. Nevertheless, prepare to take out the remaining strange vessels before they can fire their weapons again."

Unlike the flying saucers, however, the death-beam projectors atop the LuthorCorp headquarters were indeed real. Now they rotated their dishes and pointed snub-nosed antennae toward the harrying Wayne Enterprises jets that bombarded the faux spacecraft. A barrage of furious heat energy lanced out, striking two of the trailing fighter jets. The pilots didn't have a chance.

As the pair of aircraft exploded in the air, the squadron

commander snapped over his command frequency, "Evasive action—we're taking fire!" As the fighters peeled away, Luthor's death beam struck out again and obliterated a third jet.

The Batplane streaked toward LuthorCorp headquarters, arming another set of missiles. Those dishes had to be taken out.

He studied his cockpit targeting cross, adjusted the range, and primed the firing systems. He thought of the dead pilots and their families. How many children had Luthor just made fatherless? Did the man even care? Did he count the cost of human lives as just another one of his business expenses, an entry on his profit-loss statement?

The targeting crosses finally aligned, and he squeezed his black gauntlets around the firing controls, launching the three small rockets. But the rooftop energy beams discharged first.

He yanked his stick violently to one side, sending the Batplane into an evasive spin. The death beam lanced past, missing the aircraft core but vaporizing the aileron and spoiler on the wing along with the tip of the vertical stabilizer.

Alarms shrilled in the cockpit, and he fought to maintain control. The energy-beam projectors tracked him, aiming once more. If the ray hit him again, the Batplane would be vaporized in the air. In a last desperate move, he punched his rocket engine control, but the dark aircraft went into an uncontrolled dive. The flaps still functioned, but the rudder and elevators in the tail section were useless.

The dishes retargeted, pointing directly at him, and this time he knew he was in their path.

But just as another blast struck out, a blue and red blur streaked between the death beam and the Batplane. The energy ray slammed into Superman, crackling all around him like a solar corona. Kal-El reeled in the air but somehow kept himself aloft.

Layers of carbon soot covered the bold *S* emblazoned on his chest, and his red cape was singed.

Out of control, the Batplane plunged toward the skyscrapers of Metropolis. Within seconds, he would crash into the populous heart of the city. His only chance was to eject, to blast himself free and hope he landed intact on the streets. But the plane still carried armaments and fuel aboard, and he could not allow it to crash into the office towers and apartment complexes.

Through the cockpit canopy he could see himself careening directly toward the *Daily Planet* building. He ignored the bleating alarms and held on to the controls all the way down as he fought to pull up, managing to veer slightly toward the river. He strained, using every functional system, trying backup controls.

The last engine failed, and all his cockpit systems shut down. The Batplane was now an aerodynamic black rock trailing smoke and fire. Falling.

He simply *stopped* in midair. Fuselage metal groaned, and the engines roared as they struggled to ignite again. But the sleek aircraft simply hung suspended, then began to move away.

Superman had caught him. Holding the Batplane up, he flew away from the streets of downtown Metropolis to a clear landing area. Kal-El looked at Batman through the canopy glass. "My turn to rescue *you*."

CHAPTER 59
LUTHOR'S ISLAND

WHILE LUTHOR WAS BUSY TRYING TO SALVAGE HIS PLAN, Lois set her sights on a more immediate goal. Inside the crowded control chamber, she had identified a communications array with a dangling headset and microphone plugged into one of the panels.

The rest of the henchmen remained engrossed in the broadcast images of titanic battles against the extraterrestrial ships over Metropolis. She didn't think Luthor had expected to engage in an actual full-scale war but had meant to cow the world's leaders by virtue of the threat. The bodyguard Bertram and three companions clomped around the edge of the room, encased in their insectile battlesuits, acting like playground bullies.

No one paid any attention to Lois in her cleansuit, hood, and goggles. She was indistinguishable from the other workers, so long as she kept a low profile. But she wouldn't accomplish anything if she kept hiding. She had to pull out all the stops and send a warning. The choice seemed obvious to her, even if it was a brash and foolish one.

Clipboard in hand, she pretended to study the readings on

306 KEVIN J. ANDERSON

various dials and gauges as she worked her way to the communication system. Jotting notes on the clipboard, she flicked the power switches, nodded to herself, and turned the black knobs to adjust the frequency to one of the military emergency bands. No one stopped her.

An angry flush covered Luthor's face and his smooth head. He was firing deadly energy beams from skyscraper towers, but at real targets now, rather than the empty alien invasion ships. She watched in horror as the brunt of a beam caught Superman and blanketed him with a crackling discharge.

Lois bit back a cry of disbelief, but Superman quickly shook away the effects. She should have known that even Luthor's worst couldn't stop the Man of Steel.

On the screens, she saw Superman—in his usual heroic fashion—making fast work of Luthor's defenses, which elicited a string of particularly foul and furious curses from the bald man.

Good . . . that meant Luthor was thoroughly preoccupied.

When the radio gear was fully powered up, Lois picked up the headset and placed it clumsily over her cleansuit hood. Years ago, she had used a classified military band to tap into Air Force communications, trying to get a story. Her audacity had backfired, and she'd gotten into a great deal of trouble. Her father had barely managed to keep her out of federal prison for that particular breach of security, and he had warned her *never* to use that particular band again. As a two-star general, he was a fearsome figure; as an angry father, even more so.

Lois didn't hesitate a moment before dialing to that frequency. She picked up the microphone, hit the transmit button, and spoke in a rush. "This is Lois Lane, daughter of General Sam Lane and reporter for the *Daily Planet,* with an urgent message."

"Lady, get off this band! This is a classified military frequency."

Lois snapped back, "Maybe you don't understand the meaning of the word 'urgent,' soldier. I repeat, I am the daughter of *General Sam Lane*. I am being held prisoner by Lex Luthor on an island just east of Cuba." She gave a quick rundown of the mock alien spacecraft he had launched from his base and how he was controlling the attack with the energy weapons. She embellished his evil schemes a little, but not by much. Lois was so intent on her message that at first she didn't realize the shouts inside the control room were now directed *at her*.

"Bertram, stop her!" Luthor yelled. The bodyguard was already stalking forward, the hydraulic pistons in his battlesuit whirring and humming. Each footfall was the step of a giant. He crashed toward her and raised his purple-encased fist.

"Gotta go, soldier!" she yelled into the microphone, then ripped off the headset as she dodged. The man in the battlesuit swung an armored fist at her with the force of a pile driver.

Lois dodged again, her goggles falling off and hanging around her neck. Bertram moved to intercept, and she hoped the other battlesuited guards didn't join the fun. Luthor's main henchman lumbered forward with more speed and power than he seemed able to control.

"Be careful of the equipment!" Luthor shouted. Several technicians in cleansuits dodged out of the way as Bertram stomped after Lois. She threw her clipboard at him, knocked over chairs that spun about on casters. In his suit, Bertram smashed entirely through a rail, making a straight line toward her.

Lois spied a bright red fire extinguisher next to one of the blinking computer banks. She snatched it from its cradle and clanged the cylinder with all her strength against the green armor. It didn't make a scratch, though her hands and wrists vibrated from the impact.

Luthor yelled, his face red, "Bertram, you lummox! Catch her, but don't—"

Infuriated, the armored bodyguard swung at her again, his face dark with concentration and effort. He drew back his powered arm and slammed it forward, intending to smash her into a pulp. But Lois dropped to the floor, and Bertram's armored fist plowed into the control bank and power center. The gauntlet sank deep into the array, destroying the workings.

Luthor roared at the stupidity of his bodyguard, but the background explosions and sizzle drowned out his words.

Blue electric bolts skittered all around the battlesuit until the bright green armor and all its internal power systems were completely short-circuited. Though the burly bodyguard cursed and struggled, he could not move. His high-tech armor was nonfunctional, imprisoning him inside a statue.

"You missed me," she said.

Luthor stood in a dead control room, as furious as he was helpless. The smell of ozone and burning circuitry filled the air. All the monitor screens in the room went dark, leaving Luthor blind and unable to use his energy beams. Bertram was alive, unharmed, and completely immobilized in his battlesuit.

That was a lot more than Lois had expected to achieve, but when she saw the remaining battlesuited guards advancing quickly toward her, she doubted her celebration would last very long.

CHAPTER 60
METROPOLIS

WITH MANY OF THE "ALIEN" SHIPS OUT OF COMMISSION and others severely damaged, Kal-El focused on the real danger now. The false invaders continued to shoot their embedded weapons, but Luthor's energy beams from the top of the LuthorCorp tower were the greatest threats.

Kal-El darted in to intercept the next deadly blast before it could vaporize another Air Force jet, again intentionally taking the full brunt of the discharge. Surrounded by fumes and ozone, he took a moment to recover, pushing back the pain and steadying his jangled nerves. Then he dove forward.

Time to put an end to this. Now.

He shot toward the top of the LuthorCorp skyscraper, where the beam generators stood like insectile frameworks. Before they could fire again, he furrowed his brow and intensified his heat vision, pushing into the infrared until his own beam melted the insulated energy cables. Sparks flew, and the support girders bent, but that wasn't good enough for him.

Kal-El flew in, arms outstretched, fists clenched, and crashed like a battering ram into the transmitter towers. He ripped apart

structural girders, uprooted power cables, and released a shower
of lightning. The tower tipped over with a crash onto the roof of
the LuthorCorp building, looking like the skeleton of a beached
sea creature.

Only then did he take a breath.

The Batplane was safely landed, but now Batman was out of the
fight. Emergency crews and national guard squads rushed through
the streets, mounted ladders, and set up rescue stations to care for
the injured inside the damaged buildings.

The fighter aircraft continued to circle the remaining alien ships,
spattering them with small missiles or streams of hot bullets until
the supposed invaders had been neutralized. At last, Metropolis
was safe.

Suddenly the clear voice of Lois Lane startled him as her message
broke through chatter on the military command frequency. He
focused his concentration on the transmission, heard the details of
her message, and all the pieces fell together. Now he knew where
Luthor was hiding, where he had orchestrated this spectacular and
deadly con job.

And where he was holding Lois prisoner.

Kal-El didn't hesitate for an instant.

On the radio, General Sam Lane bellowed orders to redirect
F-100D squadrons southward while commanding another squadron to launch from Tyndall and Eglin Air Force bases in Florida.
But Kal-El knew they would never find the small Caribbean island
soon enough. Lois was in danger *now*. He could think of nothing
else.

She had gotten herself in trouble, tangled up in Lex Luthor's
scam, while he'd been trapped in Siberia. Kal-El hadn't been there
when she needed him.

Even if the USAF jets reached the island base at supersonic

speeds, how could they land and deploy soldiers in time to rescue her? How could anyone get on the ground swiftly enough to save her?

He could. *I'm coming, Lois,* he thought.

Kal-El streaked off, heading due south.

FROM HIGH ABOVE, HE SCANNED THE CARIBBEAN ISLANDS and keys with a growing sense of urgency, trying to locate the correct one. Kal-El crisscrossed the skies, desperate to find Lois. She had ended her transmission so quickly, he knew she had to be in deep trouble.

Lois continued to get herself into impossible situations, such as this one, but this time she had also exposed Luthor's location. In her own way, she was fighting to save the world. He felt very proud of her, and his heart pounded harder as he increased speed. He knew it was not only fear that drove him faster. It was about how much Lois meant to him, how much he *loved* her. The thought of a snake like Luthor holding her captive made him clench his fists. Not only had Luthor threatened Earth, he had threatened *her*.

He sped toward a tiny dot of an island in the middle of the blue sea. Sharpening his vision, he saw the outline of the small patch of land, the beaches, industrial areas, docks and shipyards, soot-stained rocket launchpads . . . and the control center, modern structures built around the ruins of an old Spanish fort.

Lois was in there. Her transmission had cut off abruptly, and she might already be dead.

Kal-El flew down faster than a missile, directly toward the headquarters building. He landed on the rooftop with a thud, spreading his red boots apart for balance. He bent over, cocked back his arm, and slammed his fist into the metal tiles. Battering until he smashed through the roof, he ripped away shingles and support beams and cleared an opening through the ceiling. He dropped down into the control room, landing amid the debris.

Lois was easy to spot next to a grinning Lex Luthor—who held a loaded Luger P08 pistol to her head while grasping her firmly around the waist. Though the technicians scattered as Kal-El crashed his way down into the control room, Luthor simply sneered. "You're utterly predictable. What took you so long?"

"I had to finish cleaning up your mess in Metropolis. Put the gun down, Luthor. I'm delivering you to the authorities."

"People should never presume to tell me what to do." He pressed the gun barrel firmly against Lois's temple. She looked more annoyed than afraid, but Kal-El wasn't fooled.

"Ask yourself, Superman," Luthor continued. "Is capturing me worth the price of Miss Lane's life? I really don't want her pretty brains splattered all over my suit, but . . ." He shrugged. "I can always get a new suit. Finding another Lois Lane may prove a bit more difficult."

Kal-El didn't move, careful not to endanger Lois. When her eyes met his, he saw her complete confidence in him—her love for him—and that gave him strength. "If you're the great genius you claim to be, Lex Luthor, then you've already figured out you can't get away."

"I still have alternatives," Luthor said. On cue, three battle-suited guards stalked forward to protect their master, encircling Kal-El. "I designed those suits to match your abilities. Three of them will be more than enough to squash you like a bug." He smiled at Kal-El. "These are *my* supermen."

The guards raised their gauntlets and shot small explosive rockets at Kal-El's chest at point-blank range. The detonations made him stagger backward into a wall so hard that the cinder blocks crumbled. But the weapons did not damage his suit, his S emblem, or him. Picking himself up from the rubble, he strode through the clearing smoke, taking satisfaction in the astonished expressions on the armored bodyguards.

From their arm cannons, a stream of large-caliber bullets poured out, only to bounce harmlessly off Kal-El's chest, though the deflected projectiles ripped craters in the walls and damaged control banks. Two ricocheted shots struck the paralyzed Bertram with loud *spangs*; trapped in his immobile armor, he flinched down beneath the raised collar shield. He struggled and strained, but the uncooperative battlesuit kept him imprisoned in his petrified shell.

Seeing that a ricochet could easily kill Lois, Kal-El used a burst of his heat vision to melt the already-hot barrels of their inset artillery.

When their weapons failed, the guards activated their jetpacks and launched themselves directly at Kal-El, smashing into him. All three used the most powerful engines and hydraulics, slamming piston-powered blows into Superman from all sides, hammering and hammering.

But all he could see was Lois being threatened, the pistol pressed against her head, and the pure evil in Luthor's face. Kal-El could no longer afford to be cautious.

He seized one of the guards by the front of his thick battlesuit and hurled him up through the gaping hole he had left in the ceiling. Kal-El picked up the second man bodily and smashed him into his companion with the force of two colliding trucks. The plated armor may have been impenetrable, but the reverberating impact was enough to knock both men unconscious.

As though he had just mopped up several opponents in a bar brawl, Kal-El turned to face Luthor once more, flexing his fingers.

The other man's confidence seemed to drain away, leaving him paler than usual. His expression was twisted as he held Lois tighter; now he was desperate and even more dangerous.

"Not one more step," Luthor said. "You *know* I'll kill her. Don't doubt it for a second."

"Please don't hurt me." Lois's voice shook with terror, and she wobbled against him. "Please, Lex!" Kal-El saw her give him a quick, sly wink.

Surprised at her sudden change of tone, Luthor glanced at his captive—and Lois stomped down hard with her full weight, grinding her heel ferociously into his instep. Luthor howled in pain, instinctively doubling over, and she brought up her knee. *Hard.*

Reacting instantly, Kal-El unleashed a burst of heat vision, and the Luger in Luthor's hand turned cherry red. The bald man hurled the throbbing pistol aside as Lois ducked free of his grasp. Kal-El seized Luthor easily, though the man continued to struggle and argue (it seemed a matter of pride for him).

Holding Luthor easily up off the floor, where his feet kicked and thrashed, Kal-El smiled at Lois. "The Air Force will be here soon, Miss Lane. Your father received your message on the secure military band. I'll wait here until you're safe."

Lois nodded matter-of-factly, surveying the ruined control center with a wry chuckle. "The general will be annoyed that I used that frequency again."

"It was a matter of national security, Miss Lane. I'm sure he'll understand."

"You don't know my father."

Still smiling, he took a step closer, wanting to put his arms around her, but he couldn't let go of Luthor yet. "Then I'll put in a good word. How could anyone stay upset with you for long?"

———

BY THE TIME THE AIR FORCE JETS ARRIVED AND A GROUP OF paratroopers landed on the island to secure the base, Kal-El had already done most of the mopping up and locked Luthor in one of his own cells. A U.S. Navy destroyer came shortly thereafter, dispatching marines who quickly fanned out and took up their positions to stand guard over Luthor's remaining weapons systems.

Finally, Kal-El handed Luthor over to the marines and watched as they put the scowling man into handcuffs and marched him away to the destroyer's brig.

"Good riddance," Lois said. "I've had enough of this island."

Kal-El put his hand on her arm. "I'd be happy to give you a lift back to Metropolis, Miss Lane . . . Lois . . . if you'd like to fly with me." For a minute the pair stood there awkwardly, not sure what to do next.

Then Lois smiled and took his hand in hers. "I'd love to."

He gently swept her off her feet, held her close, and the two of them were quickly airborne, flying free and alone in the empty sky. She looked into his bright blue eyes and let herself enjoy the sensation of being held in his arms again. They never once looked back down as the island vanished below them.

CHAPTER 61
THE *DAILY PLANET*

WHEN CLARK KENT RETURNED FROM VISITING HIS mother in Kansas, he congratulated Lois on her front-page story. "It must have been quite an ordeal, Lois."

"Good thing Superman was there to save her," Jimmy said with a grin.

Lois raised her eyebrows. "Give me a little credit, Jimmy— Superman and I took more of a tag-team approach. Luthor didn't have a chance against the two of us." She let out a wistful sigh. "I'm just glad I helped restore the world's faith in Superman. Some of those innuendos Luthor made . . . And now we know what *he* was up to all along! Even Senator McCarthy has denounced Luthor. He's in full-blown damage control."

"Now, Lois, I doubt the world really questioned Superman," Clark said mildly. "He's proved himself again and again with his good deeds. Isn't that enough?"

"Never a doubt in my mind," Lois said. She looked at the folded newspaper, the large-type headline, and more important, her own name on the byline. "Superman certainly doesn't slack off when people need him." She pointed to the prominent photo of the Man of Steel. "He's a real hero."

Upon returning to the bullpen, Clark was delighted to see Lorna Bahowic back at her desk, happily wading through mountains of complicated letters and compiling her next "Lovelorn" column. Clark was relieved to see her diligently tackling those crises so that he could deal with matters to which he was better suited.

"We all can't be Superman, Lois." Clark fumbled with his eyeglasses and looked away. "I wish I could have been here myself, but my mom wasn't feeling well, and I had to take care of her. In Smallville, Kansas, we're raised to think that family takes priority."

Lois's expression softened as she looked sincerely at him. "Of course, Clark. It's just . . . well, you always seem to be gone every time something exciting happens around here."

"Something exciting is *always* happening in Metropolis, Lois. And the Luthor scandal is going to last for quite a while."

Luthor faced a mountain of charges, thanks in large part to Lois's investigative journalism and all the information she had discovered about his secret island base, his energy-beam controls, the murders of many LuthorCorp employees, and his plans to dupe the human race. More than a hundred people had been killed during the attack of the fake alien battleships on Metropolis, including five fighter pilots, and Luthor would be held responsible for those murders.

But the crimes did not stop there. He had also been implicated in secret dealings with the Soviets, and the launch of the three nuclear missiles had his fingerprints all over it as well. Though the Soviet premier denied all knowledge of a general named Ceridov or the existence of any gulag in the Siberian wasteland, the computer tapes recovered in Luthor's control center told a different story.

Once his plan was revealed, Luthor didn't even bother to deny his involvement. Instead, he wanted to receive *credit* for his genius in developing the "alien" propulsion system, the invasion battleships, and the flying-saucer prototype that had crashed in Arizona. Luthor even admitted to using his high-powered energy beams to blast Sputnik out of orbit, which elicited furious demands from the Soviets to have him extradited to face trial in Moscow as well.

All together, there was more than enough evidence. Luthor wasn't going to worm his way out of this one.

"So, Mr. Kent, maybe there aren't aliens out there after all." Jimmy sounded glum. "I'm glad the invasion turned out to be a fake, but still . . . all those movies can't be wrong, can they?"

Clark sighed. "Just because one or two stories are hoaxes doesn't mean that all the rest are untrue." He squeezed the young photographer's shoulder in a gesture of friendship. "After all, it only takes one."

Jimmy grinned at him. "And we know Superman's an alien— there's no denying that."

"See? There's always hope." In the back of his mind, Clark was trying to convince himself, too. He longed to know that he wasn't alone.

Perry White stood at the door of his office, impatiently tapping his fingers on the jamb. "Is this a newfangled journalism technique they teach in school? Wait for the news to come to *you*? Come on, people—stories don't report themselves. Get out there, hit the streets, find some leads. Is it asking too much for a newspaper to have a headline *every single day*?"

Clark took up his hat and notepad, Jimmy grabbed his camera, and Lois got a brand-new pen to replace the one that had been ruined during her escape from Luthor's base. The smiling trio left the *Daily Planet* together to see what Metropolis had to offer them today.

CHAPTER 62
THE CAVE

HE KNEW THE WORLD WOULD NEVER BE TRULY SAFE—NOT from petty thieves who were willing to murder, not from corrupt industrialists who wanted to take over the planet . . . perhaps not even from the threat of alien invasion.

But Earth was secure enough, for now.

Bruce sat in the Cave, still clad in his dark armored suit, the black scalloped cape tucked behind him; he had removed his cowl and it sat like a demonic mask on the corner of the laboratory table. At the moment he was deep in thought, balanced between being millionaire Bruce Wayne and vigilante Batman, half in and half out of costume, both a corporate head and a hero. It didn't really matter which outfit he wore.

With Lex Luthor in disgrace, the future of LuthorCorp was in limbo. The man had been too narcissistic to believe his company could possibly function without him, so—unlike Thomas Wayne—he had failed to create detailed contingency plans for his demise. He had established basic guidelines for the company to continue, and it would limp along for a time, but it was obvious that Luthor had designated no heir. He did not trust anyone enough.

Many of LuthorCorp's pending R&D contracts had been transferred to Wayne Enterprises. Bruce's best researchers would continue to develop sophisticated ways to defend America, and with those profits he could devote more resources to medical research and the construction of new hospitals, which would have made his father proud.

Alfred had brought him a club sandwich and small bowl of canned peaches in syrup, a treat he had particularly enjoyed as a boy. Bruce hadn't touched either.

He regarded the empty cowl on the desktop next to him—the black pointed ears, the empty eyeholes of the mask. But the focus of his current study was the faintly glowing green rock sitting in a lab tray, the mineral sample he had taken from Luthor's mansion. Superman's Achilles heel.

If the story of Kal-El's origin was true—and Bruce had no reason to doubt it anymore—this might indeed be a fragment of the exploded planet Krypton. And through some sympathetic connection, a kind of radiation that primarily targeted someone tied to that planet, even in small doses this "kryptonite" weakened Superman. Because of the gulag's reactor explosion, the entire meteor crater at the Ariguska impact site was gone. All traces of the Siberian kryptonite were almost certainly destroyed.

He wondered if the piece here was the only sample Luthor had possessed, and now Bruce had it. Nobody else needed to know its power over Superman.

He looked at the rock one last time, then sealed it in a new lead-lined case he'd had specially constructed. He locked the case in a vault carved in the Cave's solid rock. For safekeeping.

He hoped he would never have any reason to use it.

CHAPTER 63
ABOVE THE EARTH

KAL-EL WANTED TO MEASURE HIS LIMITS. HE NEEDED TO know how far he could go. As he shot straight up into the sky, the details of the terrain below shifted from individual houses and buildings to intersecting patterns of roads and the checker-boards of crop fields, then to a blur of generalized landscape, and finally the outlines of the continents themselves, swiftly masked by thick white clouds.

The atmosphere grew thinner and colder as he flew higher, higher, straining toward the very edge of Earth's atmosphere and beyond. He had never tested himself like this before, never pushed so high.

The air became vanishingly thin until he just kissed space, where raw and unfiltered sunlight continued to give him strength. He felt as though his every skin cell was charging, like a minute battery. He felt no shortness of breath even here. He was an alien, after all.

No one had been here to teach him. He had no comrade to give him advice, no other Kryptonian to tell him about his heritage, his strengths and weaknesses. Kal-El simply drifted over Earth, gazing out toward the infinite universe. So many stars . . . so many planets. So many questions.

He focused his telescopic vision, pushing outward into deep space with a resolution greater than that of the best Earth-based telescope. From here, he could see the moon with its artistry of distant mountain ridges and round craters, the stark and lifeless terrain drawn in sharp relief by slanted sunlight. He tried to discern any signs of activity—lost cities or alien bases, domed settlements, silver rocket ships, the barest hint of an extraterrestrial civilization.

But he saw nothing. No hint of strange visitors, Kryptonian or otherwise. He silently asked the universe if he was truly alone, but the universe didn't answer.

So he turned back and looked at the blue, green, and white globe turning beneath him. From here, high enough that he could see the planet's curvature, Kal-El gained a new perspective: The landmasses showed no political boundaries, no lines delineating countries, no colors that separated Communist from capitalist. Kal-El decided he liked this view of Earth best.

He descended swiftly through the atmosphere, cutting through the clouds and soaring over continents, heading back to Metropolis. He was not alone, because the people of Earth were *his* people. And Lois. She could be more than just a friend. He'd like that, and he knew she would like it as well.

Kal-El might have been different from them . . . but all people were different from one another. Yet even with those differences, they all shared a common bond. And Kal-El—Superman—would always stay there to protect them.

CHAPTER 64
FEDERAL COURT BUILDING, METROPOLIS

LEX LUTHOR'S SENSATIONAL TRIAL PROCEEDED WITH GREAT alacrity, an example of swift and effective American justice. The news media loved it. He wasn't the least bit surprised. These little people who now accused him were incapable of seeing the larger picture.

Nobody else saw the irony in the fact that he was entitled to face a jury of his "peers." Who, in all of the United States, could be considered Lex Luthor's peer? Nevertheless, the evidence against him was incontrovertible.

With Lois Lane's persistent and thorough investigative work over the past several months, as well as Superman's repeated interference, Luthor had been caught red-handed. Because of his covert cooperation with the Soviet KGB general, Luthor was even branded "un-American." Senator McCarthy renounced any and all connection he'd ever had with Lex Luthor.

That was the most annoying of all.

Lois Lane was a permanent fixture in the gallery, sometimes sitting next to Clark Kent, covering the story daily. As Luthor glanced at her without catching her eye, he expected to see her gloating, or at least exhibiting some personal satisfaction to see such a great man brought so low. But she was a professional newswoman, and she reported the story for the *Daily Planet* with a reasonable degree of objectivity. With grudging respect, Luthor had even considered complimenting her efforts but decided that she would probably not appreciate the gesture.

He insisted on being his own legal representative, since he was far more qualified and talented than any lawyer he could have hired. Certainly no one had a greater incentive to succeed. But his conviction was a foregone conclusion—he knew that from the start. Lex Luthor refused to beg, refused to make excuses. In fact, in his cool and logical summation, he did his best to convey to the jury, and the hordes of reporters in the gallery, the breathtaking complexity and scope of his plans, his sheer genius in creating the false alien battleships and directed-energy defensive weapons. Surely someone had to admire that.

Not surprisingly, the little people of the jury took less than an hour to find him guilty, convict him of treason, and sentence him to death.

Luthor remained seated, motionless. He didn't rage, didn't curse, didn't make a scene. Of course, the government was too shortsighted to take advantage of his brilliance. In his mind, the wheels were already turning. Starting now, he had to plan his escape.

Looming over him, the portly, sour-faced judge said rather snidely, "I believe, Mr. Luthor, that our penal system uses a model of electric chair designed and built by LuthorCorp."

Not at all rattled, Luthor gave the judge a cold smile. "Then, Your Honor, I am confident it will work properly."

CHAPTER 65
GOTHAM CITY

KAL-EL FOUND BATMAN SITTING AMONG THE GARGOYLES on a rooftop in Gotham City. Hunched over, the other man looked like a gargoyle himself in his black cape and cowl. He directed his intent gaze at the streets, as vigilant as the silent stone sentinels beside him.

Drifting down in a quiet swirl of red cape, Kal-El landed next to him. Batman didn't flinch, his gaze never flickered, but he spoke in a deep voice. "Greed, corruption, jealousy, poverty—even pure evil." He turned to look at Kal-El, his eyes darker than the shadows around him. "People will always find reasons to cause harm. And the world will always need men like us."

Kal-El added his increased acuities to scan Gotham City. "I'm glad to know I won't be the only one protecting the innocent and defending against injustice."

Batman frowned. Even without any sort of superhuman vision, he seemed to see as much as Kal-El could. "I hope you aren't going to propose a partnership. *You're* the hero, Superman. I prefer to operate out of the public eye."

Kal-El frowned. "We could accomplish more together. We have the same goal—to make the world safer from criminals."

"Criminals," Batman repeated. "The Gotham City Police Department considers *me* a criminal. But I'm not going to stop what I'm doing simply because I don't fit into one of their neat categories. What exactly is a vigilante? Do *you* ask permission to rescue those people you save, or do you act on your own and follow your conscience? As long as I do what's right, I'll keep doing it." Now he did smile slightly. "Besides, I don't need a sidekick."

Kal-El was surprised. "You thought I wanted to be *your* sidekick?"

"I said I don't need one."

"Neither do I. But we don't always have to operate alone. We don't each have to *be* alone. Sometimes we'll encounter problems large enough to warrant cooperation between us. There's got to be some sort of trust."

Batman nodded. "Agreed."

Kal-El stood tall then, smiling. "And in that spirit, I promise I will never expose your real identity . . . Bruce Wayne." He had secretly used his X-ray vision to look through Batman's mask, recognizing him immediately. "You can trust me, Bruce. My word is my bond."

Now Batman rose from his crouch, an unexpected smile on his face. His black cape fluttered in the suddenly cool night breeze. "And I promise not to reveal the location of your Fortress of Solitude . . . or *your* secret identity, Clark Kent."

AUTHOR'S NOTE

Readers may have noticed that some details in this novel differ from "our" version of the late 1950s. For instance, the real Senator McCarthy died several months before the launch of Sputnik (and had he been alive at the time, he would surely have suffered a stroke to see such a blatant demonstration of Soviet superiority in the space race). Nikita Khrushchev's famous shoe-banging incident at the UN occurred years later than the similar actions by the Soviet premier in this novel. In our 1950s, no Soviet nuclear missiles were, in fact, launched at the United States, nor was Sputnik shot out of the sky.

The role of Superman and Batman in historical events is, of course, perfectly accurate.